Shee-Oak

**A road trip to redemption across
the Australian outback**

GERALDINE STAR

Cover design and layout: Green Avenue Design.

Publisher: Star Monde, Australia

978-0-6451412-0-7 (eBook)

978-0-6451412-1-4 (Paperback)

A catalogue record for this book is available from the National Library of Australia

Dedicated to my godchildren Elise, Simon, Anthony, Damien, Alberta, Joey.

Chapter 1

The nightmare of roaring noise, scooting dust, and a skidding Kombi reverberated through Mia's head, her skin was clammy, and nausea simmered. Her long hair fell limp as she peered through the window of the lifeless vehicle to the haze shrouding the land with branches and leaves littered everywhere. The stench of oil, an overheated engine and scorched clingy seats forced her to leave the van.

At least the dust storm had passed, and her surroundings were clearer.

After a few swigs of water, she fastened her pink runners and stared at the powdery skid marks made when she lost control of the Kombi on the rough road. The steering wheel had had a life of its own, and thoughts of dying had unnerved her before the van halted without warning.

She stepped down into a bowl-shaped hole, and onto something that shifted beneath her feet. 'Shit!' she screamed, as she leapt back into the van, thinking it was a snake.

With her hand protecting her racing heart, Mia closed her eyes to calm herself and tried to breathe deeply, as the dreaded counsellor had attempted to explain after the accident, but all she could do was gasp. She poked her head out the door and squinted like a meerkat in both directions and in the distance, near the roadway, she glimpsed something shining, a mailbox.

A sense of boldness gripped her as she gathered her water, useless phone, and backpack, and trudged along the isolated road for ten minutes, cursing herself for taking flight from Canberra. When she glanced behind, the loneliness of her shoe prints in the dirt spooked her. What had she got herself into? Her nerve disappeared and her steps became cautious with every sound echoing. Something flitted through the trees, and she froze, knowing she had no protection. She saw a gnarled, short stick lying near the fence, and her hands shook and her mind worked overtime as she ran, grabbed it and bolted back onto the road.

Thoughts of never being found, of dying here with no one knowing spurred her onwards in this desolate place. She bent her head and gazed at her distinctive orange T-shirt. Was orange a good omen? Would anyone be crazy enough to travel in these waves of crippling heat?

Sometime later, a speeding dot in a cloud of dust appeared on the horizon. She halted, not sure if she should flee, hide in nearby scattered bushes or wait until it approached. Her body arched in fear as she gripped the stick and felt her heart throb as the vision got closer and closer. An old, battered ute with three black growling dogs chained to the tray sped towards her.

'What in hell are you bloody well doing here in this madness?' The dishevelled driver wore a crumpled calico hat and braked the car beside her while his mate thumped the side of the vehicle and told the animals to be quiet.

The plume of dirt from the car stung her, and she cringed. 'My...my Kombi's stuck. It won't go. I can't see what's wrong.'

'Get in,' said the driver, pointing to the seat. 'We'll check the bloody van for you,'

She gulped as the passenger stepped out. His body rippled with muscle through his discoloured shirt and tattered jeans, and around his waist his belt held a holder with a knife protruding from it. The driver signalled her to sit beside him while the dogs growled.

The men might attack her, but she had no choice but to go with them. She slithered into the middle of the torn, dirty seat and a choking noise rose from her throat as she adjusted to the smell of animals and sweat. When she saw the stubby one staring at her exposed legs, she readjusted her skirt and gazed at the horizon. He must be fifty or sixty.

'I'm Bill. This is me mate, Crowbar.' The driver doffed his hat, nodded. 'Where are you from? What's your name?'

'Can...berra...Mia.'

The men howled with laughter. 'That pissy place. Who'd want to live there? Those greedy pollies,' said Crowbar.

'Where are you going?' The driver turned and glanced at her.

'...Adelaide.'

'What are you doing on this road? Didn't you see the warning at the start of the gravel?' He lifted his hat and scratched his head as he braked alongside the Kombi. 'You're miles away.' They jumped out, leaving Mia wondering what to do.

Noticing her hesitation, Bill nodded to an enormous tree with generous branches beside the road and said, 'Sit over there in the cool. Where's your key?'

Mia hesitated then threw it to Bill, and paced the side of the road, listening to the men curse and swear as they tried to work out what was wrong and wondering whether they could fix the van before dark.

'How's it going, Ivan?' said a chuckling Crowbar.

Bill grinned at him. 'Good, Milat! Wolf, wolf! woof woof!' He turned his head towards Mia. 'We're just joking, don't take any notice of us. You'll be okay.'

They laughed, then stuck their heads back in the engine.

Should I be frightened or grateful for their help? Will they leave me here when they fix the Kombi? Do they expect money or some other payment? She ran a stick through the dirt to calm her scrambled thoughts.

Next Bill climbed into the van, and Crowbar pushed. It kangaroo-hopped a few times, then leapt into action, leaving the potholes in its wake, and they left the motor running.

'All fine now.' Bill hobbled to the ute. 'You'll get lost if you drive now but don't worry, I'll find you a bed for the night.' He spoke into a two-way and when he had finished, he flicked his head at his mate, and they both started towards her.

They're out to get me, she thought as her body froze, not understanding what he meant.

Bill pointed his hand to the distant mailbox. 'Talked to the owner of the farm up there, Flea…Felicity. She's happy to have you stay the night. You'll be safe with her, got kids of her own about your age.'

Bill directed Mia to follow his ute to the cattle grid at the farm's entrance and then explained how to find Felicity's farmhouse. They tooted their horn, and the dogs yapped as they roared down the road, their beamed lights heralding the approaching darkness. She realised she'd forgotten to thank them, and her unease rose as she headed down the narrow gravel track to a faraway house.

***

Typical bloke, offloading his problems, Felicity thought, as she scrutinised the young woman in front of her. That mane of dark hair with red streaks, and all those bangles and rings made her an attractive "hippy". Too delicate to be out here. Maybe mid-twenties. Tall, slim build, a bit sexy. No wonder Bill got excited.

'Welcome to *Neerea*, I'm Felicity, everyone calls me Flea.' She extended her hand in greeting. 'Heard you had trouble with your car. Picked the wrong day to come this way, we've just had the worst dust storm we've ever had. Climate change, they say.'

'Yeah, never been so scared.' Glad to see a visitor, the three dogs jumped around and Mia tried to keep them at bay.

'Down, boys, it's alright. Sit…excellent dogs. I'll feed you later.' Felicity patted the animals as they nuzzled into her.

'Thanks for letting me come. What an inferno, wind, dust and heat. How can you live here? Do you wear dust masks?'

Felicity raised her eyes in pretend disgust and gave a rich, throaty laugh. 'Come in. Bring your luggage. People from the city can't hack the countryside at night with no streetlights. It's pitch dark and too scary.'

While Mia gathered her gear, Felicity waited on the veranda and smiled up at the Milky Way. It was something special. She agreed with that handsome TV presenter, Stan Grant, a Wiradjuri man, about wanting to wrap himself in the stars when he was in the bush. Now she was studying the heavens for any clues to tomorrow's weather. At daybreak she would be up and ready to work on the farm before it got too hot.

'Thinking of staying, are you?' joked Felicity, as Mia made two trips to bring in plastic bags and coloured luggage. 'You travel with lots of stuff.' The visitor dumped her baggage in the hall. 'Don't leave them there. You can have my daughter's room over here.' Felicity glanced at Mia. 'You'd better have a shower, wash the dirt away. But don't use too much water, the tank's low. Bathroom's at the end of the hallway. I'll get you a towel and some sheets and you can make the bed.'

Felicity grinned as she opened the linen-press in the hall and muttered to herself. 'What a muddle. Haven't played domestic goddess for a while.'

'Here, Mia.' She handed Mia a towel and beige-coloured sheets. 'You clean up. I've got to check the chooks to see they didn't blow away in the storm. Later I'll make dinner and hear about your trip.'

Felicity's eyebrows furrowed as she stomped through the dry backyard and out the gate in her riding boots. What brought this girl so far from the main road? What's she doing out here? That hell of a dust storm must have frightened her. Then to break down in the middle of it, no wonder she looked a mess when she arrived at the house.

Felicity found five chooks huddled together between the old water tank and the fence. They were reluctant to move, so she gently pulled them apart, and waved a bowl of scraps, and they scampered after her.

'Here girls, where's your randy rooster mate?' She laughed when the big black speckled hen tried to hog the food. 'Where's that fella hiding?' She closed the chook yard gate and searched for him. 'Bet he flew off in the wind like that bloody hubby of mine.'

***

The wafting smell of chops cooking, and a table covered with a checked tablecloth and set with a plate of boiled eggs, cucumbers, tomatoes and wine glasses greeted Mia as she entered the kitchen.

'I'm just reheating this bread, it's stale.' Felicity peered into the oven. 'Haven't been to the shops. Help yourself to a wine or a beer from the fridge. There's cold water in the cooler on the sink, too.'

Mia sat with a glass of water, her hair hiding her face.

'Are you okay, pet?' Her visitor didn't answer, her head still bowed. One of these sensitive, useless city types, thought Felicity. 'Now tell me what you're doing out in these back blocks?'

Mia tossed her hair. 'I'm going to Adelaide, to the music festival.'

'You're right out of your way. Didn't you see the warning on the road or did you get lost?'

Mia stared into the distance and said, 'I made an escape from those looming big trucks and the horrid open highway and took the back roads because I've never been in the Australian bush. My GPS dropped out, and I ended up on the wrong road somewhere. Didn't know where I was.' Then she turned and glared. 'How come my phone doesn't work?'

Felicity blinked and studied her. 'You should ask those damn telcos. Everything's not what it seems out here.'

Mia picked at her dinner, while Felicity sipped her wine and attempted to make conversation. At the start, Mia rattled on about how good she was at her job in the computer world, then gave curt answers to all following questions. The only concern the girl appeared to have was if her phone worked. After her second glass of wine, Felicity drummed her fingers on the table, wondering what to say next.

Suddenly Mia dragged her chair away, stood and muttered, 'I'm tired, I'm off to bed.'

'Aren't you going to help clear up?'

Mia flicked her hair away from her face, gave Felicity a withering look, and vanished down the hall to the bedroom.

'No manners,' Felicity mumbled to herself as she poured herself another drink. 'I'd kill my kids if they behaved that way. Thank goodness she's leaving tomorrow.'

Chapter 2

Discoloured photographs of laughing teenagers on the bedroom pin board were curled at the edges with age, and on the crowded antique chest of drawers there was a framed picture of Felicity with what looked like her husband and two adult children.

Felicity's daughter appeared about twenty in the photo, confident, pretty, as though there was a sparkle in her life, good times ahead. Her son, tall with dark hair, looked conservative, not Mia's sort, but still interesting. As she climbed into the cast iron bed, she wished she had happy family snaps.

Her mother had left her so long ago and her childhood memories were blurred. From her purse under the pillow, Mia slid out a worn black and white torn photo taken beside a swimming pool. Her finger ran over the exotic-looking woman who gazed out to the world with pouting lips. She closed her eyes as tears appeared; she was the scrawny nine-year-old clinging to the woman, her mother, longing for a cuddle, love, and affection.

Mia dragged the gritty curtains together and pulled the sheet over her head to escape the shadows from the dappled moonlight. The house creaked with the heat. Exhaustion.

During the night, she woke, petrified. Was it a gunshot? She sat up, her body tense, her mouth dry. Another shot, this time closer, then a deadly stillness. The back gate squeaked. A dog growled. Then footsteps in the hall. They passed her room. She reached for her phone to get some light, knocked her water bottle off the side table and it bounced on the wooden floor.

She heard the footsteps return. The door creaked and opened. Mia held her breath, her body froze, her heart stopped.

'Sorry about the gun. Thought I'd give the fox a scare,' said Felicity in a whisper, letting the hall's light into the room.

Mia burrowed deeper under the sheets, relieved her Oxys had numbed the pain as she thought of how creepy this place was. Anything might happen being so far from civilisation.

Mia woke to the sounds of birds chattering in a nearby tree and a radio blaring out the ABC news. She jumped from the bed and tugged the curtains open to see a dry-looking garden covered with debris from yesterday's wind – broken branches, twigs and severed bushes, rolled drums. Dressing in white shorts and a green T-shirt, she sat on the floor, drew her arms around her and rocked for ten minutes to lessen the intermittent pain she felt when the effects of her pills wore away. Her hair dropped over her face, and she closed her eyes, wondering what she was doing in this god forsaken place.

Her voice wavered as she called, 'Flea…Flea?' There was no answer.

Ringing alarm bells in her head was her father's motto, "In strange places, check your surroundings and exit points, you may need to escape."

Mia rose from the floor and retraced her steps from the night before back to the heart of the house, the large, disorganised kitchen where they had eaten. She investigated what lay elsewhere, moving with caution as she scanned bedrooms with their unmade beds and scattered clothes, opening the office and peering at the bookshelves stuffed with books and papers. A computer and monitors occupied the desk near the window.

The front door was ornate and set strangely in a large lounge room with an open fireplace. There were huge, curtained windows and a lonely-looking unpolished grand piano sat in the middle of the room. Shards of glass from a smashed photo frame littered the floor, and when she tried the front door, it didn't budge as they had painted it in.

Mia stepped into the laundry alley where dozens of empty wine and beer bottles lined the wall. Someone here drinks too much? The laundry led to the side yard with lots of withering vines covering two water tanks. Back in the kitchen, through glass doors, she surveyed the fly-screened veranda which ran the width of the house and contained a comfortable looking leather lounge and big wicker chairs. Her snoop complete, she had two escape routes.

A sense of relief washed over her when she spotted her Kombi parked under the tree where she had left it last night. Her nose twitched as she stepped off the dusty veranda and out to the dry garden yard ringed by overgrown bushes, tall trees, and a wire fence. In the distance she noticed a large, corrugated iron shed with water tanks. She bit her lip, and her stomach fluttered. What's that strange noise? She crept up to inspect a high wired fence and grinned. Chooks!

Back in the kitchen, Mia ferreted in the cupboards for food, switched on the kettle, dangled a tea bag in a cup and made toast and jam. On the edge of the wooden table was an old newspaper. She flicked through the pages until a photo caught her attention. Felicity, wearing sunglasses, stood with a smile, holding a trophy, and beside her was a large sheep with a first-prize ribbon draped across its ample back.

The growl of an engine interrupted her, and she frowned and tip-toed to the veranda. Who's that?

An old ute pulled up outside the yard and a tall, willowy-looking Felicity jumped out and gave her wide-brimmed hat a few bangs on her long legs. She wore a crumpled khaki shirt, blue jeans, and dirty black riding boots. Her grey streaked blonde hair was pulled from her face into a ponytail, showing small gold looped earrings. After Felicity had removed her boots and sunglasses on the veranda, Mia scrutinized her. Her eyes were enormous, deep brown, and friendly. Last night under the harsh fluorescent kitchen light she had a tired, wrinkled face, but today Felicity appeared not to be as old. Maybe in her late fifties?

'Morning. Sorry I scared you last night. I was after a fox, I sighted through the bedroom window, running off with my only rooster and now there are feathers everywhere. Did you sleep well?'

Mia sat and stared into the distance, and Felicity leant over her and glanced at the opened paper. 'Ah, a photo of me a few years ago, didn't look too bad then. When I took over the farm, my sheep won awards. Now it's too dry and there's no rain.' She strode towards the sink. 'You've made yourself at home? Coffee?'

'Yes, please. Yesterday exhausted me. I was so scared and couldn't talk last night.'

'Yeah. It can terrify people out here, especially if you are new to this part of the country. Do you want to get going soon?'

Mia gave a heavy sigh. 'I'm so tired, I need to rest. Is it okay if I go tomorrow?'

Felicity gave her an inquisitive look. 'Sure…but as long as you can do something for me. You work with computers, right? Could you have a look at my modem? You help me with my computer, and I'll give you a bed.' She grinned. 'A fair deal?'

Mia laughed and agreed to work on the computer, so after coffee Felicity led her to the office with its expensive computer and two monitors. She threw books and papers from the desk onto the sofa and shook the curtains to remove the dust. Mia swung on the office chair and swore to herself as she attempted to boot the computer.

'Every day at work I had to fix computers,' Mia said, tossing her hair.

After she turned the computer on and off at the power point a few times and jiggled the wires and worked the keys, it started.

'Thank you so much. I've tried and tried to get it to work,' said Felicity. 'It may need an update. The internet's slow and I need a new satellite dish. Bloody politicians promise the earth but never deliver.'

The tension in Mia's head diminished as she worked on fixing the computer while Felicity paid bills and organised overdue filing. They stopped and chatted every now and again. Mia welcomed the periods of silence, her mind working overtime trying to fathom what she was doing here and what Felicity was really like.

There was a silver-framed photo sitting on a bookcase, Mia pointed to it and asked, 'Is that your husband, the one with his arm around you?'

Felicity laughed, and Mia noticed a red flush creep across her cheeks. 'No way! A friend. Taken at a fundraiser about six months ago in Mildura and it was a wonderful fun night.'

'Ah, cool. He's got the hots for you, just look at his eyes.'

'Really?' Felicity gave an embarrassed grin. 'Well, that's done. You updated everything in no time, and we're back online. Thanks.'

'My phone's still out-of-range, I can't talk to anyone.' Mia's face crumpled. 'I need to speak to my friend Brad, to let him know where I am.'

Felicity groaned with frustration. 'The bloody dust storm has put this stuff out again. Those telcos can go to hell, there is no service, but they never forget a bill. My kids climb onto the old water tank and get a signal so you could try there.'

Mia looked up at the soaring platform surrounding the tank and placed her phone in the pocket of her shorts. Should she do this? Felicity held the ladder while she climbed, pausing on each step to catch her breath, her legs like jelly. At the top, she sat on the ledge, wiped the beads of sweat from her face and forced herself to focus. Dry brown paddocks and treetops swayed in the distance with no people or houses anywhere. She tried her phone, but no reception. She tried again and again, holding it near her, away from her, shaking it.

'This is fucken hopeless. He's not there, there's no connection,' Mia shouted as she raised her hands to the sky. Then she froze and couldn't move nor think, an inner force rooted her to the ledge. Fear rose through her body as she directed her gaze below, freaking out.

After a few minutes Felicity called, 'Are you okay? Are you scared of heights?' No answer. 'Why didn't you tell me?'

Felicity came scuttling up the ladder and manoeuvred herself to wrap her arms around the sobbing young woman.

'We'll just sit and talk for a while.' Felicity made herself comfortable and pointed to a yellow patch. 'See that dry patch in the garden? I stopped the water when the drought hit, rationed it so I watered only those green bits, I'm hoping everything will come back when it rains. See the dogs playing over there?' She continued to chatter until Mia stopped gasping for breath. 'I think it's time we climbed down to the ground. Okay?'

Mia half-nodded and crossed her arms over her chest.

'Watch me and I'll show you the best way.' She moved towards the ladder and Mia sniffled. 'Better put that phone in your pocket.' Felicity stepped down the ladder facing the tank and signalled Mia to follow.

Mia's teeth chattered and her heart pounded as she descended, Felicity encouraging her to take each step. At the bottom, she burst into more tears.

Felicity hugged her. 'Sorry, my kids have climbed that for years, thought it was easy for everyone. You need to rest for a while.'

'I'm still scared...' said Mia with her hands clasped across her front.

'Here sit and have some lunch, nothing fancy, sandwiches,' said Felicity.

Mia ignored her and raced to the bathroom. On her way back, she overheard Felicity talking to herself, 'She's not robust like my kids, I shouldn't have let her up there.'

Mia succumbed to exhaustion and dizziness, and she gulped a pill before laying between the cool sheets and sleeping in snatches and dreaming of falling from a high cliff. When she woke, she rubbed her eyes and gazed at the small blue clock beside the bed noting she had slept for two hours. The bed clothes were sticky, and the bathroom called.

'Getting stuck in that dust storm yesterday must have scared you, sapped your energy and made you tired,' said Felicity as she pulled out a plate of corned beef slices from the fridge. 'Here, make yourself a sandwich, homemade pickles courtesy of Bill's wife, and tomatoes I've nursed through the dry.'

Mia studied the antique green glass jug, decorated with gold leaf and blue finches on the table, then poured herself a glass of water, debating with herself whether she should take another pill from her packet to calm herself.

Felicity grabbed the small white box from the table. 'What are these? Did they affect your balance when you were up on the tank?' She hesitated. 'Oh shit, that's not my business.'

Mia snatched the packet and ran into the bedroom. When she returned, she prepared a tomato sandwich and then made a beeline for the wicker chairs on the veranda where she spent the rest of the afternoon.

At sunset she refused Felicity's offer of a beer or wine and muttered that she would have one later, so Felicity opened a bottle of red for herself and kept filling her glass as she fried steak and chips.

Over dinner, Felicity opened another bottle and continued drinking while Mia paced up and down the house, not wanting to return to her oven-like bedroom. As the evening wore on, Felicity became more garrulous and told Mia funny stories about her life as a farmer. However, Mia stiffened when she mentioned she had thrown a crystal decanter at her father's photo in the lounge room.

'I jumped up and down with annoyance at my father. This drought, the dust storms didn't help. He forced me to take over the farm to keep his sheep legacy alive, and I left a good job in the city for it,' she said, waving her hands around. 'But that's enough on my story, it's your turn tell me about your trip to Adelaide and this festival.'

Mia's face brightened. She explained how there were two different festivals and raved about people coming from across Australia and overseas to hear the music. She rattled off a list of singers and bands that meant nothing to Felicity and asked, 'Have you ever been?'

Felicity chuckled. 'Too busy shoving rams in the ute when I go to Adelaide so never catch up on what's happening. Now what's your interest in music?'

'Africa, my father grew up in Nairobi, Kenya and we lived there when I was little. The housekeeper looked after me when my mother left. I loved Anga as I called her and can still picture her, wrapped in her colourful khanga as she led me to the markets, to hear this amazing music. Those drums and the foot tapping stayed inside my head, and I've followed African music ever since.' Mia jumped up, removed her sandals, and started dancing while clapping and drumming her feet.

Felicity clapped to the rhythm and continued to sip her wine. 'Did you bring any music?' Mia nodded. 'Let's hear it. It'll get the cobwebs out of me.'

As the music filled the house, Mia moved the furniture and pulled her reluctant host to the kitchen floor. The spirit of the night captured the women with crazy dance moves, Felicity crashing against the walls and into chairs.

After half an hour Mia stopped. 'Why don't you come with me to Adelaide?'

Felicity gave a bemused smile as she raised her glass. 'I'd love to escape, to get away from those bloody sheep.' She hesitated. 'Let me think about it.'

'I'm terrified of being on the road alone.' Mia screwed her hair into a bun on the top of her head and gazed at Felicity with doe-eyes. 'We could share the driving and we wouldn't get lost or bogged. Please come.'

Felicity closed her eyes and made quirky musical movements with her hands. 'I can just imagine myself sitting on the grass, letting the music flow over me, forgetting my problems. Escape. But you want to go tomorrow, don't you?'

'I'll wait for you.' Mia drummed her feet on the floor with the exuberance of youth. 'Just need to arrive in Adelaide before next weekend.'

'Hmm, there're lots of jobs. Let me mull this over.' Felicity slurred her words as she tried to count the tasks on her fingers. 'If Bill or his son could help for a few days, then I'll get away, but I need to sort the arrangements out.' She grinned. 'I'll ring him in the morning and see what he says. Is that okay?'

Mia rubbed her hands together with excitement. She had a driver who knew the roads.

Chapter 3

'Oh, my head,' said Felicity, holding her forehead the next morning when Mia appeared for a late breakfast. 'Drank too much last night but haven't had fun like that for a long time and I agreed to go to Adelaide with you.' She threw her head back and laughed, slapping her thighs. 'And to make matters more interesting, I've spoken to Bill, and he's coming over later to get the list of jobs, so it'll happen. Yippee, I can escape.'

'You're coming?' Mia looked at her in astonishment.

'Last night, I realised I'd cut myself off from people and the outside world since Alan left and the drought hit. I've been getting more and more anxious when I look at the bare paddocks, and there is no feed for my sheep. But now I can blast myself out of here in your Kombi.' She raised her thumbs in celebration.

'Wow, I'll have a driver. Adelaide, here we come.' Mia gave an embarrassed giggle, and her host laughed.

'I've got a few jobs to do, would you feed the chooks after breakfast? Scraps are in that bucket next to the sink,' said Felicity.

Mia froze. Feed the chooks. An image of being pecked to death flashed before her eyes. She snatched the scraps, and when the dogs greeted her at the gate and ran beside her, she tried to shoo them away. They wagged their tails and looked up at her until something hijacked their attention and they growled, their noses bent to the ground.

She tugged at the crooked wire gate and stepped into the yard. The frenzy of the chooks, and their BAWK, BAWK, BAWK terrified her. Suddenly she spied a big monster lizard with yellow blotches across the yard. She screamed as it moved towards her, poked out its long tongue and made a harsh hissing noise. She couldn't move and dropped the scrap bucket on its head. Both Mia and the goanna sized up escape routes and danced, she scooted one way and the lizard on its hind legs the other, until weaving around the pen she made her get-away out the door.

The lizard's attention drifted to the chooks, and it hissed again and flashed its tongue.

'Quick, quick, there's an enormous…monster out here,' Mia shrieked as she ran to the house.

At the back door, Felicity saw the girl running, the cowering chooks in the distance, and the lizard. 'Are you okay?' she said as she pulled her through the laundry fly-screen door into the house. 'Old Fred, the goanna's a nuisance. I'll get rid of him, but I bet he's got the eggs.'

From the doorway, Mia watched with amazement as Felicity plucked meat from the fridge, strolled to the chook yard and opened the gate and stood back, coaxing the goanna out of the pen.

The goanna snared the piece of meat and ran towards Felicity, who bolted away, and the lizard scuttled off and sprinted up the nearest tree. Felicity fixed the hole she spotted in the fence by pulling the netting and staking it with an iron peg lying nearby.

'There you go, me ladies. You're okay now.' She picked up a black and white speckled hen and stroked it. 'Don't let old Fred stop you laying.'

Mia's ashen face peered from the door, and Felicity laughed. 'All in a day's work. You've seen the best of country life today. I should shoot Fred, he's dangerous, but I don't want to get a gun to him like the foxes. Bloody British brought those pests. Fred's a local, the Gugaa or goanna is a totem of the Wiradjuri people and this is their country, and he's my "pet".'

***

A ribbon of dust heralded the neighbour's arrival and the barking dogs gathered.

'Hello Flea, Mia.' Bill removed his hat as he opened the fly-screened veranda door. 'Hear you're taking the old girl on a trip to Adelaide for the weekend. Good idea. She needs a break after that arrogant, witless Alan tried to send her bankrupt. I certainly won't allow him near here, and everyone around here will look after the place.'

Felicity gave an embarrassed laugh and guided him by the crook of his arm to the kitchen. 'I'll make a cuppa while we plan how I can get away.'

As they huddled together, working through the jobs, Mia watched with interest. They seemed to be such good friends.

She was fidgety and wandered around the house and into the garden, wondering what to do.

She plonked herself into an armchair on the veranda. After a few wriggles, she found a comfortable spot, rummaged through her bag, and found a red notebook and a short stubby pencil. The words flowed as she described what happened when the Kombi broke down on the rough potholed road.

> *That afternoon, the wind roared and rocked the Kombi in bursts. I thought someone knocked at the window. Maybe the truckie on the main road who kept blowing me kisses followed me. The blood drained from my face. I peeped out the window, but there was nobody there. I curled myself as small as I could into a foetal position. Time stopped. fear became my monster. I surprised myself and slept for a while, my Oxys kicking in. When I woke, it was worse. The Kombi was a furnace. The heat drenched me. Yuck, I was sticky and smelt horrible. My imagination ran amok. I might have died. No one knew I was there. Flea wants to drive with me through this wild country and I'm so relieved.*
>
> *But there's no phone contact, it's like my arm's cut off. What will I do?*

Bill leaving interrupted her. 'There's lots to do this next week. The young fellow's still in Sydney. I'll get my mate, Crowbar, on to it.' Bill wiped his bald patch with his hand

and plonked on his calico hat, saying his goodbyes. 'Have a good time, Flea, you too, Mia.'

Felicity searched for an atlas and a road map in the over-stuffed bookshelves in her office and cleared the table. 'Paper maps are much better than GPS's and the internet, you can see the details. Suppose you used Google when you got lost?'

Mia gave a self-conscious giggle. 'There was an old man sitting on a seat at a derelict service station in this deserted place and he told me to go right at a T-junction, but I turned left at the next road and ended up here.'

Felicity burst out laughing. 'I'm not relying on your navigation skills. What do you want to see?'

'The festival starts in Adelaide at the weekend.' Mia danced around the table. 'But I had always planned to see Mungo Man and Woman on the way. Will we have time?'

'I've been to Mungo National Park a few times, it's a wonderful place, but it may be closed in the heat. Think we could get there, but the remains are out of bounds to the public. What's your interest?'

'I got to know about the Indigenous remains from my cultural anthropology studies at uni and always wanted to visit the place where they discovered them.'

Felicity's voice lightened, and she grinned as she pointed to the proposed roads. 'This route will be best, it's more direct. We must watch out for roadkill and wildlife, the animals are competing for food in this drought, we don't want an accident. I'll pack.' As Felicity danced to her room, she called, 'What'll I wear to listen to the music?'

'What?' Mia could not believe her question. 'Comfortable clothes. Bring a cushion or a fold-up chair. I'll clean the van.'

Mia pondered on the craziness of her circumstances as she stared in the hallway mirror and rubbed lipstick from her teeth. Here in the middle of nowhere, she knew no one, but she had found Felicity, the "bush-woman" to help her drive. She threw her hands in the air in surrender.

***

At twilight, a canvas of variegated red and purple with pencil-thin clouds filled the sky, its gentle shadows and movements giving way to the ghosts of the night. Felicity berated herself for her sudden drunken decision to escape. Her head told her she shouldn't leave, but her body knew it needed a break. She slipped on her riding boots and strolled through the she-oak trees near the house to her special place where she ran away to reflect, to decide.

At the trunk of a tall tree with a canopy that went forever, she ran her fingers around a deep carved scar, her mother's tree, her memorial. The one she had chosen before death hollowed her out to be remembered by. Felicity and her sister had played cubby houses and spun intricate ghost stories under this mottled shelter. She smiled when she remembered how they had once spooked themselves so much that they bolted back to the house. They had told no one as it kept the mystique alive.

Her father said the scar was a surveyor's mark, but she now believed Indigenous people carved it many years ago.

She must contact the local Wiradjuri Elders to verify what it was, and they could tell her more.

She wriggled into the soil, trying to create a comfortable possie between the tree and the hard-cracked earth, and closed her eyes, hoping her escape might bring a welcome relief from the drought. The tree gave her space as it always did, it soothed her soul as the breeze rustled its leaves, singing to her, bringing her peace. Little stars popped open like flowers in the sun. But there were no answers on the wind.

Chapter 4

Day three, Mia woke groggy and grumpy. Last night after a few glasses of wine, Felicity droned on about her two kids, who were overseas. She spoke of how her son Simon rang, chatted for hours and sent her photos but her daughter, Emily, blamed her mother for her parent's marriage breakup and had tantrums when she phoned. Felicity had laughed when she called Emily, "Daddy's girl" and as much as their relationship was difficult, she loved her.

Mia thumped the pillow as she brooded on her distant mother. 'You're a bitch,' she muttered to herself. 'Always leaving me, you flitted off after the accident, didn't help me recover.'

The low sun beaming scarlet and indigo streaks emerged from behind the trees, the leaves dappling the early rays of light. Mia calmed herself by rocking and lay listening to the birds twittering in a nearby bush. She strained to listen to Felicity talking to her dogs.

'Good boys. Now Bill's looking after you for a few days. I'll be back soon. Behave!'

She thumped her fists on the pillow again in anger. 'It's not fair.' After a while she dragged herself from the bed and stripped the sheets, a habit she had gained from the English boarding schools her father had dumped her in during his career in the Middle East. Surveying her bags, she rummaged through one and dumped the clothes she wanted to wear for the day on the floor.

'Oh, you're up, you look nice and bright,' said a startled Felicity, as Mia waltzed into the room dressed in tight shorts, a low-cut gypsy blouse and lots of bangles. 'A trough sprung a leak, I had to mend the pipe.'

'What? You're kidding. You can do that?'

Felicity raised her eyebrows with a smirk. 'Help yourself to breakfast.'

'Nope, don't feel like any.'

Mia put a bag on the kitchen table and using a large hand mirror made up her face. Felicity half watched as she finished her chores. The transformation intrigued her. When Mia had completed her makeover, she gathered the rest of her luggage, dragged it along the path and threw it into the Kombi. One of the plastic bags split, and a kaleidoscope of coloured clothes scattered across the seats. 'Shit, I'll fix it later,' said Mia.

'I'll just lock up to keep snoopy Alan out. Bill's so angry with him, I'm sure he'd get his gun out if he saw him,' muttered Felicity to herself as she grabbed an Akubra hat, turned the house key and ran to the gate with the last of her gear for the trip.

Mia sat dumbfounded in the Kombi. 'Don't you lock the veranda?'

'Naught to take. Bill will have a nap when he checks the sheep and I've left water and mugs.'

Mia held her phone in the air, trying for a signal. 'Get me out of here! I can't stand this lack of contact. Can you drive a Kombi?'

Felicity smirked as she pulled herself into the driver's seat. 'I operate tractors, trucks, semis, any type of vehicle. Ah, it's got gears, haven't driven a van like this in ages.'

The women did a high five and Felicity yelled goodbye to the barking dogs with their clinking chains.

'To the start of a fantastic trip, let's have fun,' said Felicity at the cattle grid gate. She waved to *Neerea* and spun the van left onto the road. 'First you must show me where you broke down. You'll laugh later when you remember this saga.'

'There's the tree where I sat.' Mia leaned towards the windscreen and pointed. 'Those skid marks have disappeared.'

'They're filled with dirt from the storm. An unsuspecting bastard will drop into those potholes, so I hope they don't have the same fate. Well, time to get on our way.'

Felicity did a skilful U-turn on the narrow road to head west.

As Mia dozed, she wondered why Felicity drank so much and was alone in the middle of nowhere. She understood why she locked away her expensive computer equipment, her snooping husband would have a nice fat wallet from one of those cash converters if he grabbed and sold the computer.

Mia pinched her bottom lip, realising it was a risk travelling with someone she didn't know. She would have to go with the flow and hope Felicity wasn't crazy or a prude.

'Where's the music?' asked Felicity when Mia opened her eyes and leant over her to take a selfie of them both in the cabin.

The two women bopped to the sounds of drums and stamping feet as the farms and drought-crisped Australian bush sped past. Felicity pointed out the changes in the vegetation while Mia half listened. 'See those trees over there with multiple trunks, that's mallee. Great for droughts and their gnarled roots make good firewood.'

Mia chewed gum and flicked her hair. 'When we stop, I want Maccas or KFC for lunch.'

Felicity gasped in disbelief. 'You don't understand. There's nothing like that out here.'

They were silent for the next few kilometres. Mia's patience waned. 'Where are the people, the towns? When do we get to the shops?'

'It's still early so there's no food or coffee around, but we'll break at the nearest pub, you'll be able to use your phone there.'

'What's happened to your kids, your hubby?' Mia placed her feet on the dashboard and threw her chewing gum out the window. 'Why aren't they on the farm helping you?'

'Emily and Simon are working overseas, and Alan's vanished.' Felicity's face grew red and her eyes pinched. Her hands gripped the steering wheel and after a few moments of silence, she said, 'Better gone, he never did a hard day's work.'

'You hate him?'

Felicity groaned and said, 'Our fights were outrageous and sometimes so unnecessary. Now we only speak through our expensive lawyers.'

The monotonous churn of the motor continued as Mia sat with her back turned, gazing at the desolate countryside, her mind in turmoil. She grabbed her bag, ferreted out a small tin of self-rolled smokes, lit one and blasted a cloud of smoke over the cabin and flicked the ash through the open window.

'Mia don't smoke that joint in here,' said Felicity, tapping her fingers on the wheel. 'It stinks, and I can't breathe. You'll start a fire flicking your ash outside in this heat.'

Unconcerned Mia continued to smoke. Felicity went ballistic. 'When I say stop, I mean fucking STOP.' She brought the van to a screeching halt and jumped to the hot, cracked earth. 'I'll hitch a car home if you don't quit smoking that stuff. It makes me sick.'

Mia squashed the joint and for the next part of the drive she sat with her arms folded, glaring into the distance.

They drove in silence to the nearby town. Outside a pub with a wide veranda, the Kombi's gears crunched as Felicity did a parallel park and tried to avoid a peppercorn tree. A bare-fronted man in a checked shirt, jeans and riding boots squatted on his haunches with his brown kelpie dog stretched out on the footpath beside him. He watched with interest as she parked, then rolled a cigarette and lit it.

'You catch up with the world and I'll meet you in the bar,' said Felicity, jumping from the van as the bloke tipped his Akubra and nodded to her.

Mia slid the side door open and sat on the floor with her legs dangling outside, scrolling through her messages. Becoming more agitated, she said, 'Bastard, bastard,' then locked the Kombi and stomped towards the pub, ignoring the kelpie wagging its tail in greeting. She marched into the bar where Felicity and the barman were laughing and had a look around for the toilets.

When she returned, Mia said, 'Give me a stiff drink, vodka on ice. A packet of chips too.'

She then straddled the stool beside the tall wooden bar, put her back to Felicity, and bantered and shared her crisps with another customer.

Felicity held her glass up to Mia's, but she ignored her and continued her conversation, the fella's eyes boring into her exposed front.

'Rude bugger, isn't she?' Felicity said to the barman as she finished her wine and paid the bill. She marched to the unlocked Kombi with Mia scrambling behind her.

'What's this sulking?' said Felicity, as she crunched the gears and the van roared off along the highway, scattering the galahs feeding on wheat dropped from haulage trucks.

Mia checked her phone and said, 'My boss is on the warpath.'

'He can't do much here. Why's he after you?'

She shrugged. 'He doesn't know where I am.'

'Great, a *Thelma and Louise* scenario? It's bizarre with your boss chasing you, isn't it?'

'I don't know...' The ringing of Mia's phone interrupted them. 'Hello...' She held it away and there was a shout, 'You bastard.' Mia turned it off and threw it on the floor.

***

They raced along the highway, passed an old church, a corrugated-iron hall and dilapidated tennis courts. The treeless Hay Plain was flat and monotonous, and the road stretched forever with few cars and slight bends every now and again to break the sameness of the landscape. Mia guarded her phone like a hawk, then dozed. Tiny, dry tussocks of grass and saltbushes danced in the scorching breeze on the scarred silvery grey earth while Felicity watched the intermittent willy-willys and the distant mirages wobble across the land.

'Mia, Mia, quick, quick, wake up. See this.'

A majestic blackish-brown prehistoric looking bird loomed, staring at them beside roadkill. As they climbed from the Kombi, Mia grabbed a tissue and covered her nose to ward off the rotten smell of a dead kangaroo. The wedge-tailed eagle flew off, its enormous talons and feathers on display while the two women stood, mouths open. As Felicity watched the bird soar higher and higher, something inside her stirred and rose, circling somewhere behind her ribs, as if this road trip were releasing part of herself back into the wild, to freedom.

The eagle's mate joined it, riding the thermals, silhouetted black against the sky. Felicity had read that eagles partnered for life and wondered whether they had rocky relationships like humans.

'Eagles feed on roadkill.' Felicity started the engine. 'Before they protected them, it was a sport to shoot them and string them along farm fences. As a child, I cried when I saw them pegged across the wires.'

Mia ignored her, plastered her feet on the dashboard and peeled off chewing gum and threw it in her mouth.

As Felicity drove, she thought of Mia's boss. He couldn't be threatening her? What is going on with this girl? She turned to Mia, smiled, and seized her chance. 'Now you must tell me about what's happening with your boss.'

Mia was silent. After some time, she huffed and crossed her arms. 'It's a long story. They're a bunch of slackers at my work. I do all the jobs, know what I'm doing, and the others don't like it. This trip's my gift to myself, a well-deserved break from them all.'

She stared into the distance, heaved a sigh, and continued with a quiet monotone voice. Her mother, Lisa, who she had not heard from since she was ten, appeared in Canberra to visit her from Los Angeles. She wanted to return to the places she had lived as a child.

'Even though I swore at her, told her not to drive in Canberra, she insisted. She'd paid for the stupid rented car. She thought she was still in the States and took the wrong side of the road on a corner. I ended up with serious injuries, but she walked away without a scratch. It tore me up, I was off for two months.' Mia dabbed her eyes with a tissue. 'I got sick of staying at home, silly me wanted to go back to work. The doctor told me he'd give me more painkillers.'

Mia rested her head against the window and after a long pause began again. 'They were short staffed when I returned. I love my job, but the pills buggered me, couldn't sit in front of the computer for long.'

'Hmm, that's nasty, having an accident. Where's your mother now?'

'The bitch flittered back to the States, haven't heard from her since.' Mia pulled a piece of her hair and stared out the side window.

'Who looked after you? What did you do to get better?'

There was a ring of the phone. Mia hesitated and said, 'I never did that. He's lying.' She finished the call and glared into the distance.

'Is everything okay?'

'Bastards can stick their job.' Mia wrapped her hair around the top of her head and rustled in the glove box to find combs to hold it. 'I'm here because I walked out.'

'How are you surviving…?' said Felicity as she belatedly wondered whether Mia had enough money to pay for this trip.

'Have Dad's credit card. I've always paid my way, but after the accident it was useful.'

'You landed a good father, you're lucky.'

A buzz interrupted them again. 'No, I don't owe you anything. Stick it up your arse,' Mia's voice ricocheted through the cabin and she threw the phone behind her, folded her arms and sat staring ahead.

'You are on the warpath!' said Felicity.

She always enjoyed the drive through the wide-open spaces, occasional "roll-a-pollies", saltbush, and off in the distance, the clump of trees and shimmering mirages. Road trips gave her a sense of freedom, a time to think, but Mia's tedious, ever-changing mood and the pinging of the phone and strange calls unsettled her.

The air-conditioning worked overtime, and the engine roared, scattering the birds on the highway. Mia fidgeted, and Felicity thought of the havoc Alan wreaked in the district with his affairs with different married women. And without her knowing, he had mortgaged the sheep to a dodgy broker and bought himself an expensive 4WD fitted out with leather seats and a pop-up camper so he could take off.

'Rotten swindler,' she said out loud and Mia glared at her.

Half-way across the Hay Plain, she swerved to miss a mob of kangaroos bounding from nowhere, and the Kombi rattled as she eased off the accelerator and guided the vehicle away from the ditch.

It shocked Mia out of her stupor. 'Shit, what happened there?'

There was a sudden blast from Felicity's phone. 'Let it ring out and see who it is.'

Mia grabbed it and glanced at the screen. 'Randall? That's a strange name.'

'Thanks, he's my Mr Fixer. I'm hoping to meet him for a drink in Mildura.'

Felicity smiled and navigated a convergence of long trucks with their huge loads, the drivers blasting their horns as the van with the two women sailed past. A white 4-wheel drive came whizzing towards them on the other side of the road. As it approached, a whistle came from Felicity's lips and she did a double take at the figure driving, Alan, her thoughts conjuring him into reality. When the vehicle raced passed with the occupant giving a wave, she laughed. It couldn't be him, he never waved at other cars in the bush, too mean and arrogant.

Soon they were at a dusty roundabout at Hay.

'Aren't we stopping? I need a break,' said Mia, stomping her feet.

'Can't you wait? We'll stop at a rest area closer to the next town so we can stay at Mungo tonight and see the Walls of China in the morning.' Felicity drank a swig from her water bottle. 'Not sure if they'll be open in the heat, but it's worth a try. What do you think?'

'Yeah, I want to hear about Mungo Man's return to country.' Mia stretched her arms and retrieved her phone for a brief conversation. 'I can't talk now, just organise it for me,' she said.

The tone sent a ripple of unease up Felicity's spine. She narrowed her eyes and squinted; her eavesdropping created more questions. But for now she said nothing.

'Let's see if Mungo's a goer. Get the number for the info centre at Balranald.'

When Mia rang, no one answered. 'They want me to leave a number, there's no way I'm talking to anyone today.'

'Don't worry. Ring on my mobile and leave my number. They can ring back.' When Mia got through, Felicity recited her number.

Later Felicity's phone rang, and Mia spoke to the woman, asking whether there was accommodation and a tour of the Walls of China.

'Boxes ticked. She's booked the Shearers Quarters, next to where everyone meets.' A high-pitched buzz pierced the conversation. Mia scanned the number, scrunched up her face and ignored it. 'We can tag along with a group of VIPs.'

'Wow. Who are they?'

'Didn't say.'

The Kombi swayed as they turned the corner into Balranald. Mia rubbed her eyes, wanting a rest, but Felicity insisted they couldn't stay. They were travelling west, and the setting sun made driving difficult, especially at twilight when wildlife, kangaroos, wild pigs, and birds crossing the road caused chaos if vehicles hit them. There was no one to rescue them on this isolated route.

Chapter 5

Felicity groaned, threw the keys at Mia, and watched her climb into the Kombi and roar through the main street. She signed herself into the air-conditioned club with its garish red carpet and menu of Chinese and Australian meals. After ordering lunch and a wine, she puzzled over the situation with Mia's work. It didn't ring true; a workmate wouldn't be annoyed if she was so good at her job. And what was she talking about on the phone? Why did she leave Canberra so quickly? Was there trouble?

When Mia returned, she stood for several minutes at the club's entrance, surveyed the rooms before she ambled to the bar. Strange, thought Felicity.

'What's a young woman like you doing here?' said the barman, taking her food and drink order. Felicity grinned when Mia ignored him.

At lunch Mia never spoke. She scrolled through her phone, listened to messages, swore, then drank a large glass of iced lemonade and burped, picked at her steak and salad, and left the building saying she was going for a swim.

Felicity scratched her head. This girl was all over the place. She still didn't understand her situation at work. And her bloody phone…. she was more difficult than she remembered her kids, and how did she know there was a pool? After finishing her meal, she rummaged in her bag for her mobile and after two tries at the number, the person answered.

'Hello, Randall.' She grinned and tapped her fingers on the table. 'I'm in Balranald, should arrive at Mungo this evening.' She paused. 'You want to go through those farm figures, don't you? Let's do it over a drink, then have dinner.'

There was an outburst of laughter at the other end of the phone as they made the arrangements.

'I'll be in a Kombi, and there'll be someone with me. If I haven't run over her.' She sniggered. 'No, it's not like that, it'll be better if I explain in person. See you tomorrow. Ciao!'

She grinned as she poured iced water from a jug on the bar into her bottle and stepped from the club into the heat. 'Shit!' The van had vanished, and she didn't have Mia's number or a hat.

The flies buzzed and the local dogs lay in a stupor as she stomped the streets searching for her. She marched to the river and abruptly stopped, having forgotten the beauty of the majestic red river gums that reached to the sky. She sighed in sadness; they didn't deserve to be under constant threat from politicians who wanted them logged.

As she looked around, there was a family picnicking, so Felicity inquired if they had seen her friend in a Kombi. They shook their heads.

Beads of sweat covered her face, and she cursed as she hurried across the reserve and over the highway. If she were alone, she would turn left to Mildura and leave here. Bugger that self-centred brazen girl she thought as she saw the pool in the distance, but no van.

Suddenly the roar of an engine and gravel flying from the edge of the road shattered the stillness of the day.

The driver banged on the side door and yelled, 'Hey, you, want a lift?'

'Where've you been?' snapped Felicity, baring her teeth.

'I did a few laps and feel much better after that boring drive.' She flung her wet hair around the cabin and Felicity ducked from the drops. 'Off we go in the time machine.' Mia grated the gears in preparation.

'You're not driving to Mungo?'

'Only to the turnoff.'

'It's tough going into the sunset, you need your wits about you. Visibility's low and wildlife everywhere. Someone I know hit an emu and the car was a write-off.'

Mia's face was defiant, and she scoffed as she pulled the Kombi from the curb. 'Bossy-boots, it's my vehicle, and I said I'd drive.'

'Look, it's horrendous on these roads.' Felicity put her hand on Mia's arm. 'Promise me you'll go slow and no swerving, I don't want to end up in the ditch.' The van hit a bump, and Felicity yelled, 'Shit, don't kill me yet.'

Vapour rose from the shimmering bitumen, and the van's fan struggled to keep the interior cool, and on they drove, their phones again out of range. Scrubby trees formed silhouettes against the extravagant purple and rose-coloured sky, and while the clouds softened and transformed the harsh day to twilight. The setting sun made the road ahead difficult to see.

Felicity fell silent on the open stretch, allowing her thoughts free range. She hoped to be a new woman when she returned, somehow dumping Alan's emotional legacy along the way. His constant barrage of lies and dishonesty wore her down, and his lawyers increased her stress. But their battle would have to end someday. Emily's behaviour was diabolical towards her, as damaging as her father's conduct at times. Felicity knew she would have to be patient, and her dispute with Alan had to resolve before their relationship improved.

She thought about meeting up with Randall, and her body tingled with an overwhelming urge of excitement. She smiled and squeezed her hands, determined to have fun with him after they discussed her dreary but essential financials.

During the changeover, Felicity had a few swigs of her water bottle and told Mia the staff at Mungo would leave a key out for them as late arrivals.

'The music, please.'

The Kombi rattled through the growing darkness, its lights shining like a torch into the wildness. Suddenly it veered in one direction. Felicity wrestled with the steering wheel to keep it on the road. 'Bloody hell, a flat tyre! Hope the spare's okay?'

'I... think so.'

'Bugger.' Felicity stopped the van, and rested her elbows on the wheel, her hands covering her eyes, and said in a low voice, 'Did you bring a torch?'

Mia shrugged and hesitated before she stepped from the Kombi into the approaching night with its menacing shadows.

Felicity cursed as she shooed Mia away and pulled the spare from under the chassis.

'The tyre's ripped from those rocks back there.'

'Why didn't you check this spare tyre?' Felicity threw it on the ground. 'It needs air. The light from the Milky Way won't change it.' Her sarcasm cut through the darkness.

The spooky shadows cast by the night made Mia's hand tremble as she shone the flashlight from her phone to where Felicity squatted and swore as she repaired the tyre.

When it was fixed, Felicity said, 'It'll be a slow journey otherwise we'll have no wheel left.'

Felicity shivered, placed her arms around herself and gulped three deep breaths before she climbed into the Kombi, the lights beaming into the distance. A wild goat appeared, so she dimmed them and sounded the horn.

In the night's stillness, the unanswered questions about her passenger weighed on her mind. Mia's moods swung from over the top, exuberant to angry and upset. She wanted her way no matter what, but this was only the first day of their road trip and Felicity was ready to strangle her.

When Mia whined about the speed of their journey, an exasperated Felicity told her to count the stars and that she could stay up and keep the tally going when she arrived at Mungo. Mia laughed, and they both hurrahed when the lights of Mungo appeared.

***

The high-pitched sound of a bird woke Felicity at dawn, and she couldn't place the call so stretched, rolled out of the sleeping bag and went to the veranda to look for it. Her search was unsuccessful. She threw on light pants and tossed a jumper around her neck and enjoyed her morning cuppa, sitting on the wooden steps and listening to the sounds of the breaking day – the insects caught in the night-lights and buzzing flies, hoping Mia was going to be in a better mood.

At seven o'clock she had to shake Mia to wake her. 'We've got to get going, there's an early morning tour with Barney our Indigenous guide. He's great and makes Mungo come alive,' she said with enthusiasm.

'Don't want to go... I'll stay and sleep.' Mia pulled a sheet over herself and turned to the wall.

'But you wanted to see Lake Mungo?'

Mia didn't answer.

Felicity ate her toast, then packed their gear to leave at the end of the guided tour. With a dodgy tyre and no spare, they couldn't risk driving the loop by the dry lake and the Walls of China, the 70-kilometre Mungo track.

'Too early for me.' Mia grumbled as she caught up with Felicity on her way to the visitor's centre.

'You miss the best part of the day.'

Felicity extended her hand in greeting to Barney, the Indigenous tour guide, dressed in a khaki National Park uniform with an enormous hat and a long wooden stick. He gripped her palm, clutched it to his own and said, 'Flea, I haven't seen you for ages.'

They chatted about what they had been doing, and acknowledged the many connections they had in common, his family well known in the area. He smiled as Mia appeared. 'Your offsider?'

Felicity removed her sunglasses and looked at him with a grin.

'Other fellas will be here soon, foreigners scared of country – these wide-open spaces. Think they'll get bitten by a snake or a spider.' His laugh creased his wrinkled face as he patted his ample stomach.

About ten minutes later a small bus sped up the track, halted, and seven well-dressed men of various ages in casual clothes alighted. Felicity laughed to herself as she noticed the fellows eyeing Mia and jostle to stand next to her during the introductions. She moved aside to read the welcoming sign. It explained that Lake Mungo was a meeting place where three Aboriginal groups: one from the west, one from the north and one from the south come together to care for the area and offer a welcome. Barney called her back to the group.

'Welcome to the gathering place of the Paakantji, Ngyiampaa, Mutthi Mutthi people here at Lake Mungo. Greetings to our French, Italian, American and Aussie visitors. I hope you enjoy your stay.'

To a hushed audience, Barney outlined the spiritual signif-icance of Lake Mungo to First Nation people and why the return of Mungo Man and Mungo Woman to their ancestral country was so important.

'It's over 50 million sunrises since they lived here, so they're incredibly special people to us.' He broke into an enormous smile and mentioned how pleased everyone was to have them home.

Mia asked a series of questions about the age of the artefacts and burial remains leading to a heated discussion between

Barney and the group. To resolve the issue, Mia confidently explained the technical aspects of dating materials in situ.

Adrian, the Australian leader of the group who was standing next to Felicity, pulled a face and said, 'That girl knows her stuff!'

'And I'm totally surprised,' said Felicity with a grin.

The delegation was soon laughing at Barney's antics. He produced a dead snake from a Perspex box and pointed at the various parts. The group muttered to themselves when they discovered the snake's rapid ability to kill. Barney winked at Felicity and she grinned. As he talked to the visitors, Barney mixed the mundane with Dreamtime stories. He gave them time to inspect the exhibits and there was a ripple of nervous laughter when Mia in her shorts and figure-hugging top bent to examine the ancient emu egg shards.

Fifteen minutes later Barney ordered the group together. He explained the fragility of the dunes, how everyone was to stay with one another, and he insisted that those who didn't have a hat were to take one from him. 'Stay together and drink lotsa water is the motto.'

They piled into the waiting van for the visit to the Walls of China, and Felicity sat next to a debonair Frenchman.

'Bonjour, welcome. Are you enjoying your trip?' They exchanged pleasantries, then she asked what the group intended to do in Australia.

In his broken English, he explained they were scientists; they were surveying the country as part of an important project. 'We are tourists here.' He was very cagey, vague, when she questioned him about his work. He told her they had been to Wilpena Pound and other areas of South Australia and were going to Broken Hill after this visit.

As Felicity alighted from the bus, she overheard an excited Mia say. 'But I'm married.' She shook her head in disbelief. Her words at the centre were intelligent and thoughtful, Adrian was correct, she knew what she was talking about. It baffled Felicity, how many personas did this girl have? The academic, the IT whizz or the dizzy, mixed-up girl?

She turned and focussed her attention on the horizon and gasped again at the breathtaking scenery. Each time she visited Lake Mungo, the dunes surprised her. Another world taken from an extra-terrestrial science-fiction movie lay before her, the craggy, weathered crescent-shaped Walls of China. They were similar in form to a dune but sturdier, made of sand and clay blown from the ancient lakebed, the eroded structures comparable in shape to the carved walls of a European Cathedral.

'This is surreal, spiritual,' Felicity said to Adrian, who fended off the flies with a wave of his hand.

'I agree, I'm blown away by these dunes, they come out of nowhere.'

He was a tall man with a good head of grey hair, a high forehead, and a chiselled bearded face. A person she felt at ease with as they listened to Barney together.

Barney stood everyone in the middle of ancient campfires with the soil still black and made them try to imagine what it was like for his people when the lake was full of water. He showed them shards and artefacts of former times and guided them behind the dunes where they viewed the low scrub of the surrounding district stretching to the horizon.

Felicity glanced at her watch when they returned to the bus. 'Barney, do you know where Mia is? We're going now.'

'She can't be far away, she was with us a few minutes ago.' Barney surveyed the dunes. 'Adrian, is any of your party missing?'

He did a body count. 'Yes, two of the group. Don't know where they've gone.'

After waiting for some time in the scorching sun, Barney suggested he return everyone to the visitor's centre. 'You can use the facilities and stay cool while Adrian and I go look for these bloody pests. I hope they have water.'

They jumped into the 4WD and sped off back to the lookout while those at the centre watched the Apostlebird's shenanigans as they begged for food.

'Don't feed those bludgers,' said Felicity, shooing the birds away. 'Leave them to collect their own insects and seeds, they're pests.'

She paced the veranda, her gaze darting every few minutes to the dirt road. After an anxious wait, Barney's 4WD approached and came to an abrupt halt. Everyone crowded around the truck for a glimpse of the missing trio.

The latecomers leapt from the vehicle in a buoyant mood. 'We lost our way.' Mia waved her hands as she spoke. 'I hunted for shards to photograph and all the dunes look the same, so we didn't know where we were.'

Adrian knitted his brows and crossed his arms as he ordered the group together. 'At the beginning Barney said you were to have hats, water and long-sleeved shirts, sunscreen. This is not Europe or Canberra - the sun is unrelenting. We're now behind our schedule, the bus will leave in twenty minutes for lunch at the Lodge. If you need any advice, talk to Barney, I'm helping Felicity fix her tyre.' Barney gave her his pump.

'I'll do this.' With a broad grin, Adrian nabbed the tool from her.

Felicity assessed Adrian's smooth unblemished hands, 'You sure? I do this all the time.' She watched him attach it and use his foot to increase the pressure and fill the tyre with air.

'What are you doing out in these parts?' said Adrian.

'I'm a farmer caught in this bloody drought,' she laughed, fanning herself with her hat. 'Before I had an interesting job in the scientific world, gave it up to come back to the land. But that's another story. Where are you going after this?' she asked, as she packed the equipment in its box.

'We'll do some more exploring, then go to Broken Hill. I go back to Adelaide and the rest of the group return to the US next week. We have reports to write.'

'So what are you doing out here?'

'It's for Government, international stuff, can't say much.'

'Hmm, it'd have to be dumping. Aussie governments love the vast inland. They identify it as a dump for their special projects, especially when they score points from our allies.' Felicity stood with her arms crossed and a scowl on her face. 'They have a habit of not investigating the full impact and they don't clean up their mess – look at Maralinga.'

Adrian seemed to wilt under her gaze. He said little as they traipsed back to the group where Mia made a dash to get her accomplices' contact details before they left.

He took Felicity's hand and with a broad grin said goodbye. 'You have a handful there. Good luck,' She heaved a sigh, and he laughed, reaching into his pocket for his business card. 'Here are my details. If you're around Adelaide you could give me a ring for a catch-up.'

After thanking Barney, she waved to the others and strolled to the van to wait for her fellow traveller. She made a promise to herself to research what Adrian's group was doing in the Australian outback when she got to Adelaide. It may be secret stuff, but someone would know. One of Shirley's contacts? Would she catch-up with Adrian? He was interesting...

Chapter 6

This time Felicity insisted on driving and Mia capitulated with a grunt, slamming her door. They roared off with a hoot of the horn and a last wave as they left the site. Silence spread and filled the gaps between the two women. Mia fidgeted with her bangles, her hair, her phone, then switched the radio on to find only static.

'Leave it! We're too far out of contact.' Felicity sped up and manoeuvred the van around emus with their dancing tails.

Ten kilometres later, Mia called in panic, 'Stop, I'm going to be sick.' Felicity huffed as she halted the van, and Mia leapt out to vomit on the side of the road.

'Here's your water.' Felicity threw the drink bottle, which bounced along the ground. 'Sun stroke, out without a hat and no liquids in this heat. You'll get no sympathy from me.' The pitch of her voice increased. 'Just drink that bloody water.'

Mia sat under a tree with her head between her legs while the flies hovered. After some time, she climbed slowly to her feet and stumbled to the side door, looking dazed. 'I'll lie in the back. My head hurts.'

As she drove, Felicity turned to check on the patient and her anger changed to concern as Mia appeared wan and drowsy. She tapped her forehand with the heel of her hand, trying to recall the treatment for heatstroke, and when she remembered, she pulled to the side of the road.

'Here, have sips of this water.' She lifted Mia's head and held a bottle to her lips. 'Drink lots of this, otherwise you'll get dehydrated, ill.'

'Tab…let, my head.' Mia gave a lethargic point to her bag.

'No way, it'll make it worse. Water and salt are what you need. Now lie on this side to keep the blood flowing.' Felicity helped her turn, then grabbed a small towel from her bag and soaked it with water from her drinking bottle with the parched earth gulping the excess. Mia groaned as Felicity wiped her face and adjusted the towel around her neck, laying a larger towel on the floor in case she puked.

'How are you feeling?' Mia stared at the roof and moaned. 'We need a doctor to check you so I'll drive fast, nonstop to the hospital. Keep wiping yourself with the towel and sipping this. It'll be rough going.'

Felicity gritted her teeth with frustration when it suddenly dawned on her: she was a rescuer again, and this time it was an ill, anxiety-riddled young woman.

'It's crazy, here I am rescuing someone when my own emotional resilience is low,' she muttered to herself. 'Taking on this for a long weekend of escape.'

Her friends had remarked on how stoic she was during her troubles with Alan. What they didn't know was underneath she was in turmoil and her drinking was excessive. Her only solace from the drudgery of work was to sit and contemplate under her favourite tree.

She chuckled to herself when she remembered the day, amid her dejection and despair, an old crow had hopped to her, tilted its head to the side and watched. She swore it winked and roared with laughter at her own mad situation. Her healing began.

Felicity wondered whether Mia always played these stunts of "poor me, help me" to get attention, to show her neediness. Or was it deeper than that, did she have a psychological problem which made her behave in this way?

The gears shuddered as she negotiated potholes on the bumpy road and scattered flocks of galahs and parrots as she sped through the parched terrain in the clattering van. She wriggled and hummed a tune until Mia's groans diverted her attention, and she turned to check her. 'Do you need anything?' Mia writhed in pain as her legs cramped. 'Keep drinking that water.'

Felicity wondered whether she should ring an ambulance to meet them on the way, but there was no signal when she picked up her phone. She had a flash from her childhood when sickness and death had stalked her mother for years. Her father had sped in the Holden with her frightened sister and herself in the back tugging at a blanket wondering if their mother, slumped in the passenger seat, would live or die before they reached the hospital. She still missed her mother.

When her mother died, her father relied more on Felicity around the farm, while her sister did the housework. Her father had always insisted that Felicity would take over the property. Now, with the countryside speeding past, her mind flashed. It was time to decide whether she wanted to stay a farmer at *Neerea*.

Her shoulders relaxed when they hit the sealed road, and they passed smaller farms and vineyards. She stopped the Kombi and climbed in beside her patient, whose eyes were closed and she was pale and sweaty, her breathing shallow.

'You're going straight to emergency at Mildura, they'll check you and you can decide what to do from there. Keep sipping that water.'

'Hooray,' Felicity shouted when she saw the bridge spanning the Murray River with Mildura on the other side. There was a woman wheeling a baby in the blistering sun, so she pulled into the curb and asked for directions to the hospital.

The Kombi came to an abrupt halt outside the Emergency department, and Felicity raced in and found someone on duty. The nurse organised a short young man in a blue gown with spiked hair and tattoos on his arms, to take a mobile stretcher to the van. He moved an incoherent Mia like a feather and in a matter of minutes manoeuvred her into Emergency. Felicity grabbed Mia's bag, locked the Kombi and followed the procession, explaining that she thought Mia had heatstroke.

'These young people annoy me they don't understand the harm the sun can do. I suppose she wasn't wearing a hat.' The grey-haired, thin nurse thumped her clipboard on the table. 'You must help us with the paperwork. She's in no fit state.'

'I know little about her and I'm reluctant to go through her gear,' said Felicity.

'There are worse problems. I need her full name and date of birth.' The nurse concentrated on the admission form while

Felicity rustled through Mia's shoulder bag for identification. All she could find was an old speeding fine with Mia's name and address.

'There're no details of her date of birth,' said Felicity, examining the fine print. 'She told me she was twenty-five or was it four?'

'Okay, I'll fill in the rest of the information when she's better.'

'Heatstroke, how long will she stay here?'

'We'll examine her first, maybe two nights, should be discharged then, if it goes well. Leave your number and we'll contact you.'

'I've booked myself into the hotel near the river. You can contact me there.' Felicity sighed with relief when she left the hospital. The burden had lifted with someone else taking charge of this young woman.

She pulled the van into the kerb of the palm-lined street and hurried into the hotel's reception, where large mirrors plastered the wall. She gasped and dropped her bags and ran her hand through her messy hair, tried to smooth her ruffled shirt and brush the dust from her face and clothes while she waited for the receptionist.

'You've two bookings, Madam. When will the other person arrive?' said the assistant with bright red lipstick and a beehive hairstyle who seemed to have trouble taking Felicity's details and finding the key to the room.

'I'm sorry, the other person is in hospital, you'll have to cancel her booking.'

'You must pay at this late stage.'

'I'll take this up with the manager later.' Felicity answered through her teeth. 'Where can I park?'

Hot, stale air blasted Felicity as she unlocked the door to her room. She threw her bags on the floor, turned on the air conditioning and opened the sliding door to the balcony. She was thinking of taking a long shower when the hotel phone rang.

'Yes?'

'Hello, Felicity? I'm Jenni, a nurse at Mildura hospital.' Felicity's stomach contracted with fear. 'Could you come to the hospital? I'd like to speak to you about the patient, Mia Holland, and her issues.'

'What! I'm not even related to her. Sorry, don't think I'd be of any help.'

Felicity showered and went to a deli and bought a salad roll for lunch, before she appeared at the hospital. 'May I see the nurse dealing with Mia Holland? Can't remember her name. Thanks.' The receptionist directed her to a dark-green upholstered bench in the waiting room.

A young nurse with red hair, pale skin, freckles from too much sun, and an upturned nose came into the room and extended her hand to Felicity. 'Hello... Felicity, is it?'

'Yes.'

'Good, come with me, I want to talk to you in private.' She led Felicity to a palm filled courtyard within the hospital.

'What's your relationship to Mia? She's confused but says you're the person to contact.'

Felicity frowned and paused. 'I only met her a few days ago. She arrived at my farm after being caught in a dust storm. She was on her way to Adelaide and wanted a travel companion, so I agreed to go with her.'

'Has her behaviour been strange?'

'Well… one minute she's quiet and polite, then she's angry, rude and other times okay, more like an adolescent.' Felicity frowned, struggling to explain. 'I don't know her, but she seems to be…escaping from something.'

'Um, she's suffering from heatstroke, but we think there may be more than that involved. Did you notice her taking any pills, tablets?'

'Drugs, shit…Sorry, excuse my language. I didn't notice. Why did she get you to contact me and not her family?'

The nurse's expression changed. 'Madam, I've a duty to tell you, this girl's not well. If you don't know what's going on, I'd suggest you search the car you've been driving. See what's there and let me know.' Felicity rose to leave. 'Don't you want to see her before you go?'

'No… I suppose I should.'

When they arrived in the ward, Felicity noticed six beds and the nurse yanked one with a surrounding curtain and peered in. 'She's asleep.' Mia lay on her side, her face grey and her dishevelled hair clung to the pillow. Felicity gulped a deep breath, glad there was medical care.

'I'll go,' said Felicity with relief. 'Let Mia know I'm at the hotel near the river when she's discharged. Thanks for telling me about the drugs. I'll search the van and ring you.'

As she drove away, Felicity's head spun. She slammed on the brakes at a pedestrian crossing, narrowly missing an old lady pushing a walker who glared at her. 'Sorry,' she mouthed as she turned into the hotel's car park.

Felicity sifted through the Kombi, not knowing if there was a time bomb of trouble there. She unloaded her sleeping bags, drink bottles and food and carried them to her room, leaving Mia's luggage behind.

After her last search, her knees buckled, and she sagged against the vehicle when she found nothing suspicious, and the tension further eased when she called the hospital to give an update.

Next was a trip to the car wash where she watched gushing water strip the dust and dirt from their trip, and she grinned as her body cried out for a complete makeover too. It was a startling reminder: she had locked herself away on the farm for far too long, and now she should revive her body and spirit.

Her jubilance was short lived. The stench of fumes mixed with dust made her gasp as she filled the petrol tank and asked for a new tyre.

'Come back in half an hour, you'll have it fixed and I'll check the others,' said the attendant whose face and overalls were stained black.

'Thanks for your help,' said Felicity when she returned and climbed into a safer, cleaner Kombi. Her body tingled as she drove to the hotel, her thoughts swirling around her date for the night.

Chapter 7

Under the full pressure of a warm shower, Felicity launched into her rejuvenation. She shampooed her hair and grabbed a large fluffy white towel, wrapped herself in its luxury and made her way to the balcony to enjoy the cool breeze.

From the wardrobe she took a black lace dress she had not worn for years. She drew in her breath and clutched the luxurious material to her, then little by little slipped the delicate dress over her head. Her hands moved sensuously over the curves of her body as she grinned and congratulated herself on the fit.

Mia had used a large hand mirror to plaster makeup on her face. It intrigued Felicity that a young person would go to so much trouble while driving or on a farm, but her efforts added to her attractiveness. She would adapt Mia's routine for her big night out with Randall.

Felicity began by smothering moisturiser over her dry skin and massaging it into her body. Fronting up to the mirror, she noticed her eyebrows had faded and pulled a face before she began rummaging through her makeup bag, searching for foundation and her favourite lipstick, but they had dried in the heat. It had to be powder and a stub of bright red lipstick she found in the bottom of her bag. Looking in the mirror, she laughed realising she could never match Mia's ability with makeup. After placing bergamot oil on the back of her wrists, she smiled and enjoyed the wafting scent.

She swept a brush through her hair and let the volume fall around her shoulders.

From a small, ornate, carved box she clasped a pair of peridot and diamond Art Deco earrings, their prettiness reminding her of her mother who had given them to her before she died. She worried her ears until the holes gave way and the gems danced in the light.

Admiring herself in the mirror made her lighter and happier, and she reached for her phone and snapped a selfie for her kids. They may enjoy seeing her out of her usual garb, Simon, yeah; Emily, no!

'Drink me,' said the little glittering spirit bottles in the mini-bar, and she made herself a long gin and tonic and relaxed on the grey lounge.

The TV weather forecast showed a low appearing over the state and she lifted her glass in celebration when she saw it might rain at the farm tomorrow. When the hotel phone rang, Felicity woke from her reverie and picked up her bag and breathed deeply as she stepped into the warm summer's night.

Randall sat at the bar reading the local paper with a half-mast beer. He was a tall, slim man, upright in posture, tanned, with thick and lustrous salt 'n' pepper hair, expressive ocean blue eyes and strong cheekbones and a well-defined chin and nose. He wore an open-necked pink shirt, flung over his knees was a black leather jacket, and his spotless riding boots poked from under the stool. His generous smile marked him out, and he grinned when he spotted Felicity, lifting his reading glasses and giving her the "once-over".

'Good to see you, Flea. You're looking smashing.'

'Thanks, Randall.' Her heart fluttered at the rich timbre of his voice, and she felt a thrill and excitement she had not experienced for a long time as she pecked him on the cheek.

He grabbed her in a bear hug and held her as he nuzzled into her neck 'Um, that's good, love the perfume.' They laughed, finished their embrace, and he winked. 'What do you want to drink?'

She placed her hand on his leg and manoeuvred herself onto a red bar stool.

'Sparkling wine, the best you have, thanks,' she said to the hovering barman. 'I'm celebrating my escape.'

'Cheers to old friends and adventures.' They clinked glasses. 'How was your trip?' 'Where's the driver?'

Felicity grimaced and closed her eyes. 'It's a long story. Will tell you later.'

'Is everything okay?' said Randall as she gave him a wry smile and asked what he had been doing since they last spoke.

'I've been out with the manager of my vineyard today. The drought's really taken its toll. Not good, but we're here to enjoy ourselves tonight after we do your business,' he said.

His phone rang, and he glanced at the number, nodded an excuse, and strolled to the courtyard to take the call.

Felicity watched the barman make cocktails enjoying the theatrics of his work and when Randall returned, he pulled from his pocket a list of financial issues to discuss. For the next little while they buried their heads in work. Then without warning Randall raised his hand, 'Stop, enough, time to enjoy ourselves.'

When he teased and flirted with her over a drink, she blushed and was dazed by his attention, realising it was a long time since she had this attentiveness.

'When's dinner?' Randall tapped his long-tapered fingers on his expensive watch.

'Oops, time carried me away. We should be there now.'

They hurried from the bar to the narrow steps of the restaurant on the lower floor to be greeted by a tall dark-haired waitress dressed in a white blouse and black tight skirt showing off her slim figure.

'Good evening, Madam, Sir, the name of your booking?'

The ambient atmosphere with its subdued operatic music, dim lighting and golden glow took Felicity's breath away, and she clutched Randall's arm in delight.

They checked the menu and Randall reached for the crisp roll and olive oil. 'Pity, you can't have your usual steak and three vegies,' joked Felicity. 'This degustation menu looks so delicious.'

The waitress, a young woman with dancing dark eyes and hair coiled at the top of her head, came to explain the options and matching wines in a heavy accent.

'How long have you been working here?' said Randall at the end of her explanation.

'Two months, I'm from… Italia.' She smiled and then rummaged in the cabinet for the wines for each plate.

'What a treat! Northern Italian dishes and wines.' Felicity held up her glass. 'This is what I miss, living in the bush. Salute.'

'Especially to you, Flea.' They touched glasses. 'You've lots of stamina, farming in a drought.' Randall manoeuvred his leg against hers, caught hold of her hand and squeezed it. She gulped and a shiver went through her body as she thought of what it might mean.

They laughed and toasted each other throughout the meal. Before they served dessert, Felicity sat upright, picked up the serviette and wiped the corners of her mouth. 'Now to my moment of reckoning. I've a problem and need to talk it out.'

In a subdued voice, she discussed the "Mia dilemma". She explained Mia's behaviour on the farm, and how on the road she had become more erratic, up one moment and angry the next. 'I'm still bewildered. Half-way across the Hay Plain she lights up a joint, and I went ballistic.'

'Did she offer you some,' he chuckled, but when he saw her stern look, he said, 'I remember that stuff makes you sick.'

'Don't go there!' She lay her hand over his. 'I forgot to mention, her behaviour at Mungo landed her in hospital, I could go on…I'm not sure if there's something wrong with the girl or she's into funny stuff.'

'Drugs? Are you kidding?' He lifted an eyebrow. 'How did you get yourself into that? You're supposed to be smart!'

'I have no excuse. That's what drought does to you, it muddles your head, and I thought a break from *Neerea* would help, but now I seem to have ended up in a bigger mess.'

'Interesting. Where was this magic tour heading?'

'Adelaide. I'd planned to stay at Shirl's place for a few days. We took a side trip to Lake Mungo because Mia wanted to go there.' Felicity concentrated on a small part of the tablecloth as she spoke. 'I'm not sure what to do. I need to find my way home or get to Adelaide but don't want to leave her stranded.'

Randall hesitated, leant against the back of his chair, and cleared his throat. 'Um…I might solve part of this mess as I'm off to visit my mate, Merv, out Menindee way. Not tomorrow, but maybe the next day. Life's tough for him, his wife died two years ago and now the drought. He won't come and see me so I'm going to his place and organising lunch.' Randall placed his sun-tanned hand on her arm and his eyes twinkled. 'We could drive on to Broken Hill and stay the night to give us time to work out how to get you to Adelaide.'

'One room or two?' She said nervously when his eyes lit up and he smirked. 'Sounds good, but I don't want to hear more drought stories.' She squeezed his hand. 'Let me think about it.'

'Now tell me, these sparkling earrings of yours. They're peridots, aren't they?' Randall moved his chair closer as she threw her head back and laughed, the earrings catching the light. Fuelled by more wine, they laughed and teased one another until the waitress arrived to tell them the restaurant was closing. They strolled from the restaurant hand in hand, Randall saying hello to business clients as they entered the street.

'Can see the headlines – "Randall's hitched to a new girl-friend".' He placed his arm around her. 'They're friends of my ex-wife, the town gossips. Are you shouting me a night cap?'

When Felicity returned from the bathroom, she found Randall sprawled across the lounge with wine and glasses waiting on the table.

'We'll leave early on our way to Broken Hill as I want to spend a few hours with Merv. What'll you say to your hippy?'

'I'll go to the hospital tomorrow and find out what she wants to do. They'll probably discharge her the following day.'

'Flea, you don't owe her anything. Let her be.' Randall threw his hands in the air, exasperated. 'Leave her van in the hotel parking lot, a note and the keys at reception.'

'That's too easy. See that stuff over there, the sleeping bags, Eskies, they're mine. How will I get them home?'

Randall pursed his lips. 'I'll take them. You can pick them up when you return.' He pointed to a large ice box. 'I can borrow that for Merv's place.'

'I don't want to leave Mia on her own.' Felicity paced the room. 'She's confused and not well. Someone needs to care for her when she leaves hospital.'

'Whatever you like. I'll visit Merv on my own,' said Randall with a narky voice, as he waved his hand in disgust. 'You mix in her drug world.'

A moment of silence, then Felicity gave him a steely eyed gaze. 'Okay, I'll come with you, but we must call it a night. I'm out of kilter, and I don't trust myself.'

'But...'

'No buts. It's been a fantastic night. The forecast says it'll rain tomorrow, so we may celebrate when I meet you next.'

Felicity bundled the sleeping bags and opened the door while reluctantly Randall followed with Eskies stuffed with other bits and pieces from the Kombi. He kissed her on the cheek as they left the air-conditioned room and walked with his head lowered to the 4WD.

Once they had packed his luggage into the vehicle, he hugged her. 'Flea, you're a hard woman breaking up our fun. I'll check arrangements with you tomorrow,' he said, scratching his head as he receded into the dark.

Felicity lay on the bed with her thoughts dancing through their dinner. She hadn't enjoyed herself so much in a long time. In her head, she nervously played *what if* regarding their relationship and concluded for the moment she wasn't ready for another entanglement yet? Or was she?

She grinned to herself when she thought of how her father had introduced Randall to her years ago as a trustworthy financial adviser. She had engaged him to work through her finances when Alan almost sent her broke. He was her financial saviour, restructuring her assets and saving her farm.

Retrieving their half-finished bottle of wine, she poured herself a glass and mused on her broken promise of not drinking too much. Now time to ponder on Randall.

When they worked on her finances, he bossed her around and made sure she understood the implications of her decision making on the farm. Every time they met she prised a little of his past from him. An only child whose mother raised him by working two jobs. His marriage had ended in the last couple of years, and his former wife lived in Melbourne with a new partner. He never mentioned other women, but maybe she needed to check whether there was anyone else in his life. She closed her eyes and grinned, he was fun and good company.

Felicity floated around the room and dropped her "Cinderella clothes" on a chair. She grabbed a bottle of water and climbed into the crisp bedsheets, dropping a precious earring to the floor.

Sleep eluded her. Tossing and turning, she tried to thrash out what she wanted from Randall after the battering and bruising she received from Alan's antics. A romantic relationship, just a fling or back to business? She worried over what would happen to Mia if she buggered off to Broken Hill with him.

Love, loss and guilt. A heart-breaking poignancy ran through her as she climbed out of bed and retreated to the balcony, peering through the streetlights to the park below until the buzzing of insects forced her inside.

In the morning, Felicity yawned as she brought the clock into focus. Eight o'clock, she never slept this late. From the balcony, she surveyed the day, stretched, inhaled deep breaths, and rang Bill for an update, so grateful not to be chasing sheep.

After a long luxurious shower, she read the papers over excellent coffee and French brioche toast with jam. She ruffled her hair in the mirror behind the reception desk as she asked, 'Any suggestions for a makeover today? I need the lot: a facial, a haircut, and my nails, serious pampering.'

'Well, you'll be busy.' The woman laughed and presented a business card. 'This beauty salon has a hairdresser next door, they'll coordinate it for you.'

'Thanks. Now I want to stay in my room tonight, if possible. Off to Broken Hill tomorrow.'

The woman checked the booking schedule. 'Your room's fine. Do you want to book for your friend?'

'Hmm, not sure of what's happening with my friend, she's in hospital. Can I put her van in your parking lot?' She handed over her credit card.

'Fine, give me her name, the car registration and I'll leave a note.' The receptionist smiled with understanding. 'Guess you can't do much.'

'I'll visit her today, so will let you know any changes. Thanks for your help.'

A haughty receptionist in a white coat ran through the beauty services on offer while Felicity sat uncomfortably in her chair. After she had made her choices, she sank onto the massage table. The blonde beauty therapist with bold, overarched eyebrows and caked makeup grabbed long thin brown bottles from an overhanging shelf. 'Now I think we'll use oil and another moisturiser to treat and soften your skin.'

'Best a farmer can do, I guess,' said Felicity with embarrassment.

Slap, slap, swish, swish. The woman slathered over Felicity's body layers of oil for a tough massage, and each pounding removed a layer of anxiety and distress from the past. Her old job in the science world in Sydney was interesting and demanding, but she had given it up to follow her father's wish for her to run the farm. She tensed as she relived her decision to return to the district and thought of the many naysayers who tried to pull her down. Those bastards received a shock when her sheep kept winning awards, but now with the drought there was little income to cover Alan's debts and run *Neerea*. Her bones were weary and her muscles knotted from the memories. She cleared her throat and wondered if her heart was still into battling the land on her own.

She decided not to visit Mia before her next appointment. The luxury of the hotel and the comfy bed lured her. She laughed to herself as she savoured the massage and indulged herself in lofty contemplation on a more agreeable subject, Randall.

Wash, snip, snip, foils. Time stood still while Felicity reclaimed some tranquillity. She forgot her embarrassment when the manicurist massaged her wrinkled, dry hands with their blemishes and calluses before the nail polish. Her phone rang; Randall organising a drink before his meeting.

'Wow, I love your new hairdo.' He stood up from his bar stool and touched the soft wispy layers, then pulled her to him in a hug. He whispered. 'You're looking very glamorous. Good enough to eat.'

'A day of indulgence and even have a new dress.' He grinned as she twirled and patted the colourful fabric. 'I broke my promise about not spending too much, but I'm in bliss…a wonderful feeling.' She kissed him on the cheek.

'You look fabulous. Now a wine or a cocktail?'

'A cocktail, I'm enjoying being decadent for a day!' He asked the barman for suggestions.

'Did you get to the hospital?'

'No, too busy being extravagant.' She touched him on the leg and raised her newly shaped eyebrows. 'I'll give Mia a ring tonight, explain what's happening.'

The drink mellowed her. After they had planned their trip to Merv's, she rested her hand on Randall's arm. 'I wish you didn't have to attend the meeting tonight.'

He flinched with surprise at her tone and smiled. 'Me too.' Understanding flickered between them. 'I'll bring breakfast and a coffee tomorrow. Pick you up at seven sharp.' He winked at her. 'It'll be very pleasant with you as my passenger.'

After their goodbyes, Felicity found an Italian take-away and then rang Mia. The number rang out. She called the hospital and asked for Mia's room. The phone continued to ring until the operator responded. 'Mia Holland isn't answering, you can leave a message?'

'Sure. It's important she gets this message. "Felicity called. I'm leaving early tomorrow for Broken Hill with a friend and have left your Kombi keys at the hotel reception. Have a safe trip, get better soon." Thanks.'

The operator read the message again and after Felicity ended the call, she danced around the room with her arms outstretched. Her body awake with excitement about her growing affection for Randall.

Chapter 8

Mia woke early to the movement and noise of the hospital, slipped out of bed and asked the dark-haired assistant with a tattoo peeping from her uniform whether they could discharge her.

'Don't know. I'll get a nurse for you.' She scurried away and fifteen minutes later one appeared.

'Hello, I was on duty when you arrived. You appear much better. I understand you want to be discharged?' She studied Mia's chart.

'Yes, I'm going to Adelaide today.'

'Will you travel with anyone?'

'My friend Flea.'

'Ah, I met her the other day, she was nice. A farmer,' said the nurse distracted as she glanced at the graphs again. 'It'd be better if you'd wait until the doctor does her rounds at nine, in case there are complications. You never know the full impact of heatstroke.'

'It's time for me to get going, I'm okay.' Mia pulled at her hair, finding it difficult to stand still.

'We can't stop you from leaving, but we should check you before you go. There are forms to sign.' She tapped her fingers on the chart and pinched her lips together. 'Will your friend look after you?'

'Yes, of course. Where are the papers? I have to leave.' She gathered her belongings and stuffed them into her bag.

'Have a shower and I'll have them ready at the desk.'

When she was sure the nurse had gone, she headed to reception.

'Mia Holland?' asked a nurse finishing his coffee and looking at her records. 'A message came in for you yesterday.' He hunted through the papers on the bench. 'Sorry, it was here a minute ago.'

She tip-toed along the wet corridor floor and asked a cleaning lady in a pink uniform how to get to the hotel.

'No car to drive?' The large woman rested on her mop. 'I take you to ambulance man. He helps.'

The cleaner left as Mia explained what she wanted to the lanky driver who had his legs sprawled in front of him with a tea bag dangling from his cup as he chattered to the nurse.

'We're not a taxi service. If you're discharged, you ring a cab.' He shooed her away with his hand.

Mia didn't move and her face crumpled into tears.

Surprised at her reaction, he softened. 'Okay, I'll give you a lift when I've finished this. You want a cuppa? Take a seat.'

Mia wiped her eyes with an old tissue as she thought of how she hated hospitals and the petty bureaucrats working in them. She kept staring at the nurse and ambulance driver and they soon concluded their conversation.

'C'mon, have you ever had a ride in one of these?' said the driver. 'You can sit here.' He pointed to the front seat. 'It's not far.'

Mia smiled as she climbed into the van.

'Why were you in hospital?'

Mia shrugged. 'Too much sun.'

'Ah, heatstroke. Where do you live?'

'Canberra.'

'Typical!'

When they arrived at the hotel, he helped her with her bags.

'Thanks for bringing me here,' said Mia, her teeth biting into her bottom lip as she gathered up her gear.

She flopped into a lounge chair and tried to snooze while waiting for the busy receptionist dealing with the morning surge of departures. When it was her turn, she rested her over-stuffed bag on the counter and said, 'I booked a room here. Can I use it now?'

'What's your name?' The woman glanced at the notes on her screen. 'Um, you went to hospital. Well, according to this, your bill's paid and you've checked out. Are you saying you didn't use the room?' Mia nodded. 'I suppose you can have a room for an hour or two seeing you spent the night in hospital but check out is at 10:30 am.'

Mia flicked back her hair and grinned, she couldn't believe her luck; she gave her details and inquired after Felicity. 'Oh, let me see. She booked out earlier. There's an envelope here for you.' The receptionist handed her the package and the room key and showed her the directions. 'Don't forget you must be out by 10:30. Next.'

Her hair hung over her face as she asked a cleaner, standing near an overfull trolley to direct her. The woman pointed to the third door. Mia stumbled into the room and dropped onto the bed in exhaustion. She ripped the envelope open, and the Kombi keys splayed on the bed. 'She's left me.'

Mia brooded, pouring her angst into grabbing the over-stuffed pillows and throwing them around and banging her fists on the mattress.

'You bitch, wait till I catch up with you.'

When her anger died, she lay down on the bed and tossed and turned, trying to sleep.

Later, a persistent yelling and loud knocking woke Mia, and in a daze, she struggled to the door.

'Miss, I must clean your room.'

'What's the time?'

'It's eleven fifteen and there's a busload of guests check-ing in soon.'

'Give me a few minutes. I need a good wash.'

'Okay, I'll finish another room, and come back. Please hurry.'

Mia lifted her arms, smelt the foul smell of her armpits and shirt, and filled the bath. Half an hour later there was more pounding on the door. After slipping on her dirty clothes, she snatched the hotel soaps and shampoos and threw them in her bag.

'Thanks, I've finished now,' said Mia to the cranky housekeeper.

Beads of sweat formed on her forehead and when she arrived at the office she asked, 'Where's my car parked?' The receptionist pointed to a map. 'I'm starving. Can you suggest a place to eat?'

Mia stumbled from the hotel to the parking area looking around for her Kombi, but in her lightheaded state, it was difficult to find. Once she was inside the van, she grabbed the first dress she saw and returned to the hotel, and when the receptionist wasn't watching, she slipped into the toilets to change before searching for some much-needed food.

She hid herself in the back of a cafe wearing her sunglasses, a hat and surrounded by her plastic bags. A little girl with pigtails peered over the booth and told her mother there was a funny lady in the next seat. Mia smiled at her and continued to wolf down poached eggs and toast, and iced coffee with double ice cream.

She re-read Felicity's message and muttered to herself, 'That bitch', and asked the waitress, 'How long does it take to drive to Broken Hill?'

'Sorry. My first week. I'll ask the owner.'

The boss, wearing a green apron stretched across his front, stared at her as he carried a stack of plates to the kitchen.

'Where are you going?' he said on his return.

'Broken Hill. I don't know how to get there. Is it far?'

He pointed out the door. 'Take the Silver City Highway through Wentworth, it's about three hours and a good road.' He hurried to the register to assist his customers.

Mia smirked as she thought of how she would surprise Felicity in Broken Hill. She gathered her bags, reorientated herself in the bright light of the street, and retraced her steps to the van.

There were a few wrong turns before Mia found the bridge over the Murray River and the road to Wentworth. The music thumped as she sped across the monotonous plains, beeping her horn and waving when a lone car or truck appeared and watching with awe as the kangaroos and emus moved away.

A dull, squeezing pain grew in her head and she reached for her water bottle to find it was empty. She needed sleep and skidded into the nearest rest area, leaving a gravel trail, dust, and a screeching flock of galahs. Tears of distress and anguish flowed as she locked the vehicle and lay a towel on the sticky back seat and dozed.

Something stirred outside. She waited; her heart fluttered. She heard the noise again and attempted to look through the window. Her mouth opened, but no sound emerged as her body froze.

A silver panel van had parked beside the Kombi, and a man in his forties, wearing large round glasses, sat at the wheel with the door open, and as Mia stared, he lifted them off and gave her a cheesy smile. His eyes were bloodshot and his lank, long black hair was awash in oil and his Adam's apple out of proportion to his neck. He pulled a cigarette stump from his mouth, curled the tapered figures of his other hand, and sent her a kiss.

She gasped and recoiled. Realising there was no one else in the area, she clambered from the back into the driver's seat and after a few goes at starting the vehicle, the van roared, and she rocketed up the highway.

Her heart raced as she glanced in the rear vision mirror and saw the car turn and follow her. The driver first tailgated her, then sped up, passed her, and then slowed down in front of the van. He drove at such a slow pace that she had to brake. He then moved to the other side and let her pass and repeated the manoeuvre. Mia clenched the wheel as beads of sweat dripped from her face. She concentrated on the highway ahead and didn't notice a juggernaut behind her, a big white motor home with an iridescent blue strip. It swung out beside her and the passenger shouted. 'Pull over.'

A shaken Mia pulled to the roadside and gazed into the distance as a couple ran towards her.

'Are you okay? We could see what that bastard was doing from the last rise in the road,' said the speaker, a rotund, balding man in his sixties, dressed in khaki shorts and a blue singlet. She stared at him. 'I'm Ken. Jan, you had better make some tea…'

Mia stepped from the van and her legs collapsed, sending her to the ground. When she came to, Jan helped her up and escorted her to the motor home.

'You lie here on the bed. You've had such a fright.' Jan moved to the sink, past the yellow and white curtained interior with chintzy knickknacks bolted into place. 'Sip this water, dear.' She placed a red-frilled cushion under Mia's head.

Mia dozed while Jan, who was short and built like a grey-hound with bleached blonde hair, fussed around the kitchen. When her mug of tea was ready, Mia said, 'I need to wash.'

'Of course, here's the toilet and washroom.'

The hot drink revived her, but her hands still trembled when she asked, 'Has he gone?'

'Oh, yes. As soon as he saw us coming, he disappeared. Our van swung right across the road when we tried to catch you. Didn't it, Ken?'

'It was dangerous, but we worried for your safety and had to do something. You don't mind if I ask you a question?' Jan said, and before Mia could reply, she continued, 'What are you doing out here alone?'

Mia sighed and fidgeted with her bangles as she told them she was meeting her friend Flea in Broken Hill. She then changed the subject, munching on a biscuit. 'These are nice. Did you make them?'

'Ken's the cook around here and I do the cleaning. We've been travelling for two months, left Sydney before Christmas and stopped off with the family at Griffith for a few weeks. Now we're on our way to Adelaide.' Jan dunked a cookie in her tea. 'You were lucky we came along as we were going through Renmark but changed our minds.'

Ken passed the plate. 'Another biscuit? Are you okay to travel?'

Mia lapsed into silence then whispered, 'Yes, it'd be better if you drive my Kombi, he might wait for me ahead.'

'That's true. I'll take your van, and you can travel with Jan.'

'You're brave driving on your own out here in the bush.'

'Do you have any water? My bottle's in the van,' said Mia.

'Ken, get some water. You must keep up the fluids in this hot weather.'

'Thank you, I'm much better after the tea and biscuits.' While Ken filled the bottle, she said, 'That fella scared me.'

Mia's face was flushed, her stomach fluttered, and her head was like a spinning top, as they discussed the logistics of the 100-kilometre journey and the quirks of driving her vehicle.

'Sure you're okay?' said Jan, and Mia nodded. 'Now, Ken, if you must stop, you give us plenty of warning.'

The convey crept along the highway and Mia dozed. At a turn off, Ken beeped the Kombi's horn and pointed. There, camouflaged by a tree and bushes, sat the silver panel van. While Jan honked, Mia wrapped her arms around herself and looked to the floor, rattled once more.

'He can't get away with this, you must report him to the police in Broken Hill. We've written his number plate in our notebook.' Jan pointed to a notebook on the dashboard. 'Do you feel okay?'

'Yeah, I just need some sleep.'

'We're booked into the caravan park, but where are you going to stay?'

'Not sure, I'll ring my friend later.'

Chapter 9

Clumps of mulga and spinifex interspersed the scattered carnage of sheep and wild animals on the red, cracked earth. Felicity clutched her hands as she watched heavy-hearted as they passed through the dry, desolate landscape. Life was trying for some farmers who lived and worked in the bush; dejection and despair lurked just below the surface for the proud, stoic people struggling through circumstances beyond their control. She was grateful for her escape.

Randall's breakfast of bacon and egg rolls and coffee had been a welcome treat as they left the city. She mulled over what might happen if there was a change in their relationship as they sped along the rough track in his air-conditioned 4WD.

'It's hard to imagine living out here, the isolation and lack of rain, even worse than at my place.' Felicity bounced in her seat as the vehicle hit a pothole and zigzagged across the road.

'Sorry, didn't see that coming. Yes, I'm lucky my business finances the vineyard. That stuff-up in water allocation's taking a toll on everyone in the bush.' He gave a strained smile. 'Suppose if you wait long enough, a good season might appear.' Randall offered Felicity a peach from a bag sitting next to him.

'You're organised.'

'Yes, Merv needs fresh stuff. I'm not sure he's managing too well.' He removed his cap and scratched his head. 'His sheep are on agistment in Victoria. There's not a lot for him to do, but he still won't come to town and stay a few days.'

'Sometimes you need blasting out of your comfort zone to see a different world.'

'Yes. A Kombi rocketed you out,' he said, dissolving into laughter.

Felicity bit her lip. 'Never expected it. I could see myself rotting away on the farm. Thank goodness Mia arrived to save me.' Her voice turned tender. 'I'm feeling much better since I've been on the road.' She leaned towards him and stroked his arm.

He gazed at her in surprise, then a broad grin broke across his face. He grabbed her hand and drew it to him and kissed it before resting his palm on her leg. She gasped at his touch and it sent her heart racing.

To calm herself, she pointed to a hawk swirling in the thermals, and they watched it dive on its prey before flying off with its catch. His face was soft, his lips parted as he reached over and ruffled her hair. He stopped the car in the middle of no-where and kissed her, running his hands over her body. She looked into his eyes full of emotion, and moved closer, then after a few minutes she backed away when he ran his hand up her leg.

'I think we'd better wait till after we see Merv. He'll be wondering where we are.'

His voice filled with disappointment as he adjusted himself and said, 'Why not now?'

Her hands rose in defence. 'I'm scared what this means.' She held his face in her palms and kissed him, whispering, 'Give me time.'

He started the car and roared off.

It got hotter outside, and the mirages grew until he pointed to a stand of trees in the distance.

'At last, that's his place, it's on the Darling River, the Barku, as the Indigenous people call it.' She whistled with joy and his sullen face broke into a grin. 'He loves the river, spent his childhood without shoes, running in and out with the local kids. "The best school ever", he says. Now everyone is angry because the river doesn't flow, and the fish are dying. Those Murray Cod were ancient.'

They approached the entrance, a cattle grid with a huge white drum beside it, and he reached and squeezed her leg. 'Be prepared, he hasn't cared for the house since Bet died.'

The dogs barked and growled and ran in circles to welcome the guests.

'Sit, you bastards,' yelled a big, generous looking man. He wore riding boots, a blue checked shirt just unpacked from its box with a tag hanging loose, and braces that held up his oversized jeans. Prancing next to him was a small brown and white Jack Russell. 'Welcome, don't worry, they're my working dogs.' He opened the gate and shooed the animals away.

After introductions, she followed the two men along the path with the dog pattering beside her. Lengthy runners of grass had withered as they crept across the garden beds, the bare lawn and dead trees and bushes standing like sentinels to the drought.

Merv ushered her through the front door. 'You don't mind if I call you, Flea?'

She smiled as she stepped into the long hall with high ceilings and an overabundance of carved wooden-framed sepia photos. An overwhelming stench drifted through the air and it made her retch.

Randall burst out, 'What's that bloody smell?'

'Apologies. The electricity cut out in the dust storm, so I turned the freezer off to stop it blowing a fuse and forgot to turn it on when the service returned. I opened the damn thing this morning and everything was off. I chucked it all out, but it still smells.' He stomped to the cooler and closed the lid. 'This might help.'

Felicity dropped her shoulder bag on the nearest chair and seized control. 'This happened to me once, and you need to clean it out now, or you'll never be able to use it again.'

'That's what I miss, someone to boss me around.' There was a twinkle in his eye as he towered over her and gave her a hug. 'Now what do I do?'

'Find rubber gloves, a bucket, vanilla, detergent and disinfectant, paper, anything to clear this odour.' Felicity searched under the kitchen sink and went through the big old-fashioned pantry built when the house had a cook. She remembered coffee beans, so added them to her list.

'You tell us what to do and Randall and I will scrub the whole bloody freezer.' Merv filled the bucket with water and gathered the cleaning products. 'Have a tour of the place, Flea. There's dust and mouse poo but some interesting pictures and books.'

She caught an echo of laughter as she wandered the hall, peering at the sepia photos of another era, and peeping in the rooms on either side. A dark room contained a mess of paper; a computer with a large screen attached in the middle of an antique rolled-topped desk and an intricate, dusty Turkish rug hugged the floor. Its long-sashed windows looked over the neglected garden. Merv's office?

Merv had annotated the pages of a book of Wordsworth's poems lying open on the table. She picked it up. The poet's love of the natural landscape in England was so different to the harshness of the Australian bush, she thought.

Shelves of books, some old, others more recent, covered the walls. Chewed bits of paper and a peculiar odour showed evidence of a recent mouse plague.

As she played the out-of-tune piano in the lounge room, a feeling of sadness and neglect came over her, and it pervaded the place. Dusty, stained sheets fell over the antique furniture and cobwebs hung from the ceiling. She heard the men finish their work.

'Oh, there you are, Flea. Now what do we do?'

Felicity reached into the freezer. 'Leave the paper and coffee beans in there for the next few days to get rid of that smell before you turn it on.' She held up a box of bicarb and a bottle of vinegar. 'Wipe it with this mixture and top up the bowl of vanilla. It'll be right after that.'

'Now who's for lunch? It's on the veranda where it doesn't stink as much,' said Randall, who had organised thick slices of bread, sliced meats, salad, olives and cheese, and pulled a good white wine from the Esky. The crystal glasses and plates and cutlery were heirlooms he carried from the oak sideboard, cracked from the heat.

'Here's to Flea.' Merv raised his glass. 'Didn't expect you to come here and help clean up my mess.' A warm smile stretched across her face. 'Now, I hear you've a hippy. Oh, wait a minute, I'll get the record player.'

He returned with an old box and a bundle of records. 'We must have music.' The strains of Vivaldi's *Four Seasons* filled the room. 'We'll celebrate having you both here.' They clinked glasses, and laughter echoed across the veranda.

Merv listened to Felicity's description of the drought and how the whirlwind of Mia saved her. For the next hour, the two men laughed and teased her about the decision to travel with a hippy and a Kombi to Adelaide.

After a while, she cleared her throat and said, 'I'm so glad I left with her, I was drinking too much.' She raised her glass, then placed it on the table and lowered her eyes. 'There are no awards for lasting out a drought.'

'Here, here. We'll drink to that,' Merv said, as he grabbed hold of her arm. 'When are we leaving?'

'Why don't we hit Adelaide together? Be frivolous, have fun.' Felicity raised her eyebrows and grinned at a startled Merv. 'Maybe a neighbour could look after your place for a long weekend? Mine did.'

'What about me?' Randall gave an impatient huff.

'You both could stay with my friend Shirl, Randall knows her, she's an identity in Adelaide. This festival has many types of music. Mia's drums and beat of Africa, nearly drove me mad on the way, but I'm sure we can choose what we want to hear. We all need a holiday.' She pleaded, 'Come on, say "yes".'

'Never been with a music mob in my life.' Merv scratched his head. 'The kids will think I'm going potty. But always a first for everything. Now do I know this Shirley?'

Felicity and Randall spent the next half an hour telling stories about their flamboyant friend. 'Shirl stitches up political deals and if she doesn't like you or your standing in life, she freezes you out. She's an Old Money Adelaidean and has an enormous home in a better part of Adelaide. I've been to the most over-the-top parties there, lasting until dawn. Her dress can be outlandish,' said Randall as he stood and impersonated Shirley and her walk while Merv roared with laughter.

'Now, now. Shirl has a heart of gold for her friends.,' said Felicity as Merv searched through his CD's on the sideboard. 'Her family were early white settlers, banking people or pastoralists. No convicts there.'

He cackled. 'Now you must listen to this, Gurrumul Yunupingu. He died a few years ago and is sadly missed.'

After two tracks of the haunting sound, the guests opened their eyes. 'It's such soulful music, it vibrates through your body. Amazing,' said Felicity.

'Sometimes, I go out to the paddocks at night in the ute with a CD of the music. I turn up the volume and let it bellow out to the stars. It's wonderful.'

'C'mon no reminiscing. We've got to go, there's a storm brewing.' Randall laid his hand on Merv's shoulder. 'How about you come for a drive with us to Broken Hill, have dinner and I'll drop you back tomorrow? It'll give you a break.'

'I think I need to be here if the storm hits, it's so dry.'

'Randall, you make sure he comes to Adelaide.' Felicity pointed her finger at him. 'Merv needs a holiday like me.'

There was a peal of laughter. The dog stretched under the table, ready for a stroll to the door with his guests.

As they waved and drove away, the fierce sun of the morning had given way to puffy clouds and a darkening sky in the distance. Silence filled the car as they sped along the dirt road. Felicity fidgeting with her watch as she grappled with her changing feelings for Randall.

Randall's chuckle broke the quiet. 'What are you, the Pied Piper, gathering everyone to your festival?'

'It'd be exciting. Have you been to a big concert like this?'

'No, imagine us oldies bopping and singing to the music.' Randall wiggled in his seat and patted her leg in tune to the song and hummed. 'You're right, it's different, and I'm sure very entertaining. Merv's a rascal with a deep side. The Milky Way's his passion, he's an amateur astronomer and there's a huge telescope in a special room out the back, connected to his computers. He chats to people from around the world.' He turned, their eyes dancing when they met. 'Next time we must visit overnight.'

'An interesting man, but he's... lost.'

'Merv's battling. I'll try to get him away for a few days.' He opened his window and shooed flies hovering on the windscreen. 'I've booked a room for us at the hotel,' he announced.

She gulped. 'Oh, okay!' She leant her head against the back of the seat and her jumbled thoughts massed like the storm clouds on the horizon.

Lightning streaks illuminated the menacing clouds, heavy rain beat down, and the wind formed a swirling dance on the parched earth.

Felicity stuck her head out the window, thumping the side of the vehicle. 'Thank you and praise you, God of the Sky. What a treat. More gentle stuff, please.' Randall chuckled and threw his hands in the air.

The gale and driving rain struck her across the face and forced her inside the cabin, her hair damp. 'This rain's welcome, but these heavy downpours can do so much damage. We don't want to be stranded in a flood. How far is it to the tarred road?' she asked.

The windscreen wipers worked overtime as Randall navigated potholes. They cheered when they hit the sealed highway. By the time they arrived in Broken Hill, the fierceness of the storm had passed, leaving flooded streets.

'I must ring Bill and let him know rain's coming.' They pulled to the high curve beside a large heritage building with wraparound verandas and wrought iron.

'The Imperial Hotel, Flea. If I remember, there's even a portrait of the old Russian Royal family on the wall, but no bar.' They unloaded the car and pressed the bell for reception.

While they waited, Felicity saw a row of 4WD's with water cans and camping equipment on top, and a familiar bus. 'Hey, the scientists from Mungo had that vehicle. They must be staying here too.'

Randall dropped their luggage in the large, well-appointed room. 'You clean up and I'll ask where we can have dinner,' he said as he carefully scrutinised his phone before he left.

She had a quick shower, then lay on the king-sized bed and dozed. In her half-sleep someone nuzzled up to her and fondled her hair, and with surprise she looked into Randall's big blue eyes. 'What's happening?' She sat up, startled.

'Had a beer on the veranda with the scientists and everyone remembers Mia and you. There were lots of laughs. Believe she's a good-looker.' Randall stroked Felicity's arm.

'How did they know I was here?'

'Oh, I told them. They want us to come to dinner at the club and they were pestering me to go in their snooker competition later – Aussies against the World.'

'Wow... I love it and play well.' She raised her eyebrows and gave him a big smile. 'You wait and see.'

Next, she was giggling and squirming from Randall's tickles and soon they were rolling around on the bed until she called, 'Enough, have a shower. You stink!'

Felicity sat on the side of the messy bed and rang Bill. They chatted about the farm, and she told him the good news, to expect rain as it was on the way.

Randall came into the room whistling as she finished the call. 'Who was that?'

'My neighbour, Bill. All okay, but as usual he wanted to gossip.'

With that, Randall did a flying leap onto Felicity, pinning her arms to the bed. 'Gotcha.' He discarded her dress in no time and the pair lay naked, caressing and kissing each other as the fan whirled.

Someone knocked at the door. 'We're off to dinner. See you there.'

'Oh, I told them to do that. Now, where were we?'

Chapter 10

On the outskirts of Broken Hill, Ken slowed the Kombi and signalled to the women in the motor home to stop on the side of the road.

'Heard on the news, there's a nasty storm brewing so we'll have to get to the caravan park and set up before it breaks. Mia, I suggest you drive your van into the city,' said Ken.

'...Do I have too?' Mia whined, reluctant to lose the security of her newfound friends.

'Don't worry, it's not far and we can catch up tonight.'

'Oh yes. We'd love to have a meal with you. Bring your friend,' said Jan in a light-hearted way. 'Think there's a club near the main street. Can't remember the name, but I'm sure you won't miss it. Is seven o'clock okay?'

Mia cursed as she waved the couple goodbye. She must find somewhere to stay before those thunderous-looking clouds burst. Her body ached, and her head throbbed with the blaring music as she drove through the streets searching for accommodation, swearing and banging the steering wheel with her fist as she saw "No Vacancy" signs everywhere.

After a while she found a small motel and asked the receptionist, who was focused on her computer, for a room. Mia gritted her teeth and glared at the withered pot plant in the corner as she waited for her to finish her task.

'Now let me check. You're on your own, are you?' Mia paced up and down the reception area. 'Are you okay?' inquired the woman as she looked up, Mia grunted. 'I can give you a small room at the back, No 23. It may be noisy with people jumping in the pool, but it's the only one available tonight.'

'Okay, I'll take it.'

The receptionist removed a set of keys from a board, showed Mia the parking zone, and explained the hotel's schedule.

Mia struggled with her luggage, dumped it on the floor and flicked open the blinds. 'Bugger!' Teenage boys were dive bombing and skylarking in the pool outside her window, so she closed the curtains.

In the shower, water trickled out of the taps. 'Bloody hell.' Mia rang reception and after a long delay, someone answered. 'There's no water for a shower and I've travelled for hours,' said Mia as she drew in her breath and pulled the telephone cord in anger. 'It needs fixing.'

The woman at the other end of the phone said, 'Sorry, Miss. We're in the middle of a drought and ask guests to save water, and shower with what's available.'

The shampoo didn't lather, so she threw the bottle on the tiles and liquid slowly oozed out. She bent to pick it up, but, with the shock of the first clap of thunder vibrating through the tin roof, it fell from her hands. She grabbed a towel and wrapped it around her.

There was a cacophony, the air conditioning blasted and the rain roared on the rooftop. Mia trembled as she sat on the floor with her bags. A sudden, loud thunderbolt sent her scurrying to the bed where she covered her head with the pink retro-chenille bedspread.

***

'Where are the scientists having dinner?' said Felicity as she and Randall stepped into a cool night washed by the passing thunderstorm.

'Let's eat alone. Somewhere quiet.'

He placed his arm around her shoulder, and they wandered along the street looking for a place to eat. The restaurant had a simple menu and the waiter, dressed in jeans and running shoes, hauled out his notebook and wrote their order of steak and vegetables.

'No dessert?' The waiter glanced at the only other couple eating, then finished writing their requests.

'We'll tell you later. Wine?'

'Oh, here's the list.' He tossed the plastic covered book at them and stood tapping his foot.

'This red, thanks.' Randall pointed to the most expensive item on the menu.

The waiter snapped the menus closed, picked up the wine list, and marched to the kitchen not to be seen again. The chef brought their meals.

Half-way through their meal, Randall moved his chair close to Felicity, and with a twinkle in his eye, said, 'You know I like this,' as he snuggled closer. 'I should have brought a bottle of Grange to celebrate.' He threw her a tender look. 'What changed your mind?'

She lifted her glass with a coy smile. 'You. I'm seeing how special you are, and what a wonderful time we might have, despite that wife of yours.' She frowned, wondering why she had bothered bringing up his wife.

'My ex-wife, I call her. Why did you mention her?'

His defensiveness alarmed her and fended off any further discussion. She played with his fingers and under the table rubbed her leg against his to give herself time to think.

He leaned closer and kissed her. 'After lunch, tomorrow I have to travel back to Mildura, how will you get to Adelaide?'

'Don't know.' She tapped her finger against her lip and hesitated. 'Plane or train? I'll work it out tomorrow and if I stay an extra night, I could play tourist. How far is it?'

'It takes ages on the train, about five and a half hours by road.' Randall raised his eyebrows with a cheeky grin. 'It'd be more fun at the Barossa.'

Felicity giggled, 'Maybe next time?'

'Do you want me to turn up in Adelaide?'

'Of course, chilling out, as the kids say, listening to music like old hippies. It's something I never did when I was young,' said Felicity. 'You must bring Merv. He'll enjoy it.'

Randall looked at his watch. 'We had better go, I promised we'd play pool.' He paid the bill and put his arm around her.

'He'll come, I'm sure Shirl won't mind.' Randall grinned, holding her close her as they walked the street. 'We'll have a great time.'

The scientists had returned from dinner and a delighted Adrian met them in the hotel's ornate hallway. 'Wonderful, we need you both for our pool competition.'

Felicity considered Adrian and after a moment, said, 'I'll be your partner, I love the game and I reckon we can beat them.'

'Okay, what a partnership, the Aussie team. Randall, for tonight you're in the second World team with Frenchie over there,' said Adrian, pointing to the Frenchman. 'We're the hosts so we get to challenge the winners of your round.'

Randall and the Frenchman were the World champs and pranced around boasting they would beat Adrian's team.

In the toss, the Aussies had to break the balls and Adrian waved for Felicity to begin. She chalked the pool cue like an expert, and with her shooting hand she gripped the butt of the stick, wrapping her thumb and other fingers as support around it. After a moment's concentration, she began blasting the balls away. She grinned as she noticed the stunned faces and handed the cue to Randall. Adrian was hopping up and down, hooting with pleasure as the game progressed, and Felicity dropped ball after ball into the pockets. Randall and his partner shook their heads, they couldn't keep up with her pace.

Felicity was lining up a tricky shot when she heard a familiar voice say, 'Flea, it's you!' The ball jumped on the table as she froze.

'Mia,' she stuttered, and the cue crashed to the floor. 'What are you doing here?'

'Oh, I met the men at the club, and I've been playing the pokies with them,' said Mia winking at her companion, the scientist, and laughing. 'Finish your game, I'll talk to you later.'

Felicity continued playing and while she waited for her turn, she watched Mia edge her way towards Randall, who was smiling and appeared delighted with the attention.

She whacked the last ball with rather too much force into the pocket, winning for the Aussies. Then she quickly shook the hands of her opponents, gave Adrian a big hug, thanked him and high-fived the other players.

'Randall, I see you've met Mia,' said Felicity as she gripped Randall's arm, and a puzzled look spread across his face. 'Sorry, Mia, we've had a long day so we're heading off to bed now.'

Adrian called, 'Aren't we going to celebrate, Flea?'

'Next time.' Felicity laughed and waved to the players. 'Good night, everybody.' She pulled Randall through the green sitting area with its antiques towards the stairs.

Mia followed, crashing into the furniture in the narrow passageway. 'Flea, can I talk to you?'

Felicity swivelled around and stared at Mia.

'I left some valuables in the Kombi when I went to hospital and I can't find them.' Mia knocked her leg on a chair and avoided eye contact. 'What did you do with everything?'

Felicity frowned and in a sharp tone, said, '…I gathered up the bits I needed, and the rest, Eskies, sleeping bags, Randall moved to his place. Why?'

'Think it may be in that lot.'

'What was it? I noticed nothing unusual, did you?' she said, as she looked at Randall. He scratched his head and Felicity felt a ripple of unease.

Mia fidgeted with her bangles. 'Oh, nothing much. Can we meet tomorrow?'

'Have you made any plans?' said Felicity to Randall with a sweet smile. He smirked, lifted his eyebrows, and she laughed. 'Okay, how about 10 o'clock for coffee?'

Randall clutched Felicity's hand, and they climbed the carpeted stairs together, laughing. When Felicity turned and looked back, she saw Mia rush to grab her scientist friend and head for the main door into the night.

Chapter 11

'What on earth! What's hidden at your place?' asked Felicity, as she flung her handbag onto the king-sized bed, the contents falling across the floor. 'Mia's a drama queen. Couldn't you see she had her scientist friend wrapped around her little finger?' Her eyes flashed with anger as she waved her hand at Randall. 'And she was chatting you up, wasn't she?'

He looked sheepish under the onslaught and stood with his arms crossed, struggling to find the right words. 'Um... she's certainly some girl.'

'Well, you leave her alone,' she said, as she gathered up the bits and pieces thrown from her bag.

'There was nothing strange when I packed your gear away,' he said in an edgy voice. 'But can't say I checked. What's she hiding? Either you find out tomorrow or I must do a thorough search when I arrive home. Must be drugs!'

Felicity threw herself on the comfortable leather lounge and fidgeted with her watch. 'I'm not sure about drugs, but I'm puzzled. Okay, her story and the way she behaved in the Kombi were strange.' She paused in thought. 'Once or twice she removed something from her bag. Wait... she used her water bottle each time.'

She beckoned Randall to sit next to her, but his phone blasted, and he went rushing to the huge veranda that wrapped around the hotel. Just like Mia, glued to his phone, she thought. When he didn't return for a while, she wondered who he was talking to at this time of night. Surely it can't be business, a woman?

'Apologies, now this girl, what's happening?'

Felicity drew in her breath. 'Didn't want to get you involved, but I'm not sure what to do. I don't want to meet her tomorrow.' She flung her hands in the air 'It's weird but she makes me do things I don't want to do and I can't seem to escape her!'

'Learn to say a big fat NO when you see her. Let's forget her and have a night-cap.' He dug around in his bags and produced a bottle of red and two wine goblets. 'Not classy, but it'll do.' He poured the drink, then raised his glass. 'To us, we're far more important than this stuff with Mia.' He kissed her, they clinked glasses, and he stroked her back until she finally relaxed.

***

'Spending time with a wonderful sexy woman gives a man an appetite.' Randall lifted his eyebrows and patted her on the leg in the cafe. When the waitress with purple hair and a sharp haircut arrived, they ordered bacon and eggs, toast and a large coffee for breakfast.

'They swarm over you like flies when you want to be on your own.' she whispered as the woman hovered around them.

'Yeah. I'm sorry I must go home this afternoon. Why don't you come with me and stay a few days? I'll show you the town and then we can travel to the festival together. I'd love you to come.'

'And frighten the neighbours? Imagine the wagging tongues if I appeared,' joked Felicity, hitting him with the tourist brochure she brought from the hotel. 'Look, there's a train to Adelaide in the morning, it gets in at a reasonable hour. I'll grab a ticket, see the scenery and spend a few days with Shirl before you arrive.' She patted his leg and her voice cracked. 'I need time to catch up with myself, to think about what's happened... with us.'

She leant over to stroke his face and he kissed her.

Randall glanced at his watch. 'Well, it's time for you to stand up to Mia.'

'Aren't you coming?'

'No way, I'll only make it worse so I'll give you an hour and meet you back at the hotel.'

'Okay. You're right. I must sort this out. See you soon.'

Randall left her at the entrance to the café with a squeeze of her hand and a peck on the cheek, and as she headed off, she clenched her fists in disgust, thinking of the meeting ahead. Her phone rang. It was the hotel in Mildura telling her she had dropped an earring in her room.

'Thank you, thank you so much. I didn't know I'd lost it. The earrings are the only piece of jewellery my mother gave me before she passed away.' The caller asked where to send it. 'I'll get a friend to collect it. Thanks.' She gave Randall's details and strolled the main street with relief.

Felicity swore under her breath as she continued her search for Mia and had almost convinced herself to return to the hotel when she saw her on the footpath talking to a couple wearing matching straw hats.

'Oh, Flea, these people helped me yesterday,' said Mia as she made the introductions and pointed to a nearby cafe.

After they had ordered their coffee, Ken described their run-in with a man in a silver panel van who tried to harass Mia by tailgating the Kombi. His wife, Jan, interrupted and relayed how she had taken the numberplate. 'We really think Mia should report him to the police.'

'It was quite terrifying,' said Jan, twisting her serviette. 'Mia's lucky she's still here. I didn't get to see what he looked like, but it scared me. Just as well we arrived because she fainted when she jumped from the van.'

Mia half-smiled, enjoying the dramatic retelling of the event.

'I'm so grateful to them,' said Mia, scowling at Felicity. 'When I came out of a hospital, I was alone and not well and to have this happen was unbelievable.' She pulled out a tissue and dabbed her eyes. 'Excuse me, I need to run to the bathroom.'

When she was out of sight, Jan said, 'Thank goodness you're travelling with her to Adelaide tomorrow. She needs someone to look after her.'

'What, did Mia tell you that?' said Felicity. 'I'm catching the train.'

'She has to travel with somebody. She can't drive on her own.' Ken's eyes threw daggers at Felicity. 'That girl's a butterfly, doesn't know whether she's coming or going.'

Felicity frowned and cleared her throat. 'I'm worried, do you think... there's something wrong with her?'

Ken and Jan pulled faces at one another, and she answered, 'No, just dizzy, and all that has happened has made her more distracted.'

When Mia returned, Felicity challenged her, 'Did you tell these people I was driving to Adelaide with you tomorrow?'

'Yes, we always planned to do that.'

Randall's advice about saying 'NO' rang in Felicity's ears.

'I would rather catch the train as it'd be much easier and more relaxing, and my friend, Shirl, can pick me up at the station.'

'Mia could drop you at your friend's home,' said Ken giving Felicity a steely stare. 'You'd do that, wouldn't you?'

Mia separated a sizeable chunk of her hair and twisted it, saying nothing.

'It's five hours to Adelaide, far too long for her to drive alone. Look at what happened on the road from Mildura,' said Jan, glaring at Felicity. 'If something happens, I wouldn't like that on my conscience. You would just be a passenger so that's not much to ask.'

Mia avoided Felicity's glare and kept twisting her hair.

Later, when Felicity relayed what had taken place to Randall, she shouted. 'Done over! They took no notice of me and I had to agree to when and where to meet. I'm so stupid!'

'Mia's got you by the balls, she gets you can't stand up to her,' he said, scolding her. 'You've been hiding on that farm, and you've forgotten how to say NO. Thank the stars it's not far to Adelaide and you can dump her there.'

'I tried to get rid of her in Mildura and she still turned up here.'

'Shirl won't let her stay, that's for sure,' he said as he rubbed the back of his neck with frustration. 'Drive home with me, that'll solve your problems.'

Felicity paused and closed her eyes, then pulled away. 'I'd love to, but I can't. It's too complicated. They think she's a butterfly, but I think there is something wrong.'

'You're mad. What about us? You go off with someone you don't know but won't spend time with me.' He picked up his keys. 'Come to your senses while we're sightseeing and then we can drive to Mildura.'

They drove in silence to a tourist stop, an old iron-ore mine out of the town. Rustic machinery, a few bushes, and even fewer trees surrounded the pit. As Felicity surveyed the view and the sparseness of the rocky land, she played with her watch, twisting and turning it, pondering on where her commitment lay, to Mia or Randall?

As she approached the mine, Felicity broke the silence. 'I hate going underground. It's like Hell and hot enough to be there.'

'Hah, the angels have saved you!' He chuckled as they saw a closed sign across the gate. 'Let's head to see the panoramic vista of Broken Hill from the lookout on the slag heap.' He shifted the air-conditioning in the car up a notch.

After ten minutes of driving, he asked again if she'd drive home with him and she looked out the window and said, 'I'm not ready, I need to get to Adelaide first.'

Neither of them spoke as they viewed the sprawling city encased in its dry landscape before them. On a drunken whim, she had escaped her dramas on the farm and now found herself in Broken Hill saddled with more hassles. Why was everything so difficult?

When they returned to the hotel, Randall packed his gear and embraced her with an enormous hug. 'Won't you come with me?'

With a sigh of defeat, she said, 'I can't.'

'I'm going then. Don't expect to hear from me!' He slammed the wardrobe, picked up his bag and gave her a brief smile before he ran down the carpeted stairs. She tried to catch up to him, but he jumped in his car and roared away. Randall left her standing on the curb, wiping tears with a crumpled tissue, gnashing her teeth.

Chapter 12

Felicity tossed and turned as she napped, thinking of the re-percussions of her drunken whim to come on this trip. How she had agreed to travel with THAT girl, rather than take a more romantic journey with Randall, and that girl might be into drugs. She groaned as she relived his angry departure. She hadn't even talked to him about collecting her earring. This was too much.

She called Shirley to give her the details of her arrival and after chatting for a while she gulped and said, 'By the way, I had dinner with Randall.'

'Well, did you?' teased Shirley. 'What are you trying to tell me, Flea? Have you two had hanky-panky?' After pestering Felicity for an answer, she whistled in excitement.

'What a hoot,' she said. 'You've been avoiding him for years. Next you'll say he's coming to visit too.'

There were peals of laughter.

'I've stuffed it,' said Felicity. 'He wanted me to return to Mildura with him and after I said no, he sulked and left in a huff, told me not to expect to hear from him again.'

'Ah, he must have the hots for you… Don't worry, he'll be in touch.'

'We made plans to go to the music festival, so if he contacts me, will you join us?'

'Oh no. Only the riff-raff go to that.'

'You're a snob,' said Felicity. 'It'd be fun. I didn't do that stuff when I was young and free.' She paused. 'I also invited a mate of Randall's, Merv. He's an interesting man, doing it tough on the Darling River. Do you know him?'

'Um…Think I do, sounds intriguing. Now how are you getting here?'

'I'm travelling with Mia, that girl who landed on my doorstep a few days ago,' Felicity said. 'I'm worried. She's odd.'

'Flea, none of your strays, thanks. You've got a weakness for poor down-and-outs and they never appreciate what you do.'

After their goodbyes she chuckled to herself, Shirl loves a gossip and always has a sense when something is amiss.

***

A takeaway meal and a glass of wine sat next to Felicity as she flicked through TV channels under the whirling fan in her hotel room. It startled her when her phone rang, looked at the caller and let it go to messages. After she'd finished her dinner, and fortified by two glasses of wine, she listened to Randall's stilted call. 'Flea, I've done the search. Please ring.'

She wondered whether his call was only about Mia. Perhaps he wanted another chance to talk about their relationship? Or was he still sulking? Alan had sulked, and she had hated it. She rang.

'Ah, I'm worried and thought I'd better let you know. Found a stockpile of tablets in a brown envelope inside the sleeping bag, five trays of ten doses, each wrapped in foil. That's fifty pills.'

Felicity gasped in dismay. 'Oh shit! At least it doesn't sound like heroin or cocaine, they're powders. Is it prescription medication?'

'Who knows, I'm naïve with this stuff,' said Randall. 'I'll have a chat to my mate at the pharmacy tomorrow, see what she has to say. It's a lot of pills so it might explain Mia's behaviour.'

Felicity's body tightened. 'I wonder if she's taking them or selling the damn things? Makes me think if my kids are into drugs overseas, I'd never know.'

There was a pause. 'Hm…Apologies for going so abruptly. The long drive gave me time to mull over what happened.' Randall's tone dropped, and he sounded concerned. 'I'm worried you're alone travelling with Mia. It's selfish, but I want more "Flea time" with no mishaps and lots of fun in Adelaide.'

'Thanks, that's sweet. I've missed you too, and Broken Hill will never be the same after our night there.' They both laughed. 'But I'll be okay driving with her. She hasn't been able to get pills for a few days unless she has another prescription or two. Don't know what happens when you withdraw from these tablets. I'd like to help her, but if she has addiction issues, she needs medical and counselling support.'

'You're not playing the "do-gooder" again, are you?' Felicity said nothing and waited for Randall to fill the space. 'Now, did you miss me this afternoon…?'

'Oh, I forgot. I've another favour to ask you.' She explained how her earring was found and asked him to collect it from the hotel in Mildura.

She smiled and hugged herself when she finished the conversation as the thought of seeing Randall again reignited feelings that had lain dormant for too long.

***

Felicity pounded the silent streets of Broken Hill at first light. She watched the red-orange glow transform into the rising sun and the trees and historic buildings glittering with their wash from the storm. She wasn't looking forward to the drive ahead, and it baffled her about where the lies and this stash of medication fitted into Mia's life.

Mia was in a good mood when she arrived on time to collect Felicity. 'Ken and Jan started early and will catch us on the road. The oldies always get to places before dark so they can nap.'

The day was cooler, with a bright blue sky and the gentle breeze moved the saltbush and remaining tussocks of grass. An opportune time to drive across the distinctive barren red soils of the Outback.

The further they drove from the city, the more erratic was Mia's driving. One minute she had the accelerator flat to the floor with the Kombi roaring as they sped over the plains, and the next she dropped back, causing the van to chug. When a large truck tried to pass, she forced it back into the traffic lane by going faster, and only just missed a head-on collision with an oncoming car. Shaken, Felicity demanded to drive.

'I'm driving! It's my vehicle.' Mia's voice sliced through the cabin.

Felicity rechecked her seat belt, and her body stiffened as she gripped the doorhandle. The Kombi swayed, and her heart raced with the revving engine, and Mia's swearing as she avoided birds flying into her path, reverberating through her head.

'Stop this! We'll both be dead if you keep driving this way.'

They screeched to a halt at a rest area. Mia jumped from the van and ran to the amenities block, ignoring Jan and Ken sitting under the solitary tree nearby.

'Hello Felicity, it's a better day for driving,' said Jan, putting her hand on her forehead to shield her eyes from the sun. 'We've made a pot of tea. Do you want a cuppa? Kennie, can you get the biscuits in the back cupboard?'

'Black, no sugar, thanks. Back in a minute.' Felicity hurried to the loo before Jan could find her a job.

When she returned Mia had disappeared, but two young jackaroos had arrived in their ute.

'Hot, isn't it?' said the taller one. 'Any water here? Our radiator needs a top-up'

'Maybe in the tank over there.' Ken pointed. 'I'll give you a little if you're stuck.'

They checked, found the water putrid and asked for the spare water.

As if on cue, Mia appeared. The men looked startled; she resembled an exotic bird in this dry desolate setting, with a purple top, and a short lime green skirt and thongs.

'Hello, where're you going?' said Mia, smiling as she walked towards them and they doffed their hats.

'Off to pick up supplies, it's too hot to work and when the radiator cools, we're out of here, the boss will be after us to muster sheep.'

Later their dirty ute with its bull bar and long radio aerial vroomed away onto the highway.

'Men of few words,' smirked Jan with a devious smile. 'You could tell they aren't used to seeing brightly coloured girls like you around here, Mia.'

Then with her hand she ironed out the creases of the map spread on the table. 'We're working out what we want to do in Adelaide. We can meet you both there. Mia mentioned she's staying with you so we'll get together sometime.'

Felicity gulped and her eyes and mouth opened wide. 'No, that's not right. I'm going to my friend's place and Mia will have to find somewhere to stay.' Her face was grim as she rose from the seat. 'We had better get going, so she has more time to find something. Thanks for the cuppa.' She glared at Mia. 'I'll drive, I want to arrive alive.'

'If you insist...'

African music thumped as they waved the grey nomads goodbye and roared along the highway across the dry red plains until the Kombi settled to a steady pace.

'What did you do in Broken Hill?' said Felicity.

'Oh, I snapped up a seat on the scientists' bus and went to Silvertown.' She grabbed her sparkly cap from the floor and placed it on her head. 'You'll be so pleased - I take my hat and water bottle everywhere now.'

'What's happening with your friend, the scientist?'

'He's cute. I'll catch up with him when I get to Adelaide.'

'You told the scientists you were married?'

'Now I'm a free bird.'

Felicity threw both hands in the air, the van swayed, and she grabbed the wheel. 'Why have you been fibbing? Randall found a stash of pills in your sleeping bag. What are they?'

A petulant Mia shrugged her shoulders and gazed at a faraway place. 'Ah yeah, they're my Oxys, pain stuff prescribed by the doctor.'

'You mean that?'

'What's the matter with you? I told you what they were.'

Felicity sighed with relief, at least it was prescription medication, but did she still need them now? Mia was too angry to ask.

The buzz of Mia's phone interrupted the silence.

'No… I owe you, zilch. Stick it up your arse,' shouted Mia, holding the mobile away from her as the person on the other end cursed, the diatribe echoing through the cabin.

'Turn the bloody thing off,' said Felicity. 'I can't drive listening to that nonsense.' With her tirade finished Mia turned off the phone.

As they flew over the stark plains, Felicity seethed with anger. Why did she always take on the role of rescuer? Now Mia, before that it was Davina, her old school friend, her father, then Alan and his debts. And a few others in between. There was a pattern.

After half an hour of soul searching, Felicity said in a strained voice, 'Have you organised your accommodation?'

'I'll do that when I arrive.'

Mia stuck her nose in the air, put her feet on the dashboard and threw gum in her mouth.

'Okay, do what you like. You can let me off in the centre of Adelaide and Shirl will get me from there.'

'No, I'll drop you at your friend's place. It won't take long and...'

Felicity raised her hand to stop her from speaking and pushed the accelerator. She didn't want her anywhere near Shirl's. An ominous silence filled the van for the next hour.

'Hey, this country's monotonous,' said Mia with a mouth full of gum. 'Nothing to see or do out here.'

Felicity heaved a heavy sigh and let her doze.

'How far is it now? I'm hungry.' Mia stretched and searched through her bag for something to eat.

Sensing Mia was in a better mood than earlier in the day, Felicity pointed to a brochure sitting on the dashboard. As Mia thumbed the pages, she showed her the best places to stay in Adelaide, the site of the festival, and other attractions she might visit. Mia asked where Shirley lived.

Felicity hesitated. 'She lives in a suburb near the centre.'

'Why don't we stop there? If you give me the instructions, I can find my way to the city from her place.'

Chapter 13

Working from memory, Felicity made a few false turns as she navigated her way through the outskirts of Adelaide. She curled herself over the steering wheel and wished she were arriving at Shirley's place on her own. There was no evidence of Mia taking pills, but her erratic behaviour said something was wrong.

At last, they arrived in the street with its setback houses, sandstone walls and overhanging branches. Felicity slowed the Kombi and peered through the imposing closed gate of a palatial Queen Anne bluestone villa, with its long circular drive fringed by a mature exotic garden. She parked the van outside the house, then rang the security bell.

A loud voice echoed through the intercom. 'Who the bloody hell's there?'

'Shirl, it's Flea.'

'C'mon-in, where's your car?'

'We're in Mia's Kombi…'

'Don't want that in here! Park it away from my damn place.'

'Okay, let us in. We'll work it out later,' said Felicity.

The summer scent from the overgrown garden tickled Felicity's nose, and the crunch of gravel underfoot as they walked down the driveway increased her anxiety.

Shirley, a formidable-looking woman of indeterminate middle age, opened the door. Her smooth round face and dark wavy hair rested comfortably on her large body. Her haughty speech and gestures showed someone born to money and privilege, yet she wore a faded green floral shift and tattered flat silver shoes. She peered at them through black owl-like glasses, and Felicity could see Mia squirm. An afternoon glow lit the grand entrance behind her, and caught the stylish lights and the wide hallway, its polished floorboards scattered with rich Turkish rugs. Paintings and photos lined the walls.

'Wonderful to see you, Flea,' said Shirley hugging her then stepping back and pointing to her companion. 'How long will you be sticking around?'

Mia put her hand to her mouth in surprise.

'She's searching for a place to stay,' said Felicity quickly, shuffling her feet in discomfort.

At that moment, a small fur ball scooted along the veranda and Mia bent to pat the dog. It growled, baring its teeth in reply, and Shirley scooped it into her arms for a cuddle.

'Um, you don't like this visitor. But you are a beautiful thing.' She cooed and showed him to her guests. 'This is Fluff.'

'Now, can't send you off this late, girlie, you'll have stay here tonight.' Shirley glared at Mia and asked her to follow to a small pokey room. 'If you want a bed here, you're going to have to change your clothes. Look decent when you return to the kitchen!'

Shirley berated her friend and when the tirade had finished, Felicity went in search of Mia to warn her about Shirley's attitude to her staying the tonight.

The door was ajar, so she knocked. No answer. She peered into the room and her body tensed in shock. Littering the bed before her, lay a variety of coloured pills and bottle, a Pandora's box of trouble.

'What are you gaping at?' said Mia, coming behind Felicity with her wash bag and towel.

'This stuff?' Felicity picked up a packet of OxyContin tablets. Her voice was shrill as her questions tripped over themselves. 'What are all these tablets? Why are you carrying so many? Are you taking them? Are you ill?'

Mia tossed her head and glared angrily at her. 'They're mine. Take a chill pill!' She pointed to the kitchen and wagged her finger. 'I heard her in there, she doesn't want me here.' She grabbed her bag and threw it on the bed. 'I'm leaving, not staying with two old crazy women. Get your suitcase out of my Kombi.'

Felicity's breathing was shallow as she scrunched the front of her shirt into a tight ball and watched, stunned. Mia bundled her things together, snatched the keys from the desk and marched through the house with her bag while Felicity followed her out along the driveway, trying to apologise.

'I don't understand why you're leaving,' said Felicity. 'Have something to eat first.'

Mia struggling with her gear turned. 'Get lost. You're a drunk. Get over it.'

Bewildered, Felicity stood at the iron gates with her arms hugging her body, trying to stop it from shaking while she watched Mia toss her belongings onto the footpath and throw her own gear into the van. Mia jumped into the Kombi, scraped the gears and, without looking back, drove away, swerving to miss an oncoming car.

Fluff barked as Shirley watched Felicity crunch up the driveway.

'How did you get rid of missy so fast?' said Shirley. 'What did you say to her?'

'She didn't feel welcomed, and you know you'd make her life miserable,' said Felicity, still trembling. 'I need a cuppa. I found a cache of pills on her bed, heaps of them.'

'Drugs in my place?' shrieked Shirl. 'Why did you bring her here? What an idiot, Flea. You've driven half-way across Australia with someone who peddles stuff.'

'No, no, Shirl.' She drummed her fingers on the table as she watched Shirley make the tea. 'Mia's erratic behaviour had me worried and it now makes sense. I don't think she's peddling. I'm not sure, but my instinct tells me it's medical, perhaps something to do with anxiety. There was a car accident, her mother was driving, and Mia was badly hurt and off work for two months.' She paused and reached for a biscuit. 'The doctor gave her prescription pills, but there were so many bottles and pills on that bed, and Randall found more trays in the sleeping bag she'd used.' Felicity buried her head in her hands. 'Maybe she self-medicates to cope with stress?'

Shirley shrugged with indifference. 'So glad she's gone, you can't do anything.'

'I hope she'll be okay on her own. She up and went without warning, and I'm more worried about her now.'

'Doctor Flea.'

There was a nervous laugh, and the phone rang, allowing Felicity to escape with her bags to the bedroom.

A dry, musty smell and the pink floral wallpaper in the bedroom reminded Felicity of her grandmother. Billowing organza curtains and French glass doors led to the garden and the high ceilings made the room cool and comforting, a haven in the heat and away from the stresses of the past few days.

The cascading water from the shower soothed Felicity. She crossed the floor naked, jumped into the antique bed and lay between the linen sheets and dozed, thinking about Mia and what to do. It surprised her when she woke to birds making their last call of the day and relished the peace of the big house. She dressed, obsessing about where Mia would stay for the night and whether she would be okay.

Drinks and nibbles by the pool at dusk was a long-standing tradition at Shirley's place and as they laughed and gossiped, Felicity relaxed.

'I have a surprise for you,' said Shirley, passing a plate of vintage cheese and olives from her trees. 'My new housekeeper's preparing meals for me.'

Felicity gasped, and she stared at her in amazement, remembering the burnt offerings from the last visit.

Shirley peered into the enormous fridge. 'Ah, and here it is, a chicken casserole. You can make the salad and there's a good bottle of French champagne I'll crack to celebrate seeing you, and for getting rid of that girl too.'

'You surprised me when you said Mia could stay,' said Felicity, stroking Fluff. 'I'd warned her she'd have to find a bed elsewhere. Don't know why the pills shocked me, they always say festivals are havens for pill taking.' She looked up to see Shirley standing with a frown and crossed arms. 'Anyway, this won't be the last we hear of her.'

Shirley answered with a din as she thumped plates, cutlery, and condiments on a tray while Felicity gathered the fresh produce for the salad. 'This housekeeper's good, Shirl. Don't you get bossy with her.' She wagged her finger. 'You need help. Behave.'

'Oh, they never do what I tell them,' said Shirley with self-importance.

'Remind me to do some research while I'm here about a group of secretive scientists I met at Lake Mungo. I may need your help if I can't discover what they are doing out there. Their boss, Adrian, gave me his card and told me to ring him when I arrived in Adelaide, but I have to sort out bloody Randall first. Let's enjoy tonight.'

Shirley stared at Felicity and said, 'Another man on the go? Lucky you!'

The doorbell chimed and Shirley buzzed in the guests as Felicity rearranged her hair with combs. 'Could you be the welcoming party?'

She pulled her face in surprise when she opened the door. 'Why didn't Shirl tell me you were coming tonight?'

She hugged Randall while Merv's booming voice filled the hallway. 'Surprises happen when it rains! Blame Shirl, it was her idea.'

Felicity resisted Randall's searching gaze as he gave her a warm squeeze and said, 'After Broken Hill, I drove to Merv's place and he agreed we needed a visit to Adelaide.'

She led them to the kitchen to greet their host.

'Welcome, great to see you,' said Shirley removing her apron and standing with her hands on her hips. 'I'll organise everyone first.' She grinned and pointed her finger at Randall. 'Flea will decide where you go! Now, Merv, come with me and bring your gear, you're in the bedroom next to mine. Dinner will be ready soon.'

Felicity threw her head in the air and gave Randall a hard stare. 'You can put your luggage in the third room on the right. I'm on duty.'

His phone rang as he left to find the bedroom.

When he returned, Felicity avoided him while she finished the salad and heated the casserole. He stayed close by, serving drinks while Felicity gave everyone an update on Mia's behaviour and whereabouts.

'She's some bird, flying the coop so soon.' Randall came behind her for a hug, but she backed away to get ingredients from the cupboard.

'Hard to know what's going on with her, but I'm sure we'll see her again,' said Felicity, worrying an earring. 'In her cache of pills, the only tablets I recognised were OxyContin, an opiate. I'll suss it out on the net, what it's used for and if there are any side effects.'

'You think there's something wrong with her?' asked Merv.

Felicity shrugged. The research could wait, and she didn't want the night ruined by palaver about Mia when there was other business with Randall to resolve. 'Let's have dinner and discuss it later.'

In the dining room Merv noticed the large chandelier hanging from the ceiling and the fine Australian cedar table and chairs, the informality of the meal in stark contrast to the setting.

'These must be worth a bomb, Shirl.' He winked at Randall.

'The spoils of my grandfather passed on through the generations. He was a wealthy grazier and member of Parliament.' Shirley's back was straight, and her ample chest puffed.

'Now, Shirl, what did those ancestors of yours do to the Aboriginal people to get their land and riches?' Randall goaded with a wicked smile.

'Oh, it was another time and I'm sure my family were very honourable.' Shirley huffed and her guests glanced at one another, grinning with embarrassment. They all knew many well-known families had thrown Indigenous people off the land and had them shot at the time of early white settlement. Shirley changed the subject.

Stories flowed throughout the meal. The atmosphere was congenial and punctuated by howls of laughter. After they moved to the terrace, Felicity remembered she had to make a call. 'Oops, time to ring my neighbour, he's out of bed before sunrise, so need to catch him now.'

She laughed to herself as she saw Shirley move closer to Merv and say, 'They tell me you're an expert on the night sky.'

During the call Bill recounted the rainfall, the storm's damage, and the condition of the sheep, then gossiped. Felicity told him about the journey to Adelaide and how Shirley had taken an instant dislike to Mia, but she didn't mention the pills as she wanted to be sure of what was going on before he knew.

'I'm not surprised, Flea, you're so naïve,' said Bill. 'This trip was my fault, you looked exhausted and needed a holiday, I encouraged you to go travelling with her.'

'Thanks, don't worry, she's no longer here. I'll be back home soon.' Felicity said her farewell as Randall entered the room with his arms outstretched. She couldn't talk to Bill about Randall, certainly not about what had taken place since she left *Neerea*.

She pulled away from Randall, still stinging from his behaviour to her when they were last together. 'Where're Shirl and Merv?'

'Oh, drinking expensive port in the lounge room. You're mad at me, aren't you?' he said, as she led the way down the hall. He caught up to her and tried to wrap his arms around her, but she remained stubbornly stiff.

She broke away and headed for the bedroom. 'I need a swim.'

When she returned, Randall joined her in the pool trying to keep pace, shadowing her at each end, but she turned her head the other way. After a while, she waned, so he grabbed her and held her tight, and whispered, 'I'm sorry.'

After a long pause and with a stern expression she answered, 'Don't walk out on me again.'

They found the switch for the garden lights, and with towels wrapped around themselves they wandered through the garden. She grabbed his hand and pointed to the shrubs and older trees suffering from the drought; the fronds of one palm were dipping to the ground, and a lion's head stood proud, waiting to sprout forth, but the water and golden Japanese fish had long gone.

'It's sad walking around here,' said Felicity as she showed him struggling exotic plants sown when they constructed the house. 'I remember this as a lush garden, and it's so depressing, the water restrictions have really taken their toll.'

'You realise we've been avoiding the subject of Mia,' he said.

'Other things first!'

She put her fingers to her lips and sauntered seductively through the French doors into their bedroom, raising her eyebrows and giving him a naughty wink as she slowly stripped off her swimmers, then gently removed his, before leading him to the shower. The water streamed over them as they lathered each other with soap, kissing and stroking their bodies in delight. Afterwards, Randall grabbed a large towel, and tenderly wrapped her in it, dried her before lifting her and to her surprise throwing her onto to the bed. He then made small, slow butterfly kisses over her body. She responded and they spent the next half an hour in each other's arms.

After they dressed, Felicity put her arm around him and they moved to a bench on the veranda outside in the cooler evening.

Randall interrupted their silent contemplation. 'I didn't tell you, but I came with the evidence.' Together they returned to the bedroom, and he ransacked his luggage, throwing it on the floor until he pulled out the packet he had discovered in Mia's sleeping bag.

'Here they are, OxyContin,' said Randall, passing it to her. 'My chemist friend told me these have to be prescribed.

They're opiates to numb pain, extraordinarily strong and highly addictive.'

'Mia called them her Oxys, said she got them from her doctor.' Felicity turned the packet. 'These were in her cache, but I don't know what other pills she has.' Felicity moved closer to him and played with the hairs on his arm. 'When I went to her room, she wasn't there but strewn across the bed were tablets in bottles, things in packets like this.' She held them to the light and studied them. 'I asked her about the pills and then, she ups and leaves.'

'Thank goodness she's gone. There's nothing we can do.'

She leant her head on his shoulder, and his phone in the bedroom buzzed.

'I'll leave it,' he said, but after it had gone to messages, the phone rang again. He flinched. 'I'm going to have to get this,' he said as he scrambled out the French doors onto the veranda.

Felicity strained to hear the conversation; Randall seemed to calm someone, but she wasn't sure. Ten minutes later, when she was about to join the others, he finished the call.

'Everything okay?' said Felicity as he paced the veranda and nodded. 'I've been thinking, I wish I had talked to Mia about these pills and discovered why she had so many. It would have saved so much angst for everyone.'

'Don't beat yourself up. She's gone.' He gave her a distracted kiss on the forehead. 'Let's get back to the others.'

Merv sat beside Shirley on the large, comfortable lounge with a glass of red in his hand and cashews within easy reach and entertained the group with his stories.

'I have something to show you, Flea, that will make you laugh.' Shirley moved to the antique sideboard and rustled papers until she dug out an envelope. 'I found these old photos in the garage. Remember those Bachelor and Spinster balls we drove all over the countryside to attend.'

'Oh, no. We were young and single and happy to get grog spilt over our best dresses. B&Ss were wild. Did you ever go, Randall?'

'No. Don't forget I was earning a crust while you were out playing.' He lifted his head in pretend disgust. 'But let's see how you played up.'

Roars of laughter filled the room as they studied the photos of young people hanging out the backs of utes with drunk smiles. There were groups of fresh-looking women in fancy silk dresses and men in black ties. They squabbled as names and their present whereabouts were tossed around in conversation.

'Shirl, who's this?' Randall pointed to a young woman wearing a white turban and a tight-fitting red dress. In the photo, she stood next to Felicity.

'Wasn't she your neighbour or something?' said Shirley.

Felicity gasped and put her hand to her mouth. 'It's Davina, I attended primary school with her. She lived up the road. Remember, she came with us to the ball and we couldn't find her when we wanted to go home?'

'It's a long time ago,' said Shirley. 'I remember we found her curled around the beer kegs.' She sat on the edge of the lounge and patted Merv's knee.

'That was the beginning of the end for Davina.' She passed the photo to Merv. 'This is what she looked like.'

'A stunner!'

Felicity's voice cracked, and she closed her eyes. 'Yes, I wish her life had been better. She got herself into lots of trouble. I tried to help, but it was useless.'

'She reminds you of Mia, doesn't she?' said Randall, putting his hand on her leg.

Felicity nodded in agreement and dropped her head. Tears formed and she picked up a cushion to soak them away. She sniffled. Randall wrapped his arm around her and gave her his handkerchief. The sound of deep sobbing, years of holding life firm, filled the room.

Chapter 14

The next day, Shirley sat at the wide wooden table in the kitchen dressed in a dark navy suit and bright red lipstick, wearing slippers as she hummed with the radio and read the local newspaper spread before her. She raised her dark, over-painted eyebrows and pointed at the clock when Felicity entered the room.

'Morning Flea, what a saga last night. Are you okay?'

'Didn't realise I was in such a state. Everything bombarded me, the farm, the drought, bloody Alan, Mia. I'm whacked, can't fight anymore,' said Felicity, boiling the water for a cuppa. 'I haven't cried so much in years and Randall's a darling. He kept telling me everything'll be okay, and I could only sob.'

'Don't worry, you're amongst friends. Now, this morning, I've got to visit my dressmaker and do a few jobs. Come with me then you can go to that music stuff when we return.' At that moment, Randall strolled into the kitchen, looking for Merv, and she said, 'He drove to the shops in your car. He's a cutie, thinks shopping's exciting.'

'What shenanigans happened last night?' asked Randall as he stood over Shirley and poked her in the ribs. 'So did something happen between you and Merv?'

'Never you mind. Help yourselves to breakfast,' she said with a smug smile.

Soon the aromas of coffee and toast wafted through the room. Felicity pencilled a list of food to buy, then left the other two to tease one another while she dressed.

She stared in the ornate bathroom mirror and a washed-out middle-aged woman with strained red eyes and tight wrinkled skin looked back. Screwing-up her face, she mouthed at her reflection, 'Okay, I've had better days,' and rummaged in her bag for eye drops. After moisturising her face tried to replicate Mia's makeup tricks.

As the women pulled out of the garage in Shirley's white Mercedes, they caught sight of the gardener pottering in the flowerbeds. They waved to him and Shirley mentioned he was finding the labouring difficult because of his age.

'My garden needs work, everything's getting beyond me. I need a smaller place, a townhouse or large apartment where I can shut the door and travel. I just hate real estate agents prying.' She gave a weary sigh and glanced with curiosity at Felicity. 'Do you want the job of selling my house?'

Felicity's mouth dropped open, and she hesitated before she said, 'That's strange, Shirl but I've been toying with what I'll do. Selling my place is a choice for me too.' She grinned. 'We could get rid of the lot and go travelling together.'

'Change our lives, you mean?' They glanced at each other and broke into hysterical laughter.

When they had quietened, Felicity rested her hands on her lap and reflected. 'The last few years have been bloody hard, and this morning, my neighbour rang. Alan's been snooping around the farm while I'm not there.' She struggled to find the right words. 'It's time to pay him off, get him out of my life so I can make my own decisions, put myself on track. I've been wrestling with what I need to do.'

There was a comfortable silence until the brakes screeched and Shirley missed a car as she barged through a stop sign.

'Whew, that was close,' she said. 'Now, what're you doing about Randall?'

Felicity sensed her face redden and laughed nervously. 'It's exciting and scary but who knows, too early to say.' She looked at her hands in her lap. 'I can't handle how he runs away when matters don't go his way. He spends a lot of time on his phone, and it makes him so distracted…'

'He runs a business, what do you expect?'

'Yeah, but these calls don't sound like business. I wonder if it's something to do with his ex. Either that or he's got another girlfriend somewhere!'

Shirley laughed. 'Can't you say his ex's name?' Felicity crossed her arms and glared ahead. 'Well, you'll have to ask him what's going on,' said Shirley. 'But you still want him, don't you?'

'Remember, my last romance didn't end in paradise, so it'll be slow and steady.' Felicity turned and gave Shirley an inquisitive look. 'Merv?'

They both laughed. 'Aren't we lucky to have "a bit on the side" at our age?' Shirley's wicked grin covered her face. 'Not long term, but for now it's fun.'

Thinking about Randall gave Felicity an inner glow of warmth as they pulled into the busy shopping centre.

The women roared with laughter and Felicity wolf-whistled at the sight of the men with their arms crossed, dressed like twins in their riding boots and blue jeans waiting on the veranda when they returned to the house. Merv's shirt was bright yellow with green figures in different poses doing somersaults and running, and Randall was Mr Conservative beside him in a polo t-shirt. The two women glanced at one another as Randall's phone rang and he hurried into the garden to answer it.

'You won't get lost wearing that, Merv,' laughed Shirley. 'Where did you get it?'

He shrugged. 'My son bought it for me for Christmas. Don't you like it?' He made a move to undress. 'Ah, I'll lend it to you.'

Felicity threw the groceries on the kitchen bench and hurried to dress. A glance in the mirror at her new outfit — a powder pink floral top worn over tight white pants and multi-coloured sneakers was reassuring. Her chat with Shirley had shifted her mood and ignited a few possibilities for the future. Felicity decided at the first opportunity she would ask Randall what the phone calls were about. She frowned, should she be worried?

'Wow, Flea, don't you look great,' said Merv, putting his arm around her. 'Too good to be sitting in a park listening to music. Now Shirl, won't you come with us?' He winked at Randall. 'We've spent the morning scanning the program and know what to hear. We'll have a ball.'

'You've been at me ever since you arrived. Okay, as long as you both make lunch, I'll join you.' The men clapped and whistled at her.

Merv poked around the fridge for food, wriggling his large bottom to pretend music. 'Shirl, soon you'll be dancing the night away.'

***

Shirley sped along the wide roads with Merv in the passenger seat. They were almost at the venue when Randall's phone rang, and Felicity threw him a questioning look when she noticed his face go pale. To her surprise, he turned off the call and looked out the window.

The atmosphere became more exciting the closer they got to the turnstile. People filled the place with carefree laughter and delight; family groups organised tickets and received last-minute instructions on what to do if they strayed. Colourful flags flapped in the slight breeze and in the distance canvas sails encased the stages with bands throwing their music to the crowds gyrating before them.

'This is a medieval market,' said Merv, as they moved into the key area with his arm draped around Shirley. 'I've seen nothing like this.'

The acts were so different. Angélique Kidjo's prancing and singing stunned them and they bobbed to the rhythmic sounds in front of the stage, then they found a more sedate classical music group and listened from their low folding chairs. As the heat of the day dissipated, the mood of the crowd changed, the dancing became wilder, and a decorative hue of coloured lights and lanterns glowed across the festival grounds.

'I'm starved. What does everyone want to eat?' said Merv. 'Shirl, you'll help me?'

'I saw lots of food over the back, there's even a bar.' Randall laughed, as he pulled out his wallet. 'I'll have something hot like my mate and a red.' He snuggled into Felicity's body and she whacked him.

'What do you want, Flea?'

'I'm not sure, you choose for me, not hot and spicy though, and the same wine.' She raised her eyebrows at him.

'Okay, surprises and reds coming.' Merv saluted and disappeared with Shirley.

Felicity sat with her arm interlocked with Randall's and they read the program under the light from his phone torch.

'I saw something interesting for us to watch later.' Randall flicked through the pages. 'A French group doing a singing painting act, it'll be different.'

Felicity felt his phone vibrate with an incoming call and glimpsed the name. His ex. Randall scrambled from the ground and looked more and more agitated as he marched back and forth, listening intently to the conversation.

Randall finished the call abruptly, sat down and covered his face with his hands. 'Apologies, that was Cas, my ex. She's not coping well at the moment. The boyfriend's gone.'

'You should have told me,' she said, gazing downward and fiddling with her watch, 'I was worried about all those phone calls.'

After he took a few deep breaths, he caught hold of Felicity's hand and fixed his big blue eyes on her. 'Look, I don't want to spoil our night, so let's not talk about it now. You have your own troubles. How are you after this morning?'

'Okay. Much better, the call from Bill telling me Alan had been hanging around the farm hurt.'

'Yes, that's strange. What do you think he wants?'

'More stuff to take, money?' she said with a shrug.

'He doesn't know about your other investments, does he?'

'No, but he'd love to find them. My intuition's working overtime. When I left, I double-checked my office and made sure I locked everything away. Bill said he didn't think he had been through the house.' She moved closer to Randall and kissed him. 'I hope he hasn't broken in. Let's forget our old partners and enjoy ourselves tonight. We can't do much here.'

'Hey, come back to Mildura with me on Monday? We'll get you home from there.' He stroked her arm. 'You can't stay on your own if Alan's lurking.'

Felicity sucked in a swallow of air and she steadied herself. 'Thanks. Here they come with our drinks.'

'Shirl pointed out your mate, Mia,' said Merv as he juggled with the plastic cups of wine. 'She's a good-looker.'

'Yeah, she was with a big goofy tattooed bloke. She even waved.' Shirley bent to distribute the food. 'I won't be inviting them home.'

'She can stay engrossed in her beau. I don't want her searching for me,' said Felicity, fanning herself with the program.

They laughed and joked over their meal until the next event. Randall clasped her hand as they battled the crowd to see the French performers on scaffolding chanting and singing as they painted paper screens.

'Frightening stuff,' said Shirley. 'I couldn't climb like they do. They have even scared the audience.'

Merv grabbed Shirl in a hug. 'I've seen enough, off we go home?'

Randall and Felicity laughed in agreement and he folded his arm around her, guiding her through the dispersing crowd. She had to bury her chaotic thoughts about Randall and his ex if she wanted to enjoy her break from the farm. But she was troubled. It wouldn't be easy for Randall to ignore his ex-wife.

Chapter 15

A blanket shielded Mia from a couple she didn't recognise grunting in the rear seat of the Kombi so she covered her ears, trying to block out the sounds of the passionate squeals. What are they doing here?

She remembered the pill she had taken while dancing with that guy, the touch of his muscled arms around her shoulders, the hardness of his six-pack pressing against her back as they moved to the music. Done with dancing, they must have returned to the Kombi to sleep. She shivered, everything was a blur, she didn't know him, and now he'd skipped out.

'Um, um, excuse me,' said Mia as she rose from the uncomfortable bench and stared open-mouthed at the panting couple. 'Time to go.' She turned and in a flurry of activity searched for the ignition key in the van's front.

When they had finished dressing, the young man jumped out, grabbed the long-haired blonde woman's hand and helped her to the ground. 'Thanks,' he muttered, and they swaggered down the road laughing with their arms wrapped together.

Mia bit her nails, trying to recall when she last had her shoulder bag and her wallet. She found her phone under a pile of chip wrappers near the driver's seat and wondered how they appeared there. Glimpses of the night emerged. She had clung to the guy's hand to navigate the dark streets until they joined a queue of people waiting to enter a cavernous bar with glowing lights, where she threw back nips of vodka and danced with abandon until dawn.

'No wonder my head thumps!' she said out loud as she looked in the rear vision mirror. 'What a mess.'

Mia's half-remembered image was staggering along the street until the hunk lifted her from the footpath and carried her. They snuggled into the back seat while the other couple lay on the other bench. The makeshift bed was narrow and his snore horrendous, so she left him, grabbed the rug, and stretched herself in the front.

Now her head pounded, her throat was parched, and her thoughts scrambled. She wanted sleep.

The phone rang, and she fumbled as the sun blasted through the cabin window. Not recognising the number, she turned it off and combed the floor for some water. Nothing, just empty bottles.

She ransacked the van, under the seats, in her bag, whimpering for something for her pounding head. Zilch.

Through her daze she realized the guy, whom she had only met last night, and whose name she couldn't remember, may have stripped her not only of her money but her other belongings.

Mia grabbed her clothes, bags, empty drink bottles and rubbish and tossed everything on the dry verge creating a colourful tip. When she had removed everything, she clutched herself and moaned in despair, 'They stole my Oxys!', her legs dangling out the back door.

A harassed-looking mother approached with arguing kids in tow. 'Are you okay?'

'Lost my bag, dumped everything to find it.'

'Good idea. Can I help you?'

'Please. I'd love a coffee, but some water and maybe a pill for my throbbing head will do.' Mia held out two water bottles. 'Could you fill these?'

Although the woman looked taken aback, she took them and her kids and disappeared into a nearby house while a purple-haired lady in a green apron shuffled towards Mia.

'Dearie is this yours?' she said as she held up a velvet shoulder bag. 'Someone threw it over my fence and it may have been there for months if I didn't come out to pull the dead flowers off my geraniums.' She handed it to her. 'You made such a racket at dawn, I should have called the police.'

Mia pursed her lips, realising she had a lucky escape. 'Oops, sorry. The bands were so good, we stayed late.'

'I see you found it,' said the mother, arriving with Mia's water and two tablets. She nodded to the older lady, then hurried home.

Mia searched her handbag and muttered to herself, 'Oh no, where are my keys?' She quaffed the drink and swallowed the tablets, sweat drenching her as she repacked the Kombi, taking brief breaks in between tidying it. She spread the contents of her bag across the front seat, and discovered her purse with credit cards, cash, and license was missing, along with the keys and her painkillers.

After half an hour, she hurried to the mother's house and knocked. 'Thanks for the water and tablets. My head's getting better. Do you have an old street map? I'm trying to find where a friend's staying. My phone battery's low.'

Together they studied the directory for clues to where she had dropped Felicity yesterday, and when Mia finally recognised several street names and landmarks from her travels, she clapped her hands with glee and asked a child to get paper and a pen for her to write the directions.

'Now I'll ring my friend, see if she'll help me,' said Mia. 'I hope she's there. Thanks.'

***

Randall and Felicity argued over a crossword clue as they finished their coffee. Her phone sitting on a bench in the far corner of the room rang and Merv, with Fluff resting on his lap, answered with his deep-toned voice answered, 'Hello, Merv here.'

The young woman on the other end, hesitated. 'Is Flea there?'

'Who's speaking?'

'Mia, I came with her to Adelaide.'

'Oh Mia, I've heard lots about you. Are you coming over to see us?'

Felicity made frantic waves of her arms and mouthed, 'No way. I'm not here, we'll catch up later.'

'Flea's not here. You lost the keys to your van? That's bad luck. How did you do this? Where are you?' After listening for a while, he winked at Felicity and then said. 'Bye, Mia. Hope to meet you soon.'

He laughed as he put the phone down.

Felicity glared at him. 'You bugger. Bet she wanted me to sort out the shemozzle. Now the next clue, Randall?'

***

'Bloody hell! She's not there. What's Ken's and Jan's surname?' Mia muttered to herself as she searched through her contacts and noticed the older woman again, standing with her garden secateurs staring at her, 'Busybody.'

'Oh lovey, we're in Victor Harbor tonight,' Mia mimicked them as she threw the phone on the front seat after the call. 'That bitch, Flea's the only person I know here.'

Mia dragged herself out of the van to the nearby park. She rested her back against a tree with a blanket pulled around her as she shivered in pain and continually wiped her face with a wet cloth. The day grew hotter, and the birds screeched as they played under a leaking sprinkler.

Two giggling teenagers came out of a house to the park, hopping from foot to foot, crossing the scalding road and running to the nearby swings. Mia drew her arms around her legs and watched with envy, wishing she had had a proper home and a family like these girls.

Her pounding head forced her to return to the Kombi, and she tossed the bags and the rubbish around again, trying to find a pill to drive away the pain. Nothing. She curled up on the rear seat, drenched in sweat, and tried to sleep, but flashes of her life came streaming back like a bad video.

At one stage, she sat up in fright. She remembered through the blur, her mother, Lisa's, last visit.

***

Her mother's whining voice jolted her from her sleep. Her unrecognisable face reshaped by too many facelifts, her long ponytail streaked with grey and her hippy clothing left over from another era. Lisa, Californian chic with a Texan drawl, and a whiff of her native accent.

Staring at the cracked upholstery lining on the Kombi's roof, Mia recalled the weird phone call.

'Hello, is that my gal,' said an unfamiliar American voice.

She talked over a startled Mia. 'It's your Mom. I'm coming to see you so give me your email and I'll send the details.'

Then the diatribe began.

Without drawing breath, she announced in her southern drawl, 'I don't know why your silly father allowed you to return to Australia. He doesn't work there. I suppose he stays with his crazy family when he returns. Do you see them? Out of *Deliverance* country in Victoria. Suppose mine are no better, so have nothing to do with my family. You never know what they might do to you….' Mia held the phone away from her ear and stared into the distance. 'Why haven't you come to visit me?'

Mia had enough. At the final click, she collapsed onto the nearby couch.

Within two minutes, there was another ring, and she studied the number, lay down, switched on the TV, and let the sound fill the room.

Months passed until one bleak, blustery Canberra day, a knock at her door startled her and she dropped the book she was reading. There, on the other side of the security screen, stood a strange woman with dark-brown eyes shadowed by kohl. She wore bangles and a long black skirt with cowboy boots and a tilted beret with a three-quarter maroon silver-threaded coat hanging from her shoulders.

'My darling... how are you?' The woman flung her large, purple-checked scarf around her neck.

Mia stood perplexed at the unfamiliar figure.

'It's your mom. Don't you recognise me?'

This apparition wasn't what Mia dreamed her mother would look like. She hadn't seen her since she was ten, and she was still recovering from the shock of the thriller she was reading.

'I told you I'd come,' whined the woman. 'Your father gave me your address.' Mia was slow to open the door. 'Ah, that's better. Now I want a big cuddle.'

Mia tensed her body and gritted her teeth as the tall woman folded her arms around her, but there was no warmth in the hug. For the next ten minutes, Lisa babbled; where she lived in the States, and about her new husband and Mia half-listened, made them both a coffee and put on African music to soothe the intrusion.

'Switch off that rubbish. It reminds me of living in Kenya and that dreary father of yours.'

Mia gathered her backpack and dancing shoes, and said, 'I must get to my class now. Time to go, Lisa.'

'But I want to spend time with you, my darling daughter.'

Mia hissed through her teeth. 'Sorry, Brad, my friend is coming to collect me. We'll have coffee before you leave.'

'I've lost your number. What is it?'

Her daughter wrote on a crumpled envelope and shoved it at her. 'When do you return home?'

'In two weeks but I'll visit my old haunts first, see my childhood farm and my primary school.' Lisa wrapped the scarf around her neck, making her even more theatrical. 'You could come with me.'

'I'll think about it,' said Mia in a hurry to get her mother to leave.

Her mother stood her ground and wouldn't go until Mia had agreed to accompany her on her nostalgic drive.

Mia leant against the door after she had finally departed and wailed, 'My mother? She asked nothing about my life.'

Lisa was never a mother, too self-absorbed, too selfish to worry about her and her father, and Mia couldn't remember when she called her mother, Mom.

Her father always said, when he had too much to drink, that he loved Lisa, but she married him for his money and played along until the next man came. Then his tears would flow, and as a child she had to console him with a hug, but soon got sick of that.

***

In the rented car, Mia's anxiety rose. She had slept badly and berated herself for agreeing to go on the trip. A short woollen coat, a scarf, blue jeans, and little green boots protected her against the cold, miserable weather, but not her mother.

'I'll drive...I know the roads,' Mia insisted.

'No, I lived here, I *can* drive on this side of the road,' said Lisa as she climbed behind the wheel.

There was a shaky start through the suburban streets. Mia clenched her jaw and gripped the door handle as the city gave way to picturesque farms, and Lisa displayed a renewed sense of urgency. She leaned towards Mia like a conspirator.

'Don't know why I'm returning to this horrid place. A family friend with an enormous nose abused me at twelve. You never get over it, damaged goods, as they say.'

Mia fixed her hands to her ears.

'I'll spare you the details. Yes, best told to an expensive therapist: I lay on a couch for years.' Lisa punched the steering wheel with her hand. 'Therapy's an American sport. Do you go to one?' She didn't wait for an answer. 'I flew from one man to another at uni. We all did in the seventies until I met your father who was a kind man, too good for me.'

Mia turned her head and stared out the window while her mother continued her monologue.

After they had travelled for about an hour, Lisa said, 'This trip's taking forever and I'm sure when I was a child, it didn't take this long.' She peered at a signpost when they reached a T-junction and slammed her foot on the accelerator rather than the brake.

Mia screamed as her mother spun around a corner, taking it too fast on the wrong side of the road. The rush headlong towards a brick fence was her last memory.

***

Her mother had no injuries, but Mia suffered the worst of the impact. Agony crept through her body at the mere thought of the trauma, the wounds, and the badly broken arm.

In the hospital they prescribed Mia little round white pills and she nicknamed her help mates, her Oxys. These drugs delivered a welcomed numbness to her pain and dissipated her fears, awakening a new sense of longing.

One morning while recovering, Mia asked if she might go to the cafeteria as she had missed the taste and smell of a proper brew of coffee. She sat at a chrome table in the garden protected by a giant palm and enjoyed the throngs of people coming and going.

Mia turned her body away and screwed up her face when she heard a familiar voice call, 'Darling, how are you?' Her mother darted towards her with her arms outstretched, so she shifted her broken arm with its sling to her chest to prevent the barrage. 'My gal, let me give you a hug.'

'No, it hurts too much.'

Lisa then sat beside her. 'Do you want something to eat? Another coffee?'

'A coffee.'

When her mom left, Mia searched for an escape. The restrooms? She was too slow, and her mother returned, carrying over cream donuts and meat pies.

'Thought you might like a bite to eat.'

As Lisa sipped her tea and ate her pie and dumped her life history on Mia. 'I didn't want to be a mom but didn't know how to stop it. Sorry. Dreadful thing to say. I love you and you were a gorgeous baby, but I wanted to give you away.' Mia fixed her other arm over her sling to prevent a further attack and gazed at her in horror.

'Here, have this.' Lisa shoved the purple scarf she wore the first day she arrived at Mia's place onto her lap.

Mia swallowed tears as she grabbed the shawl and threw it on the ground.

'You're not grateful? It's awfully expensive…Versace.' Lisa picked it up and stuffed it in her bag. 'I'm sorry about your injuries but I'm leaving tomorrow, get better.'

She never heard from her mother again.

***

If only she could spin the wheel backwards and start again. The thought of her mother, and the pain from the accident, fuelled her anger as she curled in the Kombi with a blanket covering her, and cried herself to a fitful sleep.

She woke startled. Her skin prickled from the clammy seat and someone banged on the side door. The old lady was standing there with sandwiches wrapped in paper.

'I've prepared something for you to eat.'

Mia hesitated, 'May I use your bathroom? I'm hot and sticky.'

'Come with me, dearie,' said the woman and Mia followed her into the musty house stuffed with antiques and creepy lifelike dolls sitting upright on chairs, and at the end of a long dark hall was an old-fashioned, green-tiled bathroom.

'Dry your hands with that towel.'

Mia closed the door with relief and eyed the mirrored cabinet, turned on the water and searched through the cupboard for pain killers, but there were only laxatives.

'Thanks for the sandwich now I must find my keys.'

Mia cringed as she banged the front door in her escape. Up and down the street she prowled, searching yards, under shrubs, in the gutter until something caught the light under a bush on the overgrown verge, her keys in their elaborate leather cover courtesy of a Bedouin tribe and a bazaar in Turkey. She held them to her heart.

'Thank you,' she whispered to the sky.

The sandwiches made her dry retch. The bread was stale and spread with margarine, so she threw them in the bin. Her uneasiness grew as she straightened her skirt and checked in the mirror of the toilet block to prepare herself to visit Shirley's place. The bastards had even stolen her make-up.

Mia wiped beads of sweat from her forehead and clutched the directions as she navigated her way through Adelaide's suburbs. On Shirley's street, she backed the Kombi to see if she had the right place, and then crept past the imposing gates to park a few houses away. Her heart raced as she stood with her hands jammed into her armpits and stared at the house.

With a pounding heart, she pressed the security-gate switch and heard the echo of the doorbell's blare and a dog barking. She pushed it again, but there was no answer. She peered through the gate's grille for any signs of someone home, rattling and pushing the gate, hoping it would open, but no one responded.

Chapter 16

Mia moaned as she sat in the driver's seat with her arms drooped over the wheel. A sudden noise from the adjacent house forced her upright, and she watched as a black limousine pulled out of the electronic gates. She held her breath as the car passed the Kombi without a sound and the puffy, fat-faced man and haughty looking blonde woman glared at her. The couple unnerved her and disappeared.

Overseas, she had lived in houses behind big fences and automatic gateways like prisons run by servants. When she moved to Australia, she had escaped this way of life and discovered a sense of freedom, a new experience for her. It would be safer retreating to the festival rather than staying in this lonely, hostile area. Maybe Felicity would return later?

The beat of the drum called as she rattled the ashtray in the front seat, hunting for stray coins. She had sixteen dollars and her wristband barcode, her ticket to the event. It would not go far, best to leave the van where she had stayed during the night so she retraced her route, checking the directions from time to time, and found a safe place for it. Dressed in a long, multicoloured skirt, she locked the vehicle and traipsed wearily to the festival grounds.

The festival's buzz and welcoming atmosphere energised her. She rested against a tree; she put a wet cloth to her forehead and moved to the rhythmic sounds. Her thoughts went to her childhood, her time in Kenya after her mother disappeared, when her father, who was incapable of knowing what to do for his daughter's welfare, often drove her to Nairobi National Park to see the wild beasts roaming freely. She couldn't get enough of the majestic lions wandering around the place or the giraffes eating from the tops of the thorn trees. The flamingos at Lake Bogoria and the many coloured birds also remained etched in her mind. She vowed never to forget them and as a child read every book on Africa she could find.

The sounds drifted over her, soothed her, as people intent on finding their next band or venue passed without as much as a glance.

Later in the day someone sidled up and squatted beside her, startling her with a tap on the shoulder and a whisper in her ear, 'Did you have fun last night?'

'Oh, it's you!' She backed off in anger, bristling with indignation as the guy from the day before sat next to her. 'Where's my money?'

'Huh. What do you mean?'

'What happened to you?'

'You were asleep, and it was too hot, so I ducked off to check my bike. I came back, but you'd left. C'mon, don't be angry, have a drink.'

'No. I've no makeup, no cash, or cards. Nothing.' She crossed her arms in front of her chest. 'They grabbed the lot and threw my keys under a bush because they could not pinch the van. Had it off together in front of me and collected everything.'

'Assholes. Are you okay?' he said as a look of concern crept across his face. 'You must be hungry.'

'My head's throbbing, I feel terrible. Do you have anything for it?'

'Nah. First aid station might have something?'

'No, I won't go there.' She brushed down her T-shirt, straightened her skirt and fluffed up her hair. 'When I woke, I thought you'd disappeared forever.' She linked arms over his shoulder and pecked him on the cheek. 'I'll have a beer.'

At the bar, they clinked their plastic glasses of ale. 'Salute.' With an embarrassed giggle, she said, 'Oops, what's your name.'

'Sam.' He raised his cup 'Bottoms up…?'

'Mia.' They both laughed.

She gulped the drink, the cool liquid soothing her throat, and had finished before he had even started.

'That's quick. A water or another one?' He chuckled when she nodded and joined the queue for drinks.

She sipped the ale as she slurred. 'I want to rest.'

'When did you last eat?' said Sam as she gazed at him.

He wagged his finger and made her comfortable at the trunk of a Morton Bay fig, where generous branches provided a refuge and ventured off for food. She bent over as her stomach churned with the smell of the nearby overflowing rubbish bins making her dry retch.

'Here, get this into you. Burgers, the best thing for a hangover. Should've had them before the beers.'

Sam sat next to her and when he caught a whiff of the garbage cans, he dragged her aside to a picnic table. She picked at the snack, eating half, her body saying no more.

'How are you?'

'Better, the food helps. Thanks,' she lied, feeling muddled.

'What do you want to do?'

'I need to regain my energy and chill out before I dance.'

'Let's get out of here.' He embraced her. 'I know a little corner in the park. No one will disturb us there.'

Sam relaxed against a tree, and she rested her head in his lap. He stroked her face and played with her locks, and soon she was dozing. In her hazy state, she cuddled into him, grateful for his care for her. Bliss.

'How do you feel?' he said as she stretched from her snooze.

'Much better, thanks. I'll have a wash then let's find the music.'

Hot and lightheaded, Mia lumbered towards the toilets, wondering where she could get pills to wipe the dizziness and pain away. Should she ask Sam? She cupped her hands under the tap, lowered her head, and drank the water from it. After wiping her forehead and hands with her long skirt, she twisted her hair to the crown of her head, pinned it there and stared into the mirror. Would he help her?

'You ready now?' said Mia when she returned.

'Coming. There's a top band at a pub close by.' Sam hoisted himself from the ground, put his arm around her, and they chatted as they strolled to the venue.

They swayed with the rhythm of the music, interlocked as one. People surrounded them and they rocked and sang the tunes along with the crowd. During a break, he lifted the comb from her hair, let the tresses fall and leant in and gave her a long, passionate kiss and she responded. They held each other until the beat immersed them, and they wriggled and stomped wildly, sweat clouding their brows.

Sam dug in the pocket of his jeans, and her eyes lit up when he produced two small silver packages. He held one and handed the other to her. She laughed and kissed him, then with care removed the lining and put the pill on her tongue. Her pupils grew larger and wider and her dancing more frenzied. Everyone gawked as she danced like a whirling dervish to the rhythm of the African drum.

Mia put her hands to her face, shuddered, then collapsed. Chaos reigned. People gathered; others fled. The manager of the hotel appeared and urged people to move aside as he rolled her onto her side. An ambulance arrived and after affixing an oxygen mask and drip, they whisked her away.

Somewhere in the mayhem, an emergency attendant asked if anyone knew the young lady. No one stepped forward.

Chapter 17

When the friends returned from the festival, they flopped exhausted on the comfortable lounge chairs. There were peals of laughter when Merv was the first to move from their stupor to begin to prepare supper.

'Outta the way, you lot make me nervous, check out the TV or do something else.'

There was a shuffling of seating and cushions to catch the television news. A young woman had collapsed at a pub and the police were appealing to the public to help identify her.

'It'd be horrible if you became ill and passed out, and no one knew who you were,' said Felicity as she leaned into Randall.

'Yes, I often think about what would happen on some of those back roads.' Randall clasped his hand in hers and gripped it as he spoke. 'If you're in your area, the bush telegraph tells everyone, but it's scary if it's elsewhere.'

'What's scary?' Merv appeared with Shirley's hand-blown glasses dripping with pieces of fruit.

'Oh, something we heard on the news,' said Randall. 'Hey, what's this, from the Cocktail of the Year award?' Laughter and a clinking of glass filled the room.

In the middle of Merv's relaxed "gourmet" supper of pancakes on the lounge, Felicity's phone rang.

Shirley waved at her. 'Leave it. They'll ring back.'

'No, no, I'd better get it. It may be Bill,' said Felicity, rummaging through her bag to find the phone. 'That bastard, Alan, could still be snooping.'

She answered the call, moving to the poolside so she could hear and had an ominous flash when the caller said, 'Mrs…?'

She braced herself. What's happened to my kids? Simon? Emily?

The woman identified herself as a nurse from the hospital, explaining Felicity's number was the last call on the phone of a young woman, who had collapsed at a local pub. She had no other identification on her. 'We think you might know her?'

After the description the caller gave, Felicity said, 'It sounds like a young woman I know, Mia is her name.' Felicity's voice whispered. 'What's happened?'

'She's in a serious condition in hospital. Do you know the next of kin?'

'Is it that bad?' Felicity gasped. She ran her words together. 'Well, I understand her dad's in Kolkata, India, and her mother's name is Lisa. I'm uncertain where she lives.' She sucked in her breath. 'Maybe the US?' The nurse kept bombarding her with questions. 'She's estranged from her mum, and her dad works for a development agency. He's high up, so shouldn't be too hard to find…No, I don't recollect if she has family in Australia. She mentioned a lawyer friend Brad in Canberra.'

'Is there anything else you can tell us?'

'Sorry, I know no more information,' she responded curtly.

'Thank you, Mrs…'

'Felicity and please contact me again if I can be of use. Is she allowed visitors?'

'Not now, ring tomorrow. She needs time to recover.' The nurse paused at the other end of the phone. 'Do you know if this young woman has any issues with substance abuse?'

With her heart racing, Felicity almost shouted, 'Sorry I have to go, there are visitors here.' She said goodbye and collapsed onto the lounge alongside Randall, who gave her a reassuring pat on the leg before finishing his dinner.

'The moment I saw that girl, I knew she was trouble,' said Shirley wagging her finger at Felicity. 'Flea, I thought your strays would get you into strife one day.'

Felicity clutched her arms to her chest. 'I don't know what to do, who to call. Poor Mia. She's alone with no-one to help her get through the medical system, substance abuse the nurse said.'

'Doesn't the hospital approach the next of kin?' asked Merv with a mouth half full of food.

'I'm sure they could find her dad on the computer,' said Randall, half engrossed in a TV program.

'Let's leave it, worry about Mia later, we can't do anything,' Merv shooed a late-night lingering fly. 'Eat up, then we'll work out what we can do.'

Felicity glared at her friends and stood, shoving the nearby coffee table away, sending her unfinished supper and the maple syrup to the Turkish rug below. 'You callous bastards.'

***

Later, sitting on the terrace enjoying a beer with his mate, Merv looked abashed as he announced he would remain a few more days at Shirley's. 'Too hot at my place and I've organised my neighbour to feed the dogs. Much better by Shirl's pool, she's a sport, even agreed to run me home. Why don't you stay for a few days, Randall?'

'I prefer to drive home with Flea.' Randall cracked his knuckles and glanced at her with his stony face.

Felicity grimaced, moving to sit with him. 'I promise we'll spend time together later,' she said in a whisper, threading her fingers through his.

'I can't wait around for you,' he said, miffed, pulling his hand away. 'There's a meeting on Wednesday I must attend, it'll be an early start.'

Felicity turned her back on Randall. 'This is a nightmare. I want to know what's going on with Mia and when it's okay to visit,' said Felicity, her words becoming more and more clipped. 'Also, somehow we have to find her van.'

'Now, I can't wait to drive this Kombi.' Merv laughed and rubbed his hands together. 'You'll be a real hippy, Shirl, when you come driving with me.'

After an uncomfortable silence, Felicity stood and suggested a walk with Randall.

'Nope, wouldn't mind a swim,' he said.

'Okay, I'll change.'

'Your stuff's still beside the pool, Randall.' Shirley raised her eyebrows at Merv.

They lapped up and down, saying nothing. Felicity waited until he caught up to her in the next lap.

'Why did you carry on?' she said as she bobbed up and down at the edge.

'What?'

'I could see where it was heading. You're running after Mia and I don't want to be part of it.' His hands rested on the side of the pool and he tapped his fingers.

'No one asked you! We don't know what's going on.'

'Hey Flea, relax, I overreacted.' He flicked water at her, and she ducked. 'I'm sure we can work it out.'

Next minute he was hugging her and whispering in her ear as they cavorted with the water lapping around them. Felicity stepped back and gave him a frank gaze as his eyes skittered away.

'Now I want to hear what's happening with your ex?'

***

A rustle of the curtains woke Felicity before dawn. She lay still, listening as she adapted to the semidarkness and Fluff emerged from the billowing drapes.

She bent and whispered to the dog, 'Shh, I'll get you breakfast.'

The house was quiet as Felicity sat on the terrace. Normally daybreak was her favourite time, and she always sat and enjoyed the early morning sounds of birds and humming bees, but today she was too unsettled by Randall's surprising admission last night about his ex and an affair.

According to him, when they had separated two years ago, Cas had moved in with her lover in Melbourne. Felicity had laughed when Randall called the man "Lover-Boy" because he was ten years younger than her. His three kids had thought it was a big joke and wouldn't visit her even though they studied in the same city.

Randall told her he was "okay" with the separation as the relationship had been floundering for some years, and he was honest enough to admit he had had an affair. But in the past few months, he had talked to Cas about getting a divorce and she was shocked, upset and had questioned their separation. She realised she may have made a mistake leaving Randall for Lover Boy, especially when Lover Boy left her.

Now she was always calling Randall, asking to return to their home in Mildura so they could talk about "things". Did this mean a reconciliation? Randall had explained there was no chance of them getting back together, but his ex was always insisting on meeting to discuss it.

Felicity had said little last night, but now, mulling it over, she realised she didn't want Randall to reconcile with his wife. He had charmed her, made her contented with her love life for the first time in years, and as she headed back to their room, she decided she wanted nothing to come between them.

Her body tingled with expectation and delight as she closed the door and gazed for a moment upon Randall, lying there so handsome and innocent. She threw her T-shirt off and snuggled in beside him, ruffling his hair, and stroking his face with her finger, and with tenderness placed her arms around him. He woke startled, pulled her to him, and their lips and tongues danced as they lingered over a tantalising good morning greeting.

'What a wake-up call.' He gently drew her into an embrace and gave her a long, passionate kiss. A devilish grin broke across her face as she stroked him. He grinned, but his hands told her his mind was elsewhere as he caressed her neck with his fingertips and nuzzled into her breasts. He whispered in her ear and desire overtook her. They laughed as pillows fell to the floor but fell silent as they found their rhythm, slow and gentle until she squirmed with pleasure and pulled Randall hard against her and he groaned in reply.

They lay intertwined as the light of the day filtered in and the birds chirped.

'A bomb's hit this place.' He tickled her, and she twisted and turned and shrieked, so he muffled her mouth, then bent and caressed her. 'I want more of this. Oh, I almost forgot.'

He climbed from their bed, dug in the pocket of his jeans, and passed a small white envelope to her. She opened it and picked out her other peridot earring. She shone with delight. 'Thanks, thanks so much. It was my mother's, and as you know, she passed away when I was young, so I'm so grateful.'

Their kiss was lingering, and then he removed the earring from her hand and helped her to position it through her ear. A mirror caught the sparkle in the early morning light. Her fears for their relationship allayed for now.

Chapter 18

Felicity glanced at the antique clock in the hallway as it marked the half-hour, 10:30. The sound of the mechanics and chimes brought back memories of her grandmother and how she had pestered her parents to buy one for their home. They promised, but it had never happened.

'Shirl, are you ready to do this search for Mia's father?' said Felicity.

'Okay, before you start, what's happening with you and Randall? Are you friends or foes?'

'You know all those calls I worried about?'

'Yeah?'

'His ex wants him back.'

'What? She ran off to Melbourne with someone. They've been apart for a couple of years. Thought they got a divorce?'

'No, he was planning to, but she wants him back.'

'Well, well,' said Shirley. 'That's certainly a surprise. What are you going to do?'

'What can I do?' moaned Felicity. 'It's his problem, he's annoyed with her but still answers her calls. I don't know what to think, but let's not talk about it now.'

They went to the study, where Felicity searched under the scattered debris on the worktable to unearth a computer mouse. 'Time to find Mia's father!'

They huddled in front of the computer, typed in his name and information and photos of him with dignitaries appeared at once.

'Not a bad sort,' said Shirley, peering at him over her glasses. 'Too busy to even think about his kid.'

'Hmm, not sure. What's the ethics here, can we approach him?'

Shirley stared at her friend. 'If your daughter was ill in hospital you'd want to know. Surely the nurses will phone him?'

'Yes, if it was Emily I'd demand to know what was happening so I could decide what to do.'

'You'd be on the next plane.'

Felicity turned away and picked at her nails. 'The nurse mentioned substance abuse, so maybe the pills we found are part of this and I'm not sure whether to ring the hospital about the medication or wait until I visit.'

'That's a dicey one, there's no harm in waiting. But aren't you going home with Randall tomorrow?' asked Shirley.

'Someone has to help Mia right now. I can't leave her on her own.'

'Ah, the good Samaritan. You don't have to do this, Flea.'

'Yes, I do, I couldn't live with myself after my friend Davina's sorry end. I'll call Bill and tell him I need a few more days here,' she said wistfully. 'I wish bloody Randall wouldn't keep going on and on about me wasting my time with Mia.'

Shirley threw her hands in the air. 'If you don't need me I'm off to chat with the gardener.'

'Okay, I'll stay here and search Mia's symptoms to see if there's a match to her behaviour.'

Felicity gazed at the meticulously filed books hidden behind glass doors calling to mind how Mia puzzled her appearing to be intelligent but so erratic. Perhaps it started with the car accident, or was she always like this?

After a deep breath, she began her research with addiction to pain medication and moved on to the symptoms of chronic anxiety and depression.

'What are you searching now?' Randall startled her as he appeared behind her and massaged her shoulders.

'That's nice.' She closed her eyes and enjoyed his gentle strokes, then said, 'I'm working out if there's a link between Mia's behaviour and certain symptoms.' She pointed at the screen. 'It could be any of these conditions or none.'

'Dr Flea let the experts do the diagnosis, with Dr Google you can be so wrong,' he said tenderly, reassuring her.

'You're right, I shouldn't be interfering, but I hate to watch the poor girl suffer.'

'Mother Teresa! When are you going to visit?'

Felicity swivelled the office chair to face him. 'I'm dreading it, I keep delaying the call to the hospital.' She hesitated. 'What if she doesn't want to see me? What if she shouts and carries on at me?'

'Why would she do that?'

'Well, we didn't part on good terms.'

'I won't visit, but Merv and I will get you to the hospital, we'll drop you off and wait in the café or in the car if there's nothing to do.'

'I'd love you to come.' Her contorted face portrayed her despair. 'Need all the support I can get for this job.'

He cupped her face in his hands and kissed her on both cheeks, and she smiled.

'I'm worried about whether to tell the nurse about the pills you found. Shirl suggested I wait until I visit.'

He shrugged his shoulders. 'Maybe she stocked up to travel, so it isn't criminal?'

'It would help with the diagnosis if they knew. Alright, I'll take them with me when we go to see her.'

'That's a good idea. Whatever your decision, I'll help you as much as I can.' Randall rested his hands on her shoulders, smiled and searched her face before he pulled her to him for a hug.

What's changed his mind, thought Felicity, he's being very supportive? Has Shirl or Merv got to him?

'Thanks, I'll just get the number for the hospital.' She dialled the number. 'Stay with me,' she mouthed at Randall as he went to leave.

'Yes, Mia Holland's here,' said the ward nurse. 'But I'm afraid she's not in a position to take calls.'

'Is it possible to visit Mia this afternoon?'

'No visitors today. Ring back tomorrow. Who shall I say called?'

'Felicity... Flea, she knows me.'

After the call, she lowered her head on her arms at the worktable and groaned.

'What's the matter?' Randall squatted beside her.

'Not sure, I'm tired and frustrated and Mia's stuck in hospital alone.' She bit her lip and sighed. 'There's no one to talk to her to help her navigate the medical system.'

'Flea.' He smoothed her back with his hand. 'She's not well enough. You can see her tomorrow.'

She smiled through her tears as Randall held her tight and ruffled her hair, planting kisses on her upturned face and she nuzzled up against him, resting her head on his shoulder.

∗∗∗

The next day they allowed Mia to have visitors. In the lift, Felicity was short of breath and her heart raced as she clutched the bag she was carrying to her chest. She had made so many visits to doctors and hospitals when her mother was ill, but she had never been desensitised to medical issues with her anxieties about them multiplying as she aged. A legacy of grief.

She asked directions at the nurses' station crowded with computer stuff, coffee mugs and half-dead flowers.

'Down the corridor on the right, Room 328.' The nurse with a man-bun rested his body against the swivel chair and whizzed it around. 'We dealt with a few cases like her the other night.'

Perhaps Mia didn't overdose? It might have been a bad batch of tablets. She had read newspaper stories about pill-taking at music festivals, politicians made huge outcries, but it had never happened to someone she knew. Why was the nurse so indiscrete?

She poked her head into a long room with a line of beds on either side, covered in blue sheets and cotton waffle blankets where patients occupied some, and curtains enclosed others. As she adjusted her gaze, she saw Mia lying still in the corner near a wall with a semi-opened curtain. A drip protruded from an arm and she was pale and wan.

Felicity approached, gazed at her and touched her hand. 'Mia, Mia, it's Flea.'

Mia slowly opened her eyes and adapted to the bright lights. She mumbled. 'You weren't home....'

'Sorry, what do you mean I wasn't home?'

'Don't ....' She turned her head, and Felicity saw her put a corner of the sheet to her eye.

'How are you, Mia?'

No answer.

Felicity cleared her throat. She didn't understand what to expect from this visit, and it was not going well. Mia's comment mystified her. What did she mean?

She looked around for a vase for the colourful gerberas she had brought.

'Mia, I'll be back in a minute.' Felicity hurried to the nurse's station to get a container. A moment of escape.

The nurse pointed to a cupboard along the corridor and said, 'You're visiting Mia in Room 328, aren't you?'

'Yes.'

'There's a note here. "If anyone visits Mia... could you ask them to contact the Nursing Unit Manager?" When you've finished your visit, I'll find her for you.'

'How are you, Mia?' asked Felicity again as she placed the bright gerberas on the bedside table so they morphed into Mia's protectors, lifting the drab room.

Mia kept her face turned to the wall. 'Why are you here?'

'I thought you'd like a visit, flowers.'

Felicity was taken aback at Mia's puffy eyelids and ashen complexion when she turned to face her and said, 'For God's sake, Flea, give up. I'm not worth it. Let me be miserable, I enjoy it. And stop being so frigging nice, you make me sick.'

'Are you kidding?' Felicity looked at Mia in dismay. 'You're the one who stuffed up your trip.'

While she waited for a reply that never came, Felicity chastised herself for what she had said.

'Mia, you may not want to talk today, but I'm here to help. Randall's waiting for me downstairs and we'll keep the Kombi safe if you give me the keys.'

Mia stirred, her face drawn and pained, and pointed to the top drawer. Felicity discovered the keys hidden at the back of the cabinet.

'I'll take these, but do you remember where it's parked?'

Mia with her back turned, muttered, 'Near the tennis courts.'

'You don't have the name of the street, do you?' Mia didn't answer. 'Okay, we'll find it. Have you contacted your parents?'

No reply.

'I'm leaving now. Do you want me to visit tomorrow? We can talk then.'

With fear in her eyes, Mia leant across to Felicity and grabbed her arm. 'Please, please come, I'll be better. Can you bring me some money, makeup?'

'Okay, bye Mia. See you.' Felicity bent, kissed her on the forehead and patted her clammy hand. When she reached the door, she turned, and Mia gave a faint wave.

Felicity sat on an uncomfortable vinyl chair in the corridor waiting for the head nurse. Her face tightened as she thought of how she hated hospitals; the atmosphere was always chilly, with plastic everywhere, and that smell of disinfectant made her stomach churn. Mia had looked older, thinner, her mouth was pale and drooped, and her unwashed hair fell loosely around her. She seemed miserable, her eyes dark, and she appeared heart-broken, such a tragic sight.

Then the lift opened and a large woman with sharply cut hair and an ill-fitting uniform alighted. She hobbled over to Felicity and introduced herself.

'You know Mia Holland?'

'Somewhat, not well.'

'She's an incredibly lucky girl. She swallowed one of those tablets doing the rounds of the pubs and festivals. Individuals react differently to pills, but this was a dodgy batch. We had young people everywhere having their stomachs pumped but she'll be okay,' she said, folding her arms over her large breasts. 'Mia's father phoned us from India and mentioned an accident or something with her mother last year. Do you know anything about it?' She adjusted her glasses but didn't wait for an answer. 'Apparently, you travelled with Mia, so he needs to talk to you. Do you have his contact details?'

'No. Mia's only an acquaintance.'

'What do you mean?' said the woman suspiciously.

Felicity drew in her breath and stammered. 'I…I only met her a few days ago.'

'Daniel Holland is her father's name, and he's on his way from India, so here's his number, you decide whether you want to contact him.'

'How long will Mia be here?'

'We're not sure as she's under observation and we have to determine if she needs to go to the rehab unit.' Her voice trailed off, and she mumbled, staring at Felicity. 'And she'll have to make a statement to the police sometime.'

Felicity gasped with horror. 'That's terrible.' Her questions tumbled out. 'Is she well enough for that? Does she have to speak to them on her own? Can she have someone with her?'

'Not sure of the procedure, I can let you know when I find out.'

The walls were closing in, Felicity wanted to run from this place and not come back. She started towards the exit. 'Thanks. I'll come back tomorrow.' At the door, she called, 'Mia was in Emergency at Mildura with heatstroke a few days ago. You should call them. Bye.' She was about to press the pushbutton when she heard the nurse say, 'Come to my office for an update when you next visit.'

Felicity stabbed the button several times, longing for escape. She rested against the wall of the lift, closed her eyes as it bumped to the ground, and her steps echoed across the hospital floor as she hurtled out the glass door. The glare disorientated and confused her until she heard Merv call and wave from the car, 'Flea, we're over here.'

'What's happening?' said Randall as she climbed into the front seat next to him.

'Give me a minute. I hate hospitals and Mia's not well. I need to catch my breath.'

After she had composed herself, Felicity had an avalanche of words about Mia's appearance, her behaviour and her father's upcoming visit.

'I couldn't explain the pills to that bastard, the Unit Manager, she was too intimidating,' she said as she waved her bag around. 'They're still here.'

'What'll you do with them?' said Merv.

'Don't know. Daniel, Mia's father, wants to talk to me when he gets here so I'll give them to him.' She rattled the keys. 'Now we must find this dammed Kombi. Only clue, it's near a tennis court.'

Randall's car phone rang, and when his ex's name appeared, he glanced awkwardly at Felicity, stopped the call, and parked the car.

'I'm assuming it'll be near the festival grounds,' said Randall as he searched the map on his phone. 'This could be the place. An action-packed adventure ahead.'

Their search took longer than expected and at last, Merv called, 'It's over there, near the toilet block.'

There was a smell of newly mown lawn, but no tennis court.

They inspected the vehicle. 'Petrol, water, tyres?' he said with enthusiasm. 'I'll fix it and find my way to Shirl's. Shouldn't be hard.'

When she returned to the house, Felicity excused herself for a nap, while Randall caught up with his work. Scenes from the hospital visit darted through her mind, making her too restless to sleep. Her head throbbed as she plonked herself on a comfortable seat on the terrace, and Shirley offered to make her a pot of tea.

Without warning there was a noisy racket from the street with Merv yelling and drumming the door of the van.

'Open the gate, open the gate.'

Shirley pressed the switch, and the Kombi swept up the driveway decorated in balloons and bunting. He jumped out wearing a red Hawaiian shirt and a straw hat, then bowed.

'A present for you ladies, gentle…man.' He handed each of them a shirt and hat, which they changed into with roars of laughter.

They romped around with Randall photographing the crazy group with his phone. 'This is the silliest gear I've worn in years. Where did you get it?' said Shirley.

'Ah, a secret…Well, there was too much doom and gloom so I was singing my way home when I saw a banner, "Variety Store Closing" and Flea needed cheering up, so I bought a few items,' said Merv as he placed his hat on his chest. 'There were a few kids hanging around, so I persuaded them to blow up the balloons and decorate the Kombi and they had fun sticking the bunting here and there, and when they got the cash, they whooped.' Merv dropped to his knees. 'Now, Shirl, you're coming to dinner with me tonight in the van. Aren't you?'

'Do we have to go in this?'

Felicity and Randall slipped away, rolling with laughter.

***

'Wow, a quiet night together,' said Felicity after a swim. 'I never thought I'd see Shirl out in a Kombi - and that Hawaiian shirt, what a shocker!'

'Merv gave us a merry laugh, just what we needed.' Randall made a salad while Felicity heated the left-over casserole. 'Let's sneak away to the Barossa,' he whispered as he crept up behind her.

Quivers shot up Felicity's spine as Randall wrapped his arms around her and kissed her neck. 'Sounds great, I'd go anywhere with you.' She turned and scanned his eyes, pleading, 'Can it wait? I need to make sure Mia's okay, it's awful what has happened to her and she's alone.' Felicity stroked his arm.

'You're not thinking of going with her, are you?' Randall pulled away, giving her a hard look.

'Sometimes in my life, I've had no one, and it's a frightening place to be. I'm not sure that girl's strong enough to survive.' She brushed his cheek, then gazed downward. 'Just give me a few days here. Somehow Mia must return to Canberra to get better.'

'Isn't her father visiting?'

Felicity sighed. 'Yes, her father's coming, but I don't know when he'll arrive. She needs someone here for her now.'

'I don't understand.' He shook his hand at her. 'I can't grasp why you can't say no to her. I'm worried about you getting involved in this girl's business as it could be more complicated than you think. Stop this patronising mother bit, our kids flew the coop years ago.'

'Look, you're disappointed, but there's no need for a hissy-fit. It's tough enough trying to navigate what to do about Mia and those pills without you making a scene.'

'What do you mean by that?'

'Oh... don't worry, you wouldn't understand.'

'Flea, I'm not interested in your strays. I want to be with you.' He glared at her. 'If you're not coming with me tomorrow, I'm not waiting around and will go this evening. There's too much work to do.' He stood rigid before her. 'Please come with me,' he pleaded as he waited for her answer. When it was not forthcoming, he turned to the bedroom to pack his bag.

There was a lump in Felicity's throat as she watched the 4WD's red tailgate lights disappear through the front gate. This relationship was like a roller coaster; one minute, they were lovey-dovey and rapt in each other, but if the situation didn't go his way, Randall found an excuse to race away. He punished her for caring about Mia, who needed help. There were glimpses of Alan's pattern of bailing out when circumstances became tight. It irked her then, and now. She stood like a statute gazing into the distance. What should she do? And there was his ex, what was she trying to do?

Chapter 19

During her third visit to the hospital, Felicity sat with a coffee and biscuit tapping her fingers on the café table, still not knowing what was happening with Mia. Did she really want to get better or was she enjoying the attention?

Her sigh was weary as she turned her attention to the buzzing hospital café. The assortment of visitors, patients, and medicos intrigued her; people whispering at tables, huddled together, drawn, and distressed; others laughing, enjoying the camaraderie of friends. It was good to be with people again after living alone on the farm.

Yesterday, an exuberant Mia had greeted her, thanked her for the flowers she had left the day before and babbled on about the future.

'I need to work and save for my business.'

'Good, what do you wish to do?' said Felicity, biting her lips to suppress a smile.

'Oh, I don't know. Travel, find a bloke, have kids.' She threw her hands in the air. 'It doesn't matter.'

'How are you going to survive?'

'I'll get money from Dad.'

'Lucky you…'

With relief Felicity had waved goodbye from the ward door. Mia was much more perky, and she had been cheerful and friendly towards her. She wished it would stay that way.

A lump formed in Felicity's throat as she thought about Randall and the fun times they had together in the past few days. But it wasn't easy. His fit of the sulks and abrupt farewell didn't augur well as he wouldn't when she'd tried to explain that Mia had no one to support her in Adelaide. And another problem was his ex ringing him all the time. What was that about? Randall hated it and was distressed, but he still hadn't clarified to Felicity what was going on.

Felicity brooded about how she attracted handsome, powerful men who wanted to control her. She despised the hold Alan had over her; he loathed her friends and always had her on trial, criticising her dress, and how she managed the house or the farm. Their relationship ran hot and cold; one minute he told her he loved her and then didn't speak to her for days. His nasty comments and manipulative moods had undermined her.

Randall's stumbling block was her attention to Mia. Surely, he could see this was only temporary, Mia would recover and return to Canberra soon. Felicity wanted her involvement with Randall to flourish, to grow, to become a true partnership. The thought of the laughs they shared made her smile.

Felicity was so preoccupied as she left the café, she almost slammed into a man walking towards the same lift.

'Ladies first,' he said and smiled when the doors opened. 'Thank you.'

The man was her age, handsome with a distinguished head of silver hair. He appeared tired and weary. He was tall, but it looked as though his height had collapsed in on itself with worry and it had crumpled his grey suit and open-necked shirt.

Surveying him through her sunglasses, she thought he must be visiting someone ill, then her thoughts returned to Randall. She wished he had come with her to visit Mia. Would she see him again?

The lift doors slid wide, and the man waited for Felicity to alight. She gave him a warm smile and stopped by the hand-gel dispenser where she massaged the bright pink slimy liquid into her hands. After a deep breath, she patted Mia's package of pills in her bag and entered the ward.

There were four cubicles with curtains enclosing two, and one containing an elderly lady lying down reading a newspaper. Mia had moved from her bed and sat beside a tall window, gazing at the variegated tree canopy outside. She wore no makeup, and her once magnificent hair was untidy and dull. Her lively face had disappeared, and she appeared dejected.

'Hello, how are you?'

'Oh, okay.' Mia's voice was thin and stretched. 'I want to leave this place today, but they won't let me go until I've got a recovery plan.' She paused and twisted the right side of her hair. 'Could I stay with you?'

Felicity withdrew, lay her hand to her chest and said, 'Look, Mia, it's difficult with me staying at Shirl's.' She hesitated. 'Bill can't manage the farm forever. I must get home....'

Mia turned away, placed her hands to her ears and stared into the distance at the same time the unit manager and the distinguished man from the lift strolled into the room. He nodded to Felicity, then crouched down in front of Mia to meet her eyes.

'Dad…' Mia flung her arms around him. He pulled a chair out scraping it across the floor, then leaned forward cradling her against his body. Felicity, not wanting to intrude, sneaked away, but he called to her.

'Flea, is it?' His face looked puzzled.

'Felicity, but everyone calls me Flea.'

'Thanks for what you've done for my girl.' He broke free from Mia's arms. 'I would like to talk to you. Can we meet up later?'

'Sure, when would you like to see me? I could wait downstairs?'

'I'd like to spend some time with Mia. May I call you?' They exchanged phone numbers and nodded their goodbyes.

***

Felicity wandered through the city, browsing in shops, enjoying her sudden freedom. A secluded café in an arcade beckoned, and she grabbed a newspaper from a pile scattered across the front bench and placed her order for lunch.

Randall, why are you so difficult? She stared into her coffee cup. It's my fault, she thought, but then grinned, it's a typical woman's response to blame yourself.

A stunning young waitress, who told Felicity she was of Lebanese descent, brought her vegetarian meal, falafels and fattoush salad. She gazed at the girl, wondering how the younger generation navigated romance, knowing she wasn't doing well in this arena. But she would like a partner, not to live with and play nurse maid to, but someone who loved and supported her. The warm memory of Randall and herself lying intertwined, talking, made her smile. A ring tone interrupted her thoughts.

'Yes, Daniel, why don't you meet me here. The food is delicious.' While she waited for Mia's father to join her, she finished her meal and spread the paper across the bench.

'Felicity – Flea?'

'Sorry, I didn't see you. Take a seat.'

Daniel explained he had arrived this morning from Kolkata and dropped his bag at the hotel before he met with the hospital staff.

He nervously played with a shiny gold wedding band as he spoke. Maybe he recently married? Mia won't like the competition of a new wife, thought Felicity.

'I told Mia not to go travelling, she was still under the care of her medical team,' he said, leaning towards Felicity. 'She's always been a bolter. If circumstances don't go her way, she quits her job, her relationship, even country. From what I have heard, her doctor, her boss, and her friend Brad had tried to persuade her not to leave Canberra, but she wouldn't listen.'

Felicity sighed and nodded her head in agreement, recognising this description of Mia's behaviour only too well.

The waitress came to take Daniel's order. 'I need a stiff drink, but they only have wine. Would you like to share a bottle?'

He gulped for air and continued. 'Mia's highly intelligent, always topped her class with no effort. Thought she might take her archaeology further, but she decided on IT.' He slumped in his chair. 'Brad, her friend, told me she was great at her job, but her colleagues didn't like how she treated them as she kept telling them how good she was. Created havoc at work and elsewhere. It appears there are a few incidents for me to sort through.'

'What's happening with Mia now?'

Daniel rubbed his forehead. 'It's a mess. With her permission, I have arranged for her doctor in Canberra to talk to the staff here. These medical matters are complex.' He clenched his hanky, then wiped the corner of his eye and blew his nose. 'There's a team meeting tomorrow at the hospital, so we'll know more.'

'I thought she was coming out this afternoon. At least she told me she was.'

'Her medication may have confused her. When circumstances get too much for her, she throws in a few lies, fibs? It drives me nuts and it could be why she's had issues at her work.'

Felicity smiled with understanding, this explained so much about Mia's attitude and behaviour.

'It's hard with me working overseas, but I assure you, I want what's best for Mia. Most of the time she's self-reliant and was going well in Canberra until that accident with her crazy mother threw her.'

His lunch and their drinks arrived.

'I was hoping you'd meet with the staff tomorrow?' stammered Daniel, looking uncomfortable.

'What do you mean?' said Felicity, staring at him.

'The doctor suggested the meeting. He thought you may have insights into her behaviour having travelled with her recently.'

She hesitated and studied him before reaching into her bag for Mia's sepia envelope, and with a slight tremble to her hand she handed him the package. 'I need to tell you about these first.'

His eyes widened as he opened the parcel, and with care he removed the contents, the trays of pills.

'Where did you get these?'

Felicity explained that Mia had accidentally left them in a sleeping bag, which ended up at her friend's place in Mildura. Randall had brought them to her when he came to Adelaide, and she wasn't sure what to do. 'Perhaps I could have discussed them with the medical staff today, but I didn't want to implicate Mia in anything. She also had other drugs, pills in bottles of different sizes. I saw them, but I don't know where they are now, so you must get Mia to explain.'

Her burden lifted as Felicity explained everything to a deflated Daniel.

***

'Well, are you going to this meeting tomorrow?' said Shirley, sharing a beer and nuts with Merv. 'Will the fibber be grateful if you go? No, of course not.'

'It's not that easy for me, Shirl. Mia's still on her own here, no doubt her dad needs to return to India. Someone will have to watch her, even if I do it from a distance.'

Shirley threw up her arms. 'You're mad, I agree with Randall, her father should make the arrangements and care for her.'

'It was strange. He's just remarried and there's a baby on the way, but he hasn't told Mia. The way he spoke, there'll be fireworks when she finds out.'

'His new floozy wants nothing to do with Mia,' Merv bellowed from the lounge. 'What do you think they've planning to do?'

'It's hard to say. Although her father talked at length, he wasn't giving anything away, so I guess there's rehab ahead. I'll find out more tomorrow.'

'So, you're going?'

Felicity smiled and gave a small laugh as if it was a joke.

'Have you heard from that mate of yours, Randall?' said Shirley.

Felicity gave her a withering look and changed the subject.

***

A doctor in dark pants, a white collared shirt with a slim black tie that tangled with his stethoscope, strolled into the tiny windowless room, crammed with five red plastic chairs. Felicity introduced herself and surveyed the space. Daniel fidgeted with his phone and the unit manager held Mia's file as though at any moment someone would steal it from her. She glared at Felicity. A person from rehab arrived late and pulled up a chair and sat between Mia's father and Felicity.

The doctor began. 'Before I speak to Mia, I wanted to meet with everyone concerned.' He acknowledged and thanked

Felicity for attending. 'We're here to pool information on what happened to her before she landed in hospital. I've spoken to her doctor in Canberra and the staff in Mildura, but I need an idea of how she was behaving every day.' He glanced at his notes, then nodded to Felicity. 'I understand you travelled with Mia and Daniel tells me you found opiates, prescription drugs. Is that correct?'

Felicity's thoughts froze, she nodded yes.

'Her doctor said Mia was in pain and prescribed tablets. She may have discovered a source elsewhere, given the number of packets you found. We'll come back to this.' The doctor twiddled his blue iridescent pen. 'It's difficult. You're not next of kin, so there's confidential information we can't discuss with you. Perhaps you could just tell us what you observed.'

Felicity squirmed and wished someone had prepared her for this inquisition. One question led to another, and all members of the group had their say. The doctor suggested they break the meeting and consider options later with Mia present. Felicity asked to leave if she was no longer required.

She shook hands with the doctor. 'Give me a ring if I can be of any help.' When the doors of the lift closed, she let out an enormous sigh of relief.

Half an hour later she was sitting, waiting for the bus back to Shirley's place when her phone rang. Daniel had just left the meeting with Mia and the medical team. He thanked her for attending and gave her an update. Then he made a proposal for Mia's recovery, a plan Mia herself had suggested, and it involved Felicity.

'What?' she groaned. 'I couldn't do that! Look, this is sudden… I'd need to think about it and get back to you.'

Daniel tried to pressure her to answer his request during the afternoon so the medical team could begin their work.

'No, this is a tremendous responsibility. I need to consider this overnight.' She threw the phone in her bag and crossed to the other side of the road to catch a tram.

At each stop, the rattle and clacking rang in her head as she passed the suburban houses and trees along the track. At the end of the line she alighted and strolled towards the vastness of St Vincent's Gulf. The wind had whipped up white horses on the waves and the sea gulls were standing with their backs against the blast. People huddled over their fish and chips, holding them tight, not sure whether the gale or the birds would attack first.

Clouds were bubbling overhead. Her floral shirt and linen pants suited this morning's meeting but were out of place on the beach. Enticed by the pale cream sand, she rolled her slacks to her knees, removed her sandals, and stuffed them in her shoulder bag. She allowed the rivulets to melt over her toes. Her body bent to resist the wind as she paddled up to her ankles in the lapping water. She trudged on, head down through the foam, passing high-rise buildings, and children's playgrounds. Oblivious.

Her mind was a whirlpool of questions. What should she do and what would happen? In her turmoil, a dog running the other way almost knocked her over. She had a brief look around for the owner and returned to her brooding.

Time evaporated. The wind strengthened and blew hard against her face, and her hair stood on end.

Without warning, she stopped. Her deliberations done. The pier she had passed at the start of her journey was now off in the distance. She retraced her steps. This time the breeze was behind her as she traipsed across the soft sand, her decision made.

Chapter 20

During the night, a rolling carousel of conflicting thoughts churned through Felicity's mind: why had she said yes, was it too late to go back on her decision? What should she do now and how should she do it? Her body ached and her head spun in confusion as she ate breakfast and prepared herself to meet Daniel at the hospital. One thing she was concerned about was that Mia couldn't be left on her own over the next few weeks if her recovery was to be successful and this would require constant vigilance.

'If you arrange tickets for tomorrow morning, Mia can fly with me to Canberra,' said Felicity, and she grinned as she watched Daniel's face light up with appreciation. 'She knows my friend's a tyrant, but I'll convince Shirl to let her stay overnight.'

'Thank you so much. Flea, I can't thank you enough,' he said as he clasped her hand in the hospital cafeteria. 'I'll get to this meeting with the Minister in Canberra now and somehow, over the next few days, discover where Mia's extra pills came from and who's been harassing her for money. You're right, she shouldn't be on her own.'

Felicity's eyes followed him to the lift, then she dialled Shirley's number holding the phone away from her ear as Shirley raved on and on about the druggy coming to stay. Felicity could hear Merv in the background trying to argue it was okay, the poor girl needed care.

There was a sternness to Shirley's voice. 'Just a night. Merv says I must be on my best behaviour.'

Felicity grimaced, there was still Mia to organise. What have I done? She gripped her hands together in prayer, then found a newspaper and waited for Daniel to ring with the flight details.

She trudged towards the ward with a heavy heart, her misgivings growing with every step as she batted her decision back and forth. Mia had no one to look after her here and had refused to return to India with her father.

'Flea, I'm allowed to leave hospital as long as I stay with you.' Mia jumped from the chair and hugged her. 'What are we going to do?'

'Let's not talk about it now.' Felicity glanced at the other patients and lowered her voice. 'I want to make sure you're comfortable with this decision.'

'What do you mean?' said Mia, flipping her hair in annoyance.

'C'mon. Where's your gear?' From under the bed, a pile of her belongings appeared. 'All those bags?'

'Mind your business.' Mia grabbed them, gave Felicity a haughty look and marched to the front reception.

Felicity gritted her teeth and waited as Mia discharged herself. When she had finished, Mia said, 'Hooray, I'm out of here and I'll see Dad again tomorrow.'

They packed the car and were on their way when Felicity said, 'Look, Shirl's cross about having you overnight, be careful.'

'That old bitch. Why doesn't she want me to stay? Scared I'll bring my mates? Take pills?'

'Are you kidding? Don't carry on.' She stopped the vehicle on the side of the road and spoke in a calm voice, 'Listen, we agreed you'd come to my farm to recover. I know it won't be easy, but I expect you to mind your manners.'

Mia put her nose in the air and ran her hand over her chest. 'What if I don't want to go?'

Felicity's body tensed and she struggled to find the right words. 'It's your choice, you either jump out now and make your own way, or come with me to Shirl's, then Canberra tomorrow, get better and move on with your life.'

She fixed Mia with a steely stare. After five minutes, Mia's shoulders slumped, and she answered with a nod. 'Okay. I'll go with you to the farm.'

Felicity scrutinized Mia's face and said, 'Okay, if you try to beat these pills, I'll try to give up alcohol. Is that a deal?'

Mia grinned and Felicity started the car and sped away, grumbling to herself about the ungrateful young woman.

***

Felicity and Mia stepped into the chaos and mumbled obscenities of Chef Merv's kitchen as he tried to undo the lid of an anchovy jar. He whooped when it opened, leaned over and tickled Shirley, his assistant, and asked her where to find the other ingredients. The clatter of pans and instructions flew across the room so Felicity escaped and sat on the terrace, watching Mia enter the pool, do a lap, then slip out the other end and run to her bedroom.

Later, the aroma of Merv's delicious pizza drew Mia from her room and she stared at the creation laden with ham, pepperoni, artichokes, mushrooms, anchovies, green peppers and black olives.

Over dinner, Merv asked, 'Mia, what's happening with the Kombi? How'll we get it to Canberra?'

She shrugged her shoulders. 'Don't know. It's only brought me bad luck.'

'If you want to sell it? I'm your man,' he said, raising his thumbs in the air. 'I'll take Shirl for another drive and get you a good price. Just leave it to the salesperson here.'

'Okay,' said Mia with a lack of interest.

'Why did you buy a Kombi in the first place?' asked Merv. Mia looked away, not answering him.

Felicity glanced at her watch. 'It's late and we're going on an early morning flight, Mia, get what you need from the van, and Merv can donate what's left to charity.'

Under the floodlights at the front of the house, they started cleaning out the Kombi until Mia's voice choked with tears and she said, 'I've got to go to bed.'

'Are you okay?' said Felicity, putting her arm around her, but Mia fled, leaving Felicity to finish the job.

'Pleased to spread the love and sort her stuff out, Flea.' Merv raised his glass of wine when Felicity returned with a pile of bags.

'Don't encourage my friend,' said Shirley. 'She's crazy taking on that pill popper. She doesn't even know her.'

Felicity gave her a wounded look and poured herself a drink. 'Okay, I'm crazy but I want Mia better.'

'You don't have to save the world or Mia,' said Merv. 'But you still haven't explained what's wrong with her.'

'Well, the car accident is a big part of the problem.' Felicity lowered her head, swirled the wine, speaking in a hushed voice, 'To complicate matters, she's been self-medicating and became hooked on prescribed opiates. She says a couple stole her pills and having no pills meant she went into withdrawal. Unfortunately, she hadn't eaten for a day or two when she swallowed that tablet in the pub and it made it all worse.'

'How could she suffer from withdrawal if she had all those pills here?' said Shirley.

Felicity struggled to say the right words before she said, 'They were the ones stolen from her van, and Randall found the other lot of her medication in the sleeping bag. Mia had none of her own pills left when she nabbed that dodgy one.' She hesitated. 'It surprised the medicos she didn't have more of a reaction seeing she was in withdrawal.'

'Wow. And you'll have her at your place? You're madder than I thought, Flea,' said Merv, playing host with another drink.

She stared into the glass as she twirled the wine. 'Yes, lots of muddy whirlpools ahead. Now it's a case of getting her off the pills and that's why I'm taking her with me.'

'And doing this in the middle of a drought?' he said, as he clutched his chest.

Felicity with a glazed look stared at him. The medicos thought the farm would be a haven where Mia could recover, with no temptation. They had worked out how to get the support of counsellors and a doctor and had given Felicity brochures and other information. Now it had to happen! She closed her eyes; she knew the cost to her own peace and sanity. But couldn't front it yet.

***

In the early morning light, Felicity and Mia climbed into the taxi and waved Merv goodbye, Shirley refusing to appear to farewell them.

As the vehicle wandered through the streets of Adelaide to the airport, Felicity asked, 'How long do you think it'll take you to gather your gear and sort out your documents in Canberra?'

'Don't know.'

'Is your dad going home on the weekend?'

'Yes, what's that got to do with it?' said Mia, with her nose in the air.

'Well, he's meeting us at the airport, then before he returns home he has to drive you to the farm so you won't have much time in Canberra.'

Mia turned and stared into the distance.

Felicity gazed at the rising sun as it released the shadows of Adelaide through the plane window and wondered what the next few weeks with Mia would bring. Yesterday when she had arrived at Shirley's, Mia had moped around, sniffling and thumping up and down the hallway which didn't auger well. She grinned to herself when she recalled Merv's advice to Mia. "When you get to the farm watch out for Flea, she's a woman on a mission. She can be brutal. Better do what she says."

On the plane Mia slept. Felicity fiddled with her to-do-list and tried to read the newspaper, but her thoughts kept bouncing. She had a real Pandora's box, allowing Randall to return home on his own and taking on Mia's complications. And this was all on top of her farm worries. She shivered, a ripple of unease running through her body.

They arrived in Canberra to the start of a shimmering hot day, and a crowded airport, with people and politicians cursing about delays. To Felicity's surprise, Mia raced away while waiting for their luggage and squealed, flinging herself at a short, balding man of about thirty-five, with a gentle face, dressed in shorts, a tee-shirt, and thongs. He embraced Mia and swung her from the floor.

Mia linked her arm through his and introduced him to Felicity. 'My big surprise, Brad. Where's Dad, he should be here?' She searched for her father and when she saw he wasn't there, she announced she would go home with her friend.

'Don't worry, Mrs ... she's not taking pills around me.'

'Don't call her Missus, she's Flea.' Mia bounced from foot to foot with excitement and her voice was loud. 'Brad's a wizard. He gets me! We'll meet you later when you find Dad. Bet he's on the phone to the witch he's just married. Told me yesterday I'm about to have a sister.' She stuck two fingers in her mouth and pretended to be sick.

Brad rolled his eyes. 'Yeah, no getting in Mia's way. Is this your gear?' He picked up her luggage. 'You have lots of stuff!' Her laugh echoed through the terminal as she stumbled with the enormous plastic bag the airline staff had allowed on the plane.

After their goodbyes, Felicity thumped her head with her hand and laughed out loud as she watched the baggage carousel spit out its load. Mia had harassed her to return to the farm because she didn't want to go to India. She hated her father's new living arrangements, his new wife, and now a baby. No longer the centre of his attention.

Her bag was the last one to arrive and as she reached for it, Daniel leapt in front and grabbed it for her.

'Sorry I'm late. Where's Mia?'

'She couldn't wait. Brad met her and they rushed off to her place.' She glanced at her watch. 'Look, I have to arrange my hire car and return home.'

'Would you like a coffee first with me?'

'I must get away. Can I check off Mia's recovery list with you?'

He moved closer as she dashed through her list. 'First, sort out the local doctor then the counselling service; investigate the access line too, and Facebook groups for both of us. I'll be ready...' In jest, she gripped the front of her neck with her hand as though she would choke herself.

'Flea, I can't thank you enough. Yesterday, I told Mia about the baby, her stepsister, and she flew into a rage. She went berserk, tried to hit me and swore, using language I haven't heard in a long time. It'll be rough going over the next few days.' He fiddled with his phone. 'Mia must get off those pills.'

Felicity placed a reassuring hand on his arm and said, 'Let me know when you're heading to the farm with Mia and good luck.'

She jumped in the hire car, used the rear vision mirror to apply her lipstick, and whistled as she drove. Escape, her last opportunity for freedom. What had she let herself in for?

Her mind whirled with thoughts of the agitation and confusion awaiting Mia over the next few weeks as she withdrew from the pills. She was not looking forward to Mia's challenging behaviour, which the medicos had warned could be difficult. With a heavy heart she drove to her favourite bookshop, realising she would need both strength and bucket loads of wisdom to negotiate this time.

The high bookshelves loomed over her as she began her search for books to help her understand what Mia was going through. The doctors had given her advice, but she needed more information on what she could do. Nothing seemed to match her needs, so she went to the front desk where an attractive young blond woman stood playing with the name tag around her neck.

'Excuse me,' said Felicity, 'I need your help, please.' The assistant gave her a wide smile. 'Do you have any books on substance abuse or drug addiction; helping someone to come off prescription pills? What to eat, what to do, those sorts of issues?' Felicity fidgeted with her watch and whispered, 'I'm taking care of someone who's in recovery.'

'Um, that's difficult. There's not much I'd recommend. I had a friend who was going through a divorce and was hooked on something her doctor prescribed to calm her nerves.' She gave Felicity a sympathetic nod. 'I didn't realise she had a problem until she told me and it's no fun coming off the stuff.' She burrowed into a pile of books sitting on a table.

'This book on Chinese medicine talks about wholesome food and exercise.' The assistant found other resources. 'These books are useful, but I recommend this one. It's about change and having confidence in the future. The exercises are fun.' In a hushed tone, she said, 'You need a team of medical and other backup people involved and be careful the person doesn't go from one addiction to another, like my friend. There's no panacea.'

'Oh, yes. The doctor part is okay, and we have a referral to the local Drug and Alcohol Access line. It's knowing what to do daily.' Felicity leant towards the assistant and chuckled. 'Guess I must watch my drinking too and pick my battles.'

'Don't forget online resources, apps on anxiety, depression, you name it. How about learning to meditate?' She bowed her head and put her fingers together, and both women laughed.

Felicity patted the woman on the arm with gratitude as she said thanks, paid and gathered up the books, wondering if they would give her enough solace and wisdom for the days ahead.

***

While Daniel waited for Mia to pack her gear for the farm, he gazed at a series of photos scattered across a notice board in her apartment. She stood behind him and pointed to a photo of them on the Great Wall in China.

'Remember this, Dad? You were trying to hug me, get me to look at the camera, and I was off in another direction.' Her voice became quieter, 'Yes, you had just told me was to be dumped again in that boarding school while you went off to your next job.'

The mantle of abandonment wrapped itself around Mia's shoulders and the pain rose in her throat. Daniel looked sheepish and was about to say something when a picture of Mia's mother distracted him. Someone had pinned the photo upside down with a black cross across it.

'When was this?'

'Don't talk about that!' Mia pouted and flung her head in the air. 'Mom! Taken the morning before she almost killed me. That bitch.' She flounced to the bedroom and returned with pictures of her life in Canberra.

'Here, Brad,' she said, handing him the photos as he sat waiting on the sofa. 'You look so handsome in your evening suit. We were such a cute couple and had so much fun dancing.'

'Yeah, that little glittery number you're wearing looks great.' Brad turned and pointed to her coloured plastic bags and luggage scattered across the floor. 'Are you leaving here forever?' He rubbed his pate with frustration. 'C'mon, Mia. Your father's ready. I have a spare key and will bring anything else you need when I visit.'

Mia stood rigid as a prima donna in the middle of the lounge room. 'I don't want to leave. I'm staying in Canberra.' She flicked her hair. 'I'll be too lonely on a farm, there'll be zilch to do.'

'What! You've been telling me the past two days how healthy and well you'll be at Flea's place because there's no temptation. Now you're baulking at going.' Her father wagged his finger at her. 'Enough's enough! You can't change your mind every five minutes. What are you going to do?'

'Nothing involving you and that Jezebel wife of yours, she's even worse than my mother.' She spat out words, 'That poor child hasn't got a chance.'

Daniel's face turned ashen, his lips contracted, and his hands curled into fists.

Brad glared at him, put his hand on Mia's shoulder and whispered, 'You can't stay here. There's no one to care for you, Mia, your father's going home. We both know this will be a bumpy ride, but you're strong and you just need time to recover. Don't throw away your life by staying here.' He gave Mia a peck on the cheek, picked up the luggage and nodded his head at Daniel. 'Where's your car?'

Mia followed him down the stairs in tears.

Chapter 21

The buzzing of a phone echoed through the silent house late in the night. Drowsy Mia, half-asleep, over-heard strands of a disagreement, Felicity's voice growing louder and sharper as the conversation moved on. 'Mia's not like that…, she's not a drug addict', but Mia couldn't make out the context of the words. Maybe it was one of her children or her husband annoyed at Felicity for allowing her to stay. She flicked on the lamp and rummaged through her bags, hoping a pill lurked hidden in her luggage, but no luck. She pulled the sheet over her head, anxiety and loneliness eating into her, and her tears flowed.

***

The next day, Felicity watched a spider hanging from its silvery fine-spun web on the office ceiling. It was stalking an insect, and the creature was going crazy trying to get untangled. She saw herself as the bug and laughed in understanding of its plight.

That phone call from her daughter, late last night, had rattled her. During the chat she discovered Alan had been up to his old tricks of lying and undermining her, which made the situation worse.

Emily had called from London. She was smart, sensible, and seized her place in the world with ease but when she found out Mia was staying on the farm it had riled her.

'Why is a lunatic you don't know sleeping in my room?' said Emily angrily.

'You're living overseas, what difference does it make to you?'

'But it's my bed, it'll have bed-bugs crawling in it.'

'Emily! Don't carry on like that. You haven't lived at home for years.'

'Dad says she's a drug addict. Are you mad?' She yelled. 'Mum, I can just imagine what's happening to you. You've gone feral, picked up one of your waifs again.'

'Calm down and listen. You know from experience, stories from your father are not always true.' She tried to change the topic, but Emily wasn't interested.

'Well, if she isn't a druggy, what is she?'

Felicity paused, trying to find the right words. Slowly she explained how Mia had an accident and how she had become reliant on pain killers while recovering. She was staying on the farm because she needed to recuperate and had no family in Australia to support her.

'Why is she in my bedroom? She'll go through my stuff.'

She groaned inwardly as she wondered what made Emily so jealous to behave like a little kid.

'Dad said you've found a boyfriend. Is that true?'

She sat on the office chair, cocked the phone between her shoulder and head, and gave a weary sigh. Closing her eyes, she said, 'On my way to Adelaide, I met an old friend. We had a great time and you needn't worry, I haven't heard from him.'

'Aren't you and Dad getting back together?'

Felicity noted the hopefulness in her daughter's tone, and a ripple of unease sped up her spine.

'Did your father say we were?' She hesitated. 'Your father and I had many good years, but the move to the farm broke us apart. He thought he was a wealthy grazier and spent money we never had. We'd be destitute if he had his way, and you wouldn't want that.' Her voice quivered. 'Your father's bloody hard work and his stories hurt. I don't know what he told you, but we won't be getting back together.'

The phone went dead.

***

Mia and Felicity grated on each other like sandpaper. For the first week, a listless and defensive Mia only appeared from her bedroom to get something to eat, and she complained of not sleeping and feeling bloated and uncomfortable. In Adelaide, the doctor's advice was to wean Mia off the pills by a gradual lowering of the dosage, and if she cared for herself and followed directions, she may be off them within weeks. Both the doctor and the counsellors had warned about the lingering reliance on old habits and behaviours, so time was needed and there was the ever-present danger of a relapse.

The staff on the local access line were supportive and gave Felicity tips to weather the "Mia storm". In a fit of sociability, Mia had shown her the Facebook page and the many apps available and told her how useful they were when she was feeling anxious.

Felicity had experience with unwell people. As a child, she had helped nurse her mother when she was dying, then when her father was older, she had assisted him. The meals she prepared for Mia were plain, nutritious, and included lots of soups. She made her herbal teas and hot packs for muscle pain and encouraged her to sit in the garden or on the veranda. Sometimes her patient was quiet and complacent, and at other times restless and troubled. The memory of helping her parents however didn't match the reality of looking after Mia.

'Why this horrid tea? It tastes like cat pee.' Mia's eyes challenged as she stamped her feet.

'Well, you must keep up your fluids, otherwise you'll dehydrate.' Felicity placed the mug on the table. 'They told you it wouldn't be easy, and the Chinese herbal book says these teas support your immune system.'

'Absolute crap! That's witch doctor stuff.'

Taking a deep breath, Felicity patiently said, 'Look, there's no magic wand, nutritious food and lots of liquids help. It's bloody hard for me too, I'm craving for a grog so it's difficult for both of us, but we're doing the best we can.'

'No, you old cow. You don't care for anyone. Hubby fled and your kids vanished. Now you're trying to buy my love. You need to control me, own me. You bitch.'

'I won't accept that in my home.' Felicity gritted her teeth and with a red face pointed her finger at Mia. 'Where's your family? You must have pissed your father off. He hasn't rung to find out how you are, nor your mother.' A knot of fear played in her stomach as she watched Mia's eyes go wild.

Mia flicked her hand in front of Felicity's nose as if to get rid of an odour. 'Don't speak to me about my parents, they live in other countries, so how can they help?' Her hands shook and beads of sweat appeared on her forehead. 'You think you are so bloody special giving me a place to stay, yet you treat me like a child. You fucken cow.'

There was an icy pause. Mia glared at Felicity, gave a hysterical laugh, and bolted to the bedroom and banged the door.

***

Felicity tried to keep love, harmony, and compassion as her catchwords, as she yearned for signs of change in Mia. She put her lack of appreciation and ability to help around the house down to her withdrawal. She knew Mia was suffering, but her behaviour made life exhausting.

Felicity rested her head on her hands as she sat at the table with a cup of tea. She missed her kids, the laughter and mischief, and the companionship they provided as they got older. But this didn't explain why she had taken on this arduous task, supporting a young woman recovering from too many pills. Too kind and generous. But for Felicity there were holes of pain papered up within her she couldn't face. Alcohol had disguised them, and now she had gone "cold turkey" it had unleashed the monsters.

By the end of the second week, Felicity tossed and turned in bed each night her level of patience and compassion for

Mia plummeting. She didn't understand where she was on the roller coaster. Mia was a perfect angel one minute and with no warning a devil the next. She blamed Felicity when her phone was constantly out of range. Bitter enmity grew.

'Mia, could you get the dinner tonight?' said Felicity at breakfast. 'Bill and I are mustering the sheep and it'll be dark when we finish.'

'No. I won't cook in anyone else's kitchen.'

'Just bloody well do it. You've been loafing around for two weeks. I can't have you here if you're not willing to help.'

Mia gave her a disdainful look and stepped away as she continued to bite into her toast.

'Look at me when we're speaking,' hissed Felicity.

Mia turned back and stared at Felicity with her face puckered in loathing.

Felicity shook her fist. 'I want dinner on the table when I get home tonight. I don't care how you do it.' She strode out of the kitchen to move the sheep, muttering, 'Ungrateful bitch!'

Bill climbed from his ute in Felicity's back paddock and lifted his crumpled calico hat in greeting. After he had rolled his motor bike from the back onto the ground, he leant against his car, folded his arms across his substantial belly and chatted about the unseasonal hot weather and lack of rain.

'How's the company at home, Flea?'

'You mean Mia?' said Felicity. 'She's a lazy, indolent thing and I've tried going easy with her, but it's impossible.' She threw her hands in the air. 'I asked her to get dinner tonight and didn't she carry-on? Said she wouldn't cook in other people's kitchens.' Growling, she flicked her hat to chase the flies. 'Stays in her bedroom all the time while I run around playing maid. She'll be out of here and back in Canberra within days if she keeps this up.'

'Is she any better?'

'Who knows! We've organised a counsellor's appointment but I'm the one that needs the pills.' They laughed and joked together.

'That bloke you went off to Broken Hill with, what's his job?'

'Oh, he's still working,' said Felicity, trying to distract Bill from his desire for a gossip. She didn't want to volunteer any ammunition to be used against her.

'Who is he?'

'Randall, a friend of Dad's. He's well known in the finance area,' she said as she tried to hide her blush by shooing imaginary flies. 'He runs a business in Mildura.'

Bill removed his hat and wiped his brow. Felicity instructed him on the next tricky manoeuvre. They had to muster the mob of sheep from a paddock full of trees, fallen logs and bushes, with lots of hidden potholes, then draft and count them ready for sale in the morning.

'This drought, I wish I didn't have to sell my girls.' Felicity poured water from a thermos and raised her mug to meet his as a starting gesture to the muster.

'Yeah, I hope it rains again.'

The dogs barked, circling the growing mob of sheep, the dust cutting the visibility. Bill on his bike and Felicity in the ute were an excellent team. She worked with the mob while he brought in the strays.

When they finished at the yards, Felicity invited him back to the house. 'Beware. I do not know what Missy might have done since I left.'

Mia greeted them with a big smile. She produced a beer for Bill and laid out cheese and biscuits, ignored Felicity and flattered Bill with a show of attention. He offered Felicity a drink, but she said no, smelling her underarms.

'I'll shower, get rid of the dust and smell of sheep.'

When Bill had left, Felicity asked Mia about dinner.

'Oh, I made a salad for you. It's in the fridge. I've had enough to eat today.' She crossed her arms and sneered. 'I rang Randall.'

The shock vibrated through Felicity's body. She stared at her and stuttered. 'You... what?'

'Rang Randall, you heard me the first time. Thought he needed a bomb under him.'

Felicity gritted her teeth and controlled her tone. 'Why did you think that Sweetheart?'

'Don't call me Sweetheart, that's for your old lover. Bet he has a young tart on the side because you're so cranky.'

'He's none of your business.' Felicity jabbed her finger at Mia's face. 'Why would you interfere with my life, seeing yours is such a mess?'

'My mess! What about your muddle — no rain, no kids, no hubby, boyfriend missing in action?' Mia flounced out of the room.

Felicity's mouth opened, but she couldn't speak. She flew to the fridge, snatched the salad and without as much as glancing at it, threw it in the bin. This cannot be happening.

Felicity's face tingled with embarrassment as she thought of what Mia might have said to him. *How dare she interfere in my personal life?* The TV babbled on while she simmered and fumed for the rest of the evening.

***

A few nights later, Felicity chuckled when Mia surprised her by agreeing to clean the dishes. She slipped away to her office, closed the door, and with trepidation dialled a number.

'Flea, how are you? Great to hear from you,' boomed a distant voice. 'I'm about to see Ginan.'

'What's that, Merv?'

'The smallest star of the Southern Cross. One of the Aboriginal groups in the Northern Territory says it's a dilly bag full of knowledge to pass on.'

'I need buckets of wisdom, not a dilly bag.'

'Before you get too excited, Ginan's now officially recognised.' He chuckled. 'Any news for me?'

'Yeah, my sheep topped the sale yards and while it wasn't a record price, under the circumstances, it was a good one.'

They continued on about prices, the weather and what they might do to counteract the drought until he said, 'How's Mia? Has she driven you mad?'

'Yes, she's driving me crazy and I've no sense of what to do about her.'

'Thought it was the case. Withdrawal from any addiction must be hard. Mia's a bright girl, but free-range with a dippy mother and a father who cares but is all over the place. Like you, he doesn't know what to do. When she comes up against people who want things a certain way, there are sure to be fireworks.'

Felicity smiled to herself; he understood the troubles she was having with Mia.

'Yep, my young fella was troppo there for a while. Had to lean on him, to get some sense into him. You're not family, so there'll be a few more screaming matches. No use being good-hearted, Mia will walk over you.'

'Need a new set of lungs?'

'That's it, I can call the battle lines.' They both dissolved into laughter and in rapid fire he changed the subject. 'Has my mate, Randall, been in touch?' Felicity's stomach sank. 'He's going through a hard time with his old partner. I don't know how much he has told you, but she can be challenging. Cas is driving Randall nuts, wants him back and won't give up. He responds to her because I think there's a bit of guilt in there, it's not like he's been a saint.'

'Yes, he told me he had an affair.'

'Oh, there was a woman, but he said it was never serious but who knows. When Cas dumped him, he later broke up with the other woman and to me, Randall seemed sort of relieved. Anyway, that's all history. He's only got eyes for you now and he's a decent bloke, Flea, bossy but hang in there. Wants me to visit Mildura, but there are too many storms to leave here. Gotta run, see my lovely Ginan.'

Felicity muttered her goodbye and drew her arms around herself, her thoughts growing dark and muddled. Another woman, his ex and her issues, where do I stand in all this?

Merv says he's a decent bloke, but there's a lot of baggage there. Bloody Alan's enough of a complication, and there's stroppy Mia. It's all too much.

She stepped outside to gaze at the night sky awash with the Milky Way, locating Ginan and asking the little star to give her wisdom and strength to survive Mia's tumult. What should she ask about Randall?

Chapter 22

Two weeks later there were flickers of early morning light as Mia struggled to open her eyes. Her throat was parched and her stomach was doing somersaults as she pulled the sheet over her head and burrowed deeper, pretending she was invisible as a distant voice called her.

The sound loomed closer, and Felicity flung away the bedclothes. 'Get up, girl. It's getting hotter and you agreed last night you'd help me do the sheep work.'

'Take care of your own bloody animals. I'm sleeping,' she said, tightening the surrounding sheet.

Felicity's words were muffled and garbled as she bolted from the room. 'No, you're… not.' Next minute she returned with a glass of water, which she dribbled on Mia. 'Get up and get going. I'll wait in the kitchen.'

No one treats me this way, thought Mia indignantly. At no time in their discussions in hospital about her recuperation on Felicity's farm, did she understand she was signing up to a boot camp? Bloody bitch. Mia switched on the bedside light, fumbled for clothes borrowed from the cupboard and stomped to the bathroom complaining to herself.

'Morning Mia,' said Felicity with a startled look. 'Did you raid Emily's drawer?' Mia, dressed in her daughter's shorts and a sleeveless top, scowled, and turned away. 'You'll need long pants to do sheep work.'

Mia poured herself a hot black coffee and closed her eyes as the liquid soothed her throat and she imagined she was far from this stinker of a place.

'Have some toast?' said Felicity. Mia snorted with disgust. 'Suit yourself. You can't go without breakfast. Too much heavy work to do.' Felicity stacked her plates in the sink. 'I'll get ready and meet you at the gate but wear those black boots on the veranda as I don't want you treading on snakes.'

Mia arched her eyebrows and grunted.

Later, as they drove to the hay shed, Felicity said, 'Please shut your window, the dust is everywhere.'

Mia turned her body to the open window, closed her eyes, and allowed the dirt to roll over her while Felicity grumbled, 'I need you to help me feed the sheep. We'll put the hay in the back, and you drive slow while I throw it to them.'

Mia's face tightened, and she crossed her arms as she muttered a half incoherent reply. '…bloody well think.' Then she made a half-hearted effort to help lift a bale but let her side fall to the ground. As tears formed in her eyes, she ran to the ute, banged the door, and sulked while Felicity struggled to load the hay.

'You bitch,' Mia swore under her breath.

With a full load in the ute, Felicity drove to the next paddock and Mia jammed her hands under her armpits. Her body shook with fear and she refused to open the gate as the sheep bunched together and swirled like bees, baaing and stamping their feet with expectation.

'Okay, why don't I open it?' sneered Felicity. 'You steer. If you go slow, they'll run away, out of your path.'

Mia inched her way into the paddock and as she drove, some sheep fled and others eyed-her-off and stood their ground. She smirked realising sheep were as stubborn as she was.

Felicity shouted, 'Drive over to the acacia tree.' She pointed to a tree in the distance. 'I'll feed the old girls from the back of the ute. Go slow.'

For the next hour, Mia hop-jumped in the ute, listening to Felicity talking to her sheep. 'Patsy, don't go stamping your foot like that, you'll get enough food', and shouting, "Stop! Start!".

'Thanks,' said Felicity. 'Now head to the dam over there and we'll see if the pump is working.'

Mia gripped the wheel as she navigated trees, fallen branches, and potholes.

'Oh, no,' cried Felicity when they saw a sheep bogged in the mud. She jumped out of the ute and ran across the cracked, dry bottom of the dam with a small pool of water in the middle.

'What a pitiful cry. I'm not sloshing around in there,' mumbled Mia, flopping her arms on the steering wheel. Now and then she darted a look at Felicity, who was trying to loosen the animal, and she heard her tenderly willing the sheep to break free as it raised its head and bleated. Mia stiffened, worried about the poor animal surrounded by so many flies, and she flinched each time Felicity pulled to release it. A sense of helplessness encased Mia, the same feeling she had when the Oxys gripped her.

Felicity startled her when she returned to the vehicle. 'We have to head home. I have to get something.' She wiped her eyes with the back of her hand and hopped in the ute and sped across the paddocks.

***

At the house Felicity jumped from the ute, banged the door, and strode onto the veranda, leaving her riding boots on to enter the kitchen. Mia's mouth flew open and her heart raced as she saw Felicity reappear with a gun.

'Don't worry, it's not for you, I won't shoot you. You stay here.' She leapt into the vehicle and sped off.

Mia shook and little beads of sweat appeared on her forehead. Felicity had a rifle to kill a sheep. What might happen if she went crazy. She stared into the distance and after a few minutes found her phone.

'Brad? I'm spooked, Felicity's taken her shotgun into the paddock.'

After a gasping Mia told him what had happened, he reassured her it had more to do with the sheep than her. 'Mia, stop it! You're living on a farm. Life and death are on the doorstep, and Felicity knows what she's doing. She hasn't used the gun on you before, has she?'

Mia nodded, lost for words; there was no sympathy from Brad.

'How are you?'

'I'm gutted, miserable. Flea doesn't make it any better, she buzzes everywhere. We fight and she dripped water on me this morning.'

'What for?'

'To get me out of bed at 5:30 to help with her stupid sheep.'

Brad roared with laughter. 'Mia, I don't believe you. You're never up that early.'

Mia half-smiled. 'I'm missing everything – you, my Oxys, Canberra, even my work. Can you visit me, please, please?'

'Um, will try to get there, but my weekends are precious with this new man I've met. Better get back to my job and I'll ring you in a few days if you haven't had a bullet,' he said, laughing laughed at the other end.

Mia threw the phone on the floor, collapsed onto a chair and sobbed, 'No one cares, why does this always happen to me?'

'What's the matter now?' said Felicity as she marched into the kitchen.

'Brad's obnoxious.'

Mia sniffled and ran to the bathroom with tears in her eyes. On her way to the bedroom, she stopped and through the open door of the office, she saw Felicity embed the gun in its special niche and try the lock three times before the key slid into her pocket. She doesn't trust her.

When Felicity stepped into the hallway, Mia confronted her. 'What did you do to that sheep?'

'I shot it, had to. The poor sheep was struggling, had lost the will to live. No matter how hard I tried, it would not help me get it out of the bog. Had a choice between shooting it or letting the crows peck out its eyes.' Felicity's hands were shaking as she explored the contents of the fridge. 'I need something strong to drink after that, a pity a cuppa will have to do after my pledge to get off the grog. Do you want lunch, a drink?'

'No. I'm catching up on my sleep.'

'Your body's out of whack so keep up the water in this weather otherwise you'll fry your brain and get lots of headaches.'

'Fry your brain, keep up the water,' mimicked Mia to herself as she lay on the bed and tossed and turned. 'She's the one giving me headaches.'

She interpreted the symbols in the intricate ceiling patterns, a habit she had started at boarding school, to distract herself.

Brad. It hit her how much he meant to her. They had met at her first job in Canberra; they had a dragon of a boss and bonded over lunches and dinners to escape the pressures of work. Brad had made her laugh and showed her how to enjoy life in Australia. Their dance classes were hilarious and as dancing partners they clicked. She could rely on him; and now he had a boyfriend. She froze, rooted to the bed, wondering whether he would still want to be her best friend.

Without warning, Mia stopped moaning and sat on the bed. She clenched the pillow, pounded it, and gave a muffled yell. 'I must get over this or I'll be dead like that sheep. Arsehole.' Her jaw was rigid, her chest tightened, and her heart beat fast with sweat trickling from her temples.

She fell back to the mattress and lay staring at the ceiling, thinking of what she could she do. In the past, her first response was to go to the internet, but these days her attention span was zilch and phones, computers, books, or even the TV didn't interest her. These devices filled her life before anxiety and Oxys swamped her.

Without warning, a thought flashed through her mind. Maybe the way out lies within and running away from this nightmare makes it worse. She had glimpsed something about this in one of Felicity's books, and it might give her clues about what to do to change her life. She drummed the pillow again and again, trying to escape from herself.

Am I responsible for my recovery? The thought agitated her, and in her half-sleep she went to her default position dreaming of Nairobi, of her mother and father, laughing and enjoying each other's company. Her dad and wild animals beckoned as he clasped her hand to soothe her as Mummy was no longer there. She whimpered and sobbed, waking with a drenched pillow and sheet from the afternoon heat.

The cool of the bathroom called. She needed a luxurious soak so turned the taps to max and watched the slow, brownish water fill the pink tub, spurting in gasps, gurgling, splashing. In a tizz, Mia combed through her bags, searching for something exotic to take away the dirty colour and smell. The white and gold jar looked expensive, and the instructions promised relaxation and an end to anxiety.

Mia grabbed hold of a large handful of salts and let them swirl under the tap, releasing their fragrance. She looked in the mirror as she undressed, taking time to massage her body and study it from different angles, and sighed as she thought of the last occasion she had bathed with a lover. From her perch on the edge of the tub, she slid into the murky water.

She lay in the bath with her eyes closed for the next half an hour with her anxieties dissipating.

'Mia, where are you?' yelled Felicity from the back door.

'I'm in the tub.'

'What! It must be putrid. We don't use the bath, that water's only for the garden, I switched the pipes for the shower not the bath.'

Mia leapt from the tub and fled down the hall with a towel half-draped around herself, almost knocking over Felicity, who was laughing, leaving trickles of water in her wake.

***

The night was oppressive and hot. Sweat streamed down Mia's body and a lone mosquito's buzz persisted, no matter how many times she shook the sheet. She waited until Felicity had gone to bed, and silence filled the house before tiptoeing to the kitchen for water and stepping onto the veranda to catch a breeze. The darkness enclosed her, and shadows lurked. Noises she didn't recognise bombarded her brain. Without warning, something panted and rubbed against her leg. A scream rose in her throat until she recognised the coat of a dog nuzzling into her.

'What are you doing here, Whiskey?' She looked into his big generous eyes and ruffled the fur behind his ears and stroked his back.

'Here, I'm going to lie on this.' She patted the lounge.

Mia lay down and helped him up beside her and whispered to the dog in the darkness, telling him about Brad, Felicity, her childhood, her anxieties, her hopes, her future. He rested at her side with his nose peeping over her breasts. He slept, but from time to time he stared at her as though he heard, and then he burrowed in next to her body. At last, she lapsed into a deep sleep.

In the first glow of the morning, Whiskey stretched and shook himself as Felicity strolled onto the veranda. Through her bleary eyes Mia saw her put a shush sign to her lips and smile, realising she meant it for the dog. When Felicity returned from inside, she had meat in her hand and signalled to Whiskey to follow, and the dog trailed after her as she tiptoed down the path, and Mia turned and slept.

Half an hour later Mia staggered into the kitchen, rubbing her sore body.

'Feeling stiff, are you?' said Felicity boiling the kettle. 'Whiskey's a delightful companion. He doesn't answer back, but he's smelly. Did you let him in the house yard?'

'No, I couldn't sleep and cleared off to the rear lounge. He came out of nowhere and scared me.' Mia squeezed a smile. 'He's good company, I talked to him for hours, then fell asleep.'

Over the next few days, Mia and Whiskey were inseparable. In the evening's coolness, she sat on the veranda steps and either chatted or stared into the distance with him by her side. As her courage grew, she found the shadows less intimidating and walked along the track to the main road. Mia and the dog formed silhouettes in the day's twilight as the birds did their last dance.

Chapter 23

The phone's ring broke Felicity's thoughts of the easy working life in her office in Sydney, when her calluses and brown sunspots didn't exist. She gave a half-hearted shrug as she filled the washing machine with clothes and yelled to Mia, who was playing with Whiskey on the veranda to answer it, and when she asked who it was, Mia ignored her.

'Better wash those hands,' Felicity scolded. 'Don't want Whiskey's germs. Now did I see him slink out of your bedroom early this morning?'

Mia smiled and skated along the kitchen floor to the bathroom.

Felicity remembered how distressed Mia was when she first arrived at *Neerea*. Her behaviour infuriated and scared her. It was nothing like what she had experienced in her children's moody adolescence. Mia threw tantrums one minute, sobbed and was sorry for herself the next, then played the "good girl". Their relationship was fraught with her choice in music echoing her moods as she swung from the depths of despair to over-the-top elation. Now there were fewer hissy-fits and life was much calmer, but she was still over-sensitive.

She smiled, she was enjoying having a younger person in the house again and there were lots of giggles and laughter. Mia's attachment to her phone had gone and when it didn't work, she wasn't concerned. Whiskey was her constant companion, and each evening they strolled to different parts of the property, Mia talking to him along the way. He slept in her room, which annoyed Felicity, but she tolerated Whiskey staying inside because he did wonders for Mia's recovery.

'I'm going to town to tomorrow. Do you want to come with me?' said Felicity.

Mia picked up the knives and forks to set the table. 'No, there's nothing there, it's boring.'

'Okay. By the way, Bill's son is coming to get parts for a tractor from the shed.'

'Is he?' She saw Mia's eyes light with interest. 'The engaged one?'

'No, Ant's been studying, he's back for a visit. A gorgeous young man – a good catch. You might find yourself a mate,' teased Felicity. 'Whiskey will be so jealous.'

Mia screwed up her face, and they laughed with affection and understanding.

'Bloody men. Have no luck with them. At least I know where I stand with Brad.' Mia stood with her hands on her hips watching Felicity prepare the vegetables. 'Met this cool man in England, we clicked, but I was on my way to Canberra and he didn't want to come to Australia. What's it called, "ships passing in the night"?'

'Hmm. There'll be someone else. You're young, attractive, and much livelier now. Are you feeling any better?'

'Let's say, I'm improving. No fast food, all that herbal stuff you give me and walks with Whiskey. He doesn't answer back, even dreaming of handsome blokes again. Must be in good shape.'

Felicity raised her thumbs. 'Take your time with men. I married forever, but it didn't last. Told my daughter the other night it was over between her dad and myself, and she hung up on me. Not happy.' She paused for a moment and stared out the window. 'It's lonely on your own but you don't have to accept the rubbish that goes with a miserable marriage.'

After Mia poured water for them both, she called for a toast, 'To all wicked men, may they rot in hell.' The two women danced through the kitchen with their glasses in the air.

'What would you do if Randall returned?'

Felicity hesitated and clamped her hands on her drink. 'I don't know…I like him, just wary of getting hurt again.' She raised her glass and grinned. 'The wings of fate?'

'He's okay but a bit old and scratchy, a good sort for you. What will you do, Flea?'

'There's too much going on around here to worry about Randall,' said Felicity, detecting a twinkle of mischief in Mia's eyes and pausing paused with suspicion. 'What's this sudden interest in him? What have you been up to, Mia? Have you been ringing him again?'

Mia could not contain her laughter. She held the chair, giggling and pointing her finger at Felicity. 'Guess who rang?'

Felicity squealed. 'Randall? You bugger.' She chased Mia around the kitchen with a tea towel and onto the veranda where the chorus of dogs joined the fun.

Mia ran out the gate and taunted Felicity. 'He'll ring back again tonight.'

Felicity overcooked the chops and let the vegetable water boil to nothing, and when she had half-finished the shrivelled dinner, the phone rang. 'Missy, you can get that, seeing you're so smart.'

'It's for you, Madam! I'll eat with Whiskey.'

***

When Felicity returned from town with a load of groceries and farm stuff, she couldn't find Mia, so she carted the food to the kitchen, and admired her appearance in the hallway mirror on the way. Her hairdresser had squeezed her in for a cut and colour, with a pedicure and a manicure. Looking at her painted nails, she remembered the wonderful pampering day she had had in Mildura and the difference it had made and laughed at the thought of chasing sheep with painted nails.

She grinned, recalling Randall's call and how after the first embarrassing pauses, they were soon in tune and chatted into the night. When she suggested they get together, the tone of his voice changed, and he proposed a visit to Canberra. It was neutral territory, but was she too pushy about suggesting a get together? Ah, life's too short, she thought. A few days' break was long overdue.

Randall had suggested bringing Mia with her to Canberra to give her a trial run back in her own home, but Felicity was half-hearted in her response. She needed a break from

Mia but wasn't prepared to admit it, and there was also still a twinge of doubt about trusting Mia and Randall together.

'Yeah, I'll ask if she wants to come, but she's very attached to Whiskey. She won't want to leave him,' she had said.

That night while eating their take-away dinner from town, Felicity asked Mia if she wanted to come with her to Canberra for the weekend.

There was a prolonged pause. 'I'm staying here to look after Whiskey. I'm not ready to go home yet.'

'Good,' said Felicity with relief. 'You watch over the farm, but I hope you won't be scared on your own.'

Mia leant back in her chair with hands behind her head with an unperturbed air. 'My dog, he'll chase everything away.'

'Bill's nearby, you can always ring if you have any problems and I'll be back on Sunday.'

'Okay. Bill's son didn't come today?' said Mia, helping herself to more chicken.

'Ant will appear when Bill needs the parts.'

Over the next few days, Felicity's heart sang, and she whistled while she worked. Mia announced during lunch she would prepare their dinner every night. Surprised, Felicity dropped the plate in her hand, and it shattered on the floor.

'Mia, I'm so pleased you want to cook. It's the best present for me,' she said, as she hugged her.

Disaster hit the first time, a fiasco, the rice burnt to the bottom of the pot, the chicken was under-cooked and covered with an indescribable sauce that made Felicity retch. Even Whiskey wouldn't eat the food. Once Mia's mojo returned, her cooking improved. When Felicity came in from the farm and dinner was ready, she clapped her hands in excitement. Then Mia announced she would make a cake for Randall.

Felicity's tone changed, 'Nice thought, but I don't think it's such a good idea.'

***

As Felicity drove to Canberra, she opened the car window and allowed *Handel's Anthems and Fireworks* performed by the Australian Brandenburg Orchestra, to blast through the dry, undulating farmland. She tapped the steering wheel to the music brimming with happiness, having escaped the routine of work and Mia's woes and anxieties.

When she arrived in the city, she stopped at a lingerie boutique she had discovered on the internet and touched the beautiful silk fabrics and breathed in the heady perfumes wafting through the shop. She bought a black see-through bra and knicker set with a gorgeous soft luxurious nightie to match. Heaven sent.

By the time she navigated the streets to the hotel where she would meet Randall, she was fluttering with excitement.

Felicity arrived early and waited on a grey-checked chair near the café, watching Randall check-in with the receptionist.

'Yes, my partner and I'll stay two nights,' he said.

Felicity giggled to herself at his formality and kept her distance. His phone rang, and he took the call while completing the transaction.

If that's his ex again, I won't let her spoil my weekend, she said to herself as she watched him walk up and down the foyer, oblivious to everyone.

When he had finished, he looked around, and she came behind him and wrapped her arm around him.

'Randall, is everything okay?'

He stepped back in surprise, then his face cleared, and he grinned.

'A business matter, all sorted now so we can enjoy the weekend,' he said as he encased her in a bear-hug.

***

In the early evening, they left the hotel in his 4WD to go to an Indian restaurant. As they drove, Felicity said, 'This is a tough decision, but I've decided not to drink tonight. Have had no grog since Mia arrived and think I'm much better without it.'

'Okay,' he said, patting his chest and laughing. 'I'll restrain myself with difficulty.'

When they got out of the car, she shivered in the autumn wind, so he wrapped his arm around her, and they scurried up the stairs hand in hand and the waitress guided them to a corner seat where they could see the other guests. There was a group of people enjoying themselves, and the Indian women at the table outshone everyone as they wore stunning-coloured saris and Kurtis embellished with beads. Those in western clothing were less colourful.

'It's good to see another life beyond the farm,' said Felicity, as Randall ran his fingers over hers. 'Those women look so elegant I'm underdressed beside them.'

He kissed her hand and gazed into her eyes. 'You're great just as you are.' He fondled her earlobes. 'Love the earrings. Aren't you glad they found the other one?'

They chattered and waited for the delicious samosas, colourful curries, and vegetables, and Felicity soon forgot the long dreary days of battling Mia.

When they returned to their room, Randall retrieved an expensive bottle of champagne he had hidden in the mini fridge. 'Let's celebrate?'

'Oh, no!' She bounced her fingers on her lips. 'This will break my not-drinking.' She made an Hmm noise in her throat, then said with a soft voice. 'Suppose a glass or two won't hurt?'

He cracked the bottle open and when the bubbles and froth had subsided, he made a toast, 'To us, many good times.'

They sipped their drinks intertwined on the lounge with their feet raised on the coffee table. Later, without warning, Randall placed their glasses on a nearby cabinet and massaged her toes, her legs and edged up her body, gently removing her clothes as he watched her between his butterfly kisses. Felicity murmured her delight.

'Wow.' He gasped in surprise when he exposed her raunchy lingerie, her bra glittering under the light and she giggled as he slipped it off and threw it to the floor. She closed her eyes while he stroked her and burrowed his head in her breasts. He picked her up as though she was a feather and pecked her on the lips for each step he made to the bedroom. She laughed, whispered in his ear, and held on tight. On the oversized bed, she arched her back in pleasure as he caressed and kissed her body. She ruffled and pulled his hair and tossed and turned in ecstasy. 'This's so g....' Her words swallowed by his mouth around hers.

||*

The next morning, through the open door of the bathroom, Felicity watched fascinated as Randall shaved, the foam removed as the blade scrapped over his skin. His gestures refined and gentle, just as he was as a lover. I might fall for you, she thought. He saw her stare and came and kissed her, rubbing the half-finished soapy stubble against her cheek and teasing her until she turned away in mock disgust.

'Yuck, I only had good thoughts about you. I take them back.'

Over a leisurely breakfast, Randall suggested a visit to the National War Memorial and grinned as he poured the tea from a green coloured pot. 'You know, there's a fine line between bravery and foolishness. You're either brave or mad for taking on Mia.'

'Madness!' Felicity threw up her hands. 'She's much better, I suppose calmer, more consistent, and she prepares dinner every night. But at the beginning...' Felicity closed her eyes. 'A nightmare.'

'You know she rang me?'

Felicity drew in her breath and her fingers touched her lips. 'Yes, the bugger mentioned that. When did she call you?'

'Not sure. Did you give her my number? She rang twice, talked and talked, and I said little. She told me silly gossip the second time, and I went mad so she didn't ring again.'

'There was no way I'd give her your number. Why didn't you ring me…tell me?' Felicity glared at Randall.

'Didn't think about it.' He scratched his head. 'I was a sounding board. You were scrambling just to care for her.'

'So, you were supporting Mia not me?'

'No…' Randall grabbed Felicity's wrists and struggled to look into her eyes as she turned her head. 'Look, you're a busy woman and it cheesed me off when you took Mia to the farm. Suppose it caused a rift between us.' He released her hands. 'That didn't mean I wasn't helping. I was supporting you without getting too involved.'

'Funny kind of support,' said Felicity. 'She must have flattered you with that attention. "Daddy gets a call from his favourite girl".' She fixed her thumbs in her ears and mimicked him.

Randall's mouth fell open, he stammered. 'What's happening? This is ridiculous, you're too confusing for me.' He grabbed Felicity's arm. 'Okay, Mia's older than my daughter, but I'm sure she sees me as a father figure. Her own father's absent when she needs him most, so she rings me. I treat her like I would my girl, listen to what she says and support her, nothing more.'

Felicity flinched. 'It may have been all right if you'd bothered to talk, now it's sly and underhanded and I can't trust you if you go behind my back.' She frowned, crossed her arms, and examined the table. 'I'm not sure what to think.'

He moved his chair closer. 'Please don't let this spoil our time together. I found out what you were up to by talking to Mia. I…missed you.'

She fingered the pearl drop she was wearing. 'Why didn't you bloody well ring?'

Silence waited like a chess piece for the next move.

After a while, Randall said, 'Sorry I hurt you, I thought it was the right thing to listen to Mia's troubles. I'm puzzled you're so upset and I won't let her do it again.'

His gaze was warm and pleading, sending shivers up her body and touching her heart.

'Hmm, I'm not sure.' She snickered.

'What'll we explore next?' Randall, catching the shift in her mood, patted her leg and gave a salacious wink.

'No… we won't go there! Let's drop by the art gallery.'

'Yes, have a look at that painting *Blue Poles*. Cost the taxpayer a mill in Whitlam's time, now worth $350 million, but didn't everyone carry on, so many outraged people.'

'Life changes.' Felicity lowered her head and interlocked her hand with Randall's. 'I've been on a roller coaster, tossed from side to side since my fateful decision to have a break in Adelaide. But the big plus is us.' When he pulled her to him and kissed her on the cheek, his alluring scent caught her by surprise, and she nuzzled into him.

***

The next day Randall trooped to the car with an arm draped over Felicity, and in the other hand he carried her bag.

'I'll miss you, Flea.' He lay the luggage on the rear seat. 'I realise I did the wrong thing talking to Mia behind your back, but she brought us together.' He reached out and grabbed Felicity and flashed her a knowing smile. 'When's our next rendezvous, soon I hope?'

'Think your ex-wife is requiring more of your attention at the moment,' she said in a caustic tone.

He pulled her into an embrace, and she squeezed his arms.

'Look, don't worry about my ex, she's going through a rough patch. Unfortunately, my kids told her I was going away for the weekend.' He held her tighter and whispered in her ear. 'How about I come out to the farm in the next few weeks?'

She gave him a seductive smile. 'I'll line up the jobs, but no "wife calls" allowed. I had a wonderful time, thanks.'

They clung to each other until little tears formed and she turned her head.

Chapter 24

Mia with Whiskey by her side, was cutting tomatoes for lunch with a sharp knife when there was a bellow from the back gate, 'Hello, anyone home?'

Not recognising the man's voice, she rested the knife on the table within easy reach and stepped through to the veranda and folded her arms.

A young fellow her age, of good height, stood on the back step with a big grin on his face. He wore cut-off jeans, and a decorated pink no-sleeve top, which showed off his well-defined muscles. He lifted his cap to show his man-bun and placed his dark sunglasses on his head. 'Hello, I'm Ant, Bill's son. Is Flea home?'

'No, she's in Canberra,' said Mia in a hushed tone, overwhelmed by such a hot-looking guy.

'That's okay. She left stuff in the shed. I'll get it, come back and have a chat.'

He roared away in his father's ute and within half an hour he returned and entered the house. Her scream was piercing when she saw an unknown presence silhouetted against the kitchen door.

'Sorry, I should have yelled out to let you know I was here.'

'I'm not used to seeing people anymore,' said Mia, her hand over her heart.

He leaned against the cupboards and asked, 'Do you mind if I have a snack?'

'Go… for it,' she stammered. When her breath returned, she asked, 'A coffee or a tea?'

He nodded, 'Coffee.' He ate the overfilled sandwich and spoke with a half-full mouth, asking how she was enjoying country life.

'It's slow, boring, but I'm getting used to it. I take walks with Whiskey in the evening, he chases the birds, I watch the sunset and this is the highlight of my day.'

'How do you get on with Flea?'

Mia pulled a face, and she sniggered. 'Depends on the time. Sometimes we fight, other days we're fine, but she always wants help to do jobs.'

'Don't worry, my father's the same. He lines up every job he has until I arrive and forgets I work and come home for a break. It drives me mad.'

'You're the first new person I've met since I arrived here.'

'Guarantee everyone knows you're here even though you've never seen them. That's why I enjoy the city, I'm anonymous in Melbourne.'

'You think so?' She stood with her arms folded. 'What do you do there?'

'Bit of study, dabble in music, work part time, other stuff.' He picked up the other half of the sandwich. 'No money but fun. Don't come home often. And you?'

'Live in Canberra, it's okay, slow sometimes.' Mia flicked a rogue hair from her face as she thought of how nice he was, the grin and his soft eyes intrigued her.

'What work do you do?'

'I'm into computers. Worked out how to use them when I was a kid and kept learning so can always get a job in any country.'

Ant glanced at the wall clock. 'Oops, better be leaving, Dad's waiting for these parts.' They walked together to the veranda door and as he strolled the pathway, he turned. Mia could see his eyes twinkling, the smile on his lips, and then his words stumbled out. 'How about coming with me to the pub tonight? The weekend's busy, there's a BBQ and you'll get used to mixing with people again. It's nothing upmarket.'

'Oh..., okay. What time?'

'I'll pick you up...say at seven?' He waved his cap and drove away, the ute raising a plume of dust.

Mia was in a tizz. She grabbed her bags, opened the drawers, and tipped clothes onto the bed, rummaging through them, throwing possibilities into a pile. She swore there was nothing suitable, her coloured gear too flamboyant for people she didn't know. Amongst Felicity's daughter's belongings she found a more conservative white cheesecloth dress which fitted, but it was far too short.

Wrapped in a towel, she brushed and caressed her long tresses until they shone like gold, then she tried different hairstyles, a plait, a chignon, finally letting her locks fall free.

Mia kept glancing at the clock and obsessing about what people would say about her, behind her back. Bastards.

Her heart missed a beat when she saw Ant strutting to the door, dressed in cream moleskins emphasising his thighs, a tight black T-shirt which defined his torso, a brown leather belt and riding boots. In his hand he carried assorted garden flowers, the names she didn't know, surrounded by gum branches.

He held the bunch out to Mia with a careless grin. 'Pinched these out of Mum's yard. Enjoy them. Not much to choose from, it's so dry.'

Mia's eyes widened, and her lips formed a silent, Oh, no. 'Thanks.'

With a frown he looked at her, dressed in shorts, a long loose light blue top, and thongs. 'Are you ready?'

Mia sucked in her breath. 'I'm not feeling well so I don't want to go and there'll be too many people.'

Ant studied her with a pleading look. 'You sure? I'll look after you.'

'I can't…' Mia turned aside, holding the flowers to her chest.

He came towards her and touched her gently on the arm. 'That's okay, another day.' He bowed and mumbled. 'Said I'd meet my friends there so will go now.' He waved and roared off along the track with the cacophony of dogs barking behind him.

Whiskey licked Mia's hands as she covered her face on the veranda step, her bottom lip trembling and she was soon wiping tears away. 'Ant's too good for me — he's polite, handsome, comes from a normal family.' She sobbed. 'Oh, what can I do?'

Mia tried to ring Brad, but he didn't answer. It's Saturday night and there was no one at home except herself, stuck in the bush with no pills, and no people for kilometres. No one loved her, and her father had not rung for weeks. She threw her arms in the air and berated herself for being a basket case and revolting. Everyone deserted her at the worst time of her life.

Solace in bed. Mia curled herself beside Whiskey and cried herself to sleep. The bush flowers and their newspaper wrapping lay next to her, a symbol of love denied.

***

The radio blared as Felicity sped along the road thinking of Randall. She squeezed herself and let the warm sensations flow through her body. What a wonderful weekend they had together and her niggle about where Mia stood in Randall's world was resolving, she now believed he had tried to help them both by listening to Mia's woes.

However, she was still struggling with Randall's ex's calls because they were persistent and every time she called, Felicity grew more and more concerned. There was no way she would ring Alan, and she couldn't even remember when they had last spoken. She had planned to talk to Randall about his wife before the weekend but had enjoyed herself for the first time in ages and didn't want to mar their time together, so they didn't discuss it.

Mia greeted her with a grunt in the kitchen, hunched over, staring into a cup of tea, the remnants of her meals beside her and the room a mess with unwashed dishes and pots.

'How was it alone?' said Felicity as she shooed flies from the windows.

'Okay, I had Whiskey.'

'Did anyone call?'

'Ant came.'

'He's nice, isn't he?'

'I couldn't go with him.' Mia put her hands to her head at the table and her hair covered her face.

'What do you mean? Did he ask you out?'

A dejected Mia turned away. 'Yeah, to the pub. I wanted to go, but it scared me. Too many people, they'd chat about me.'

'That's a pity. Ant's a great kid, should I say a young man. I'll just pick up the rest of my bags, then we can talk.'

When she returned, she made herself a tea and listened to Mia explain how she had lost her confidence to go out with Ant. 'I've forgotten how to mix, living out here.'

Felicity put her arms around her. 'Don't be too hard on yourself. It'll be better and when you return to Canberra, you'll enjoy seeing people again.'

With a sad smile on her face, Mia gathered up the plates, loaded the dishwasher and dashed to the bedroom.

'I forgot, Ant gave me these. Flowers from his mother's garden.' She thrust the blooms at Felicity and beamed. 'They're special because there's a drought. He's so thoughtful.'

'Wow, beautiful, what a gentleman. When's he returning to Melbourne?'

'Tomorrow he said.'

'What a pity.' Felicity hesitated, not knowing how to broach Mia's calls to Randall. With a deep breath, she held back the words she really wanted to say, and then her phone rang. From the lounge on the veranda, she chatted to Randall for over an hour, trying to cover the squeals of laughter at his seductive remarks. When they finished the call, she stood, put out her arms and spun herself around in happiness. She was not discussing him with Mia. Life's too short.

***

Over the next week, Felicity was back and forth across the farm every morning, rotating the sheep to different paddocks, making sure they had enough food and water. She laughed at the antics of the small birds chasing the magpies and crows, and the stubborn animals who stamped their feet at her as she tried to muster them to another paddock. Even Mia's anxiety and trauma about not going to the pub with Ant had subsided.

Her favourite haunt, her tree with its unusual glow, called. Under its protective branches, her eyes grew moist as she thought of how her relationship with Randall had strengthened and how they spoke each night. There was still no rain, but as she stretched her legs, she realised she was more energetic and less in need of alcohol to get herself through the days. She was happier and more content.

With gratitude she reflected on the Wiradjuri people whose care for the land was so important, part of their culture.

They had taken what they needed from this tree but had left it intact all those years ago. Her parents had had protected it, preserved this sanctuary, a special place for them.

Sadly, her family and those before them had plundered other trees nearby, tearing away groves of tall majestic white and yellow box, apple gums and bushes to make way for machinery and crops that scarred the land forever. She had planted saplings and watered them with a bucket when she arrived at the farm but had lost many in the drought.

Whiskey stirred, nuzzling up to her and bringing her back to the present. She thought of Randall and wondered what part he would play in her future life. If their relationship continued, she would have to introduce him to her children. How would they cope with him as her partner? Her friends had mixed stories of introducing their new beaus to a family.

'Where were you?' Mia stood with her hands on her hips. 'Randall's been trying to get hold of you. Wants you to ring him.'

'Okay, I'll chat to him after dinner.' She caught a whiff of Mia's cooking. 'That smells delicious. Is it ready now?'

They ate in silence.

In her office, Felicity flipped the internet to a city paper and moved documents to plant her feet on a box to prepare for a long conversation. She dialled the number.

'Thought I lost you,' laughed Randall at the other end of the phone. 'Had a choice between your message bank or Mia.'

She smiled and said, 'What's happening?'

'Good news.'

'Yeah. What?'

'I couldn't tell you on the weekend in case I jinxed myself. But I'm branching out.' He paused. 'I've bought a share in a business in Adelaide.'

Silence.

'Aren't you pleased for me?' said Randall, taken aback by her reaction.

Felicity blurted out, 'You'll be even further away.'

'No, I'll live here but go to there more often. Become a "Shirley boarder" like Merv.

'I hope not,' she said in a stern tone. 'Merv's more than that when he visits.'

'Don't be so cross. The organisation has been going on for months.'

'Sorry, I was thinking of myself. Congratulations. We'll celebrate when you come next weekend.'

'Good idea.'

She interrupted their conversation as she heard a pitter patter on the corrugated tin roof, and it grew stronger and louder.

'Randall, it's raining!' yelled Felicity, jumping up and down with excitement. 'Gotta make sure I've covered everything. Bye, darling.' She raced through the house into the garden and raised her hands to the sky, letting the water soak through her hair and over her body. She wrapped her arms around herself and thought how the rain was heaven, and Randall was such a sweetie.

Mia switched on the back light, and yelled, 'You're a drenched ghost and fucken mad.' The deluge became heavier as she continued her dance to the gods with her hands raised to the sky.

Chapter 25

A furious frenzy hit the house as Felicity removed limp cobwebs from the ceilings; swept, mopped, vacuumed floors. Layers of dust and dirt detached from windows and furniture; cushions washed and fluffed, and the rotary clothesline groaned with an overload of curtains, blankets, and bedcovers. She harangued Mia and soon a new home emerged with a freshness not seen at *Neerea* for a long time. A makeover in tribute to Randall's upcoming visit.

Secateurs, axes, hoes, and shovels next appeared in the yard as Felicity pruned or discarded weary drought riddled plants and trees. She had tried to protect her extensive garden as dry conditions caught hold, watering less and less, but her ever shrinking oasis helped to keep her sane and manage the snakes coming closer to the house to survive.

'Mowing the lawn is our last job,' said Felicity, dressed in jeans, a long-sleeved shirt, wraparound sunglasses, and a huge floppy green hat. 'Should take me an hour, it'll be trimming dirt in parts. How about a celebration tonight?'

'Wow, what fun,' laughed Mia as she curtsied. 'For you, a gourmet dinner.'

Felicity began her methodical rounds of the garden on the sit-on mower. After a while, she noticed a rusty drum had rolled across the lawn from the fence. She muttered to herself, 'Bugger, why didn't I get rid of this before I started?'

The motor idled as she jumped off to remove it and as she moved, she tripped on the side of the machine, her arm twisted under her, taking the brunt of the fall.

Agonising pain leapt through her shoulder as it popped from the joint.

'Mia, Mia,' she yelled, the mower's engine roaring through the desolate yard and Felicity laying on the lawn writhing. The agony rippling through her body. An old crow made a series of eerie caws and the blazing sun stood still, suffocating her.

Her voice was distant, hoarse as she screamed, 'Mia, Mia'. After a while she thought she heard, through her tears and groans, the dogs barking, creating a loud continuous racket.

'What's the matter?' called Mia from the back veranda, and next minute Whiskey came bounding towards Felicity, licking her face, then lay whimpering with his head close to the grass, watching her.

'Flea, what happened?'

Felicity contorted her mouth, trying to suppress the pain. 'My...my shoulder's popped. Turn off...' She could say no more.

Mia fumbled with the key as Felicity's moans sounded like a wild animal in distress.

'What can I do?' said Mia in a panic.

'Ring ambulance...' Felicity gasped for breath through her half-closed eyes and tugged at Mia's sarong. 'Help me....'

Mia fastened her arm under Felicity and helped her to a sitting position, then to stand, taking great care not to jar her injured shoulder.

'That,' wailed Felicity as she pointed at the dress repeatedly and kept waving her good hand across her body to show Mia what she wanted her to do.

'You...want me to wrap this around your arm?'

Felicity nodded and Mia removed the sarong to reveal a pair of upturned breasts and styled pubic hair grinning in her nakedness and the thongs on Mia's feet made the figure even more bizarre.

'Oh my goodness,' said Felicity, grimacing through the blur of her pain.

Mia tried to immobilise the shoulder by wrapping her sarong around the upper part of Felicity's body as the agony seared. She then helped her to the car and ran inside to dress and ring the ambulance. Felicity rocked herself back and forth on the seat and screamed with her eyes closed, 'This's worse than childbirth. Why didn't I get painkillers?'

After what seemed like forever, Mia returned with Felicity's bag and through her haze Felicity saw she was no longer naked and her fitted purple T-shirt stood out. Mia jumped in the car and they sped off.

'Slow...slow.' Felicity wondered what would kill her, a dislocated shoulder or Mia's driving as she passed a vehicle at top speed with her hand resting on the horn.

'Did you ring the ambulance?'

'Yeah.'

Tears of pain formed and reformed as the car's suspension struggled and the pothole jolts sent her into fresh rounds of excruciating pain. Her thoughts flew to the many journeys she had made along this road to the hospital during her mother's illness. Then the car had sped through the day or night with her mother slumped in the passenger seat. She read the fear on her father's worried face and wondered whether they would ever make it. The silence always haunted her and now she was in agony, her screams coming in surges echoing through the vehicle as the spasms became worse.

'Sing… sing, Mia,' said Felicity, trying to distract herself from the waves of pain.

Mia started in a self-conscious way, then belted out some tunes.

After a while, Felicity groaned, 'Stop,' Then when Mia stopped, she said, 'No, sing.' Mia continued her songs.

When the sealed road began, Felicity wept with thanks and directed Mia through her tears along the back roads to the hospital, not wanting Mia to be caught for speeding.

Felicity gave a sigh of relief as they drove into the area reserved for ambulances as one was backing out. Mia wound the window and shouted, 'Bit late mate, we're here.'

The driver scratched his head as he put the van back into its space.

Felicity tried to get out of the car, but the makeshift sling made it difficult. Mia raced to her side and guided her to the door in Emergency, its harsh fluorescent light illuminating Felicity's tortured face. The woman on duty stared at her in the colourful drape, readjusted the files, and threw the paperwork at Mia.

'Fill these out and get her to sign them and you need her Medicare number,' she said officiously.

Mia grimaced, dug into Felicity's bag and found the yellow purse with the card, then picked up a pen from the counter and began the laborious task of filling out the form. Felicity sat moaning, rocking her body back and forth and holding her arm.

Ten minutes later, an irate Mia pushed to the clerk's desk and said, 'Can't you tell my friend's in agony. When's someone coming to help her?'

The woman turned aside as a nurse with a brown manbun walked behind her chair.

'Sorry, we're waiting for the Doctor. There's a breech birth.'

'But isn't there something for the pain?'

'No, that's up to the doctor.'

'How much longer will she be?'

'Not long, he's scrubbing up now.'

Mia returned to Felicity and tried to comfort her by putting her hand on her other arm, but she recoiled.

***

The nurse noticed Mia hesitate not knowing what to do and ushered her behind the cream curtains into the small, improvised cubicle where Felicity lay.

'Well, Flea, didn't expect to see you in here,' said the short dishevelled white-haired doctor as he examined the injury. 'How did you do this?'

The nurse fiddled, trying to remove the sarong with its strange bows. 'Please help me, Miss.'

Mia undid the makeshift sling and explained what happened while Felicity alternated between heavy breathing and moaning.

'Hold your horses, Flea,' said the doctor. 'We'll get you a drip, pain killers and work out what we can do.'

Mia bit her lip when Felicity's breathing changed as the drug snared her, and her face relaxed.

'This'll only take a minute, it'll hurt and then be finished.' Mia saw Felicity focus on his pink polka-dot bowtie as he gathered a towel and with the aid of the nurse grabbed her arm, and with precision and force, snapped the shoulder back into the joint socket.

'Thanks, Doctor,' murmured a dazed Felicity.

'Here, Flea.' He snatched an arm-support and sling lying on a table behind the curtain and adjusted it. 'Now I know you won't like what I have to say. Your arm's immobilised, it's important you wear this for two weeks, maybe more, so don't go lifting sheep or other heavy objects.' He laughed as he looked over his tortoise-shell glasses. 'No driving for the first few days as you need rest to heal this injury. There are exercises, but we won't start these until I see you next week.' He wagged his finger at her. 'Behave, have a break and do nothing stupid, otherwise you'll do irreparable damage.' He signalled for her to follow him into the ward. 'Here, lie on this bed for half an hour, it'll help you over the shock.' He turned to Mia and with a twinkle in his eye, said. 'Miss, make sure she does the right thing. I know she'll test you out.'

'I'm a tough boss, she won't be doing anything,' said Mia with her head in the air and a grin on her face.

Felicity groaned.

'Here, I'll give you a prescription for Felicity to manage the pain.'

Mia blushed as she could see Felicity scrutinise her from the bed.

Felicity whispered, 'The over-the-counter stuff will be fine, I promise to rest. That was the worst pain I have ever had.'

'Are you sure?' The doctor yanked his script pad from the pocket of his white coat. 'Won't take me a minute.'

Felicity waved him away. 'No, thanks.' She closed her eyes.

The nurse guided Mia to a waiting area with a grey lounge, plastic chairs, and old well-used magazines. 'Did you bring your mother into town on your own?'

Mia grinned and nodded.

'You did a good job,' the nurse said as he smiled. 'Your mum must be proud.'

Her expression lit up, and she beamed; they laughed, and Mia noticed his gentle blue eyes.

'Bye.' He winked. 'I'll see you later.' He disappeared into the ward.

Mia sat curled on the lounge, half reading an out-dated glossy magazine. She chortled to herself about how well she had handled the accident. And the cute nurse thought Felicity was her mother.

Later, the nurse returned and beckoned to Mia. When they came back to the room where Felicity rested, he said, 'Your daughter's here, ready to take you home.'

Understanding flashed between the two women. Mia's face shone and her heart fluttered.

'You were good to get me here so fast.' Felicity slowly manoeuvred herself from the bed and Mia put her arm around her. 'You cared for me so well. I love you. Thanks.'

***

Later, when the evening shadows appeared, and Felicity's drugs had worn off, they sat on the veranda and laughed at the half-finished lawn. Felicity sighed, 'What a bizarre experience. One minute, mowing the grass, the next racing to the hospital, then being drugged and my shoulder manipulated back into shape. The lawn's so much better where I mowed, Randall will have to finish it as I can't afford to have you out of action now.' Mia noticed she looked resigned to her fate for a few weeks.

***

"You're not allowed to do that. The doctor told me I'm the boss." Mia's catch cry as she set about organising the house, the food, and the cleaning. She drove Felicity around the farm and even listened to instructions about how to fill the water troughs.

'I can see you've a new chief, Flea,' said Bill, handing her a beer one evening after he had shown Mia how to feed the sheep. 'Watch out, you'll be out of a job.'

'Yeah, she stepped up, I couldn't do without her and she's much happier too,' Felicity whispered from the veranda lounge. 'Hope this bossing around doesn't go to her head.'

He pointed to the sling. 'That must drive you nuts.'

'It sure does, and I'm not a good patient.' Felicity clenched her fist. 'Boy, do I get frustrated! Just finished reading Virginia Woolf's *A Room of One's Own*, I meant to read it years ago and she certainly made me think about women's lives and how they often get dismissed.'

Bill paused and studied her with a peculiar smile. 'Don't know about that.'

Felicity could see this conversation would go nowhere, so changed the subject. 'Randall's visiting this weekend, he'll entertain me and do a few of the jobs.'

Bill's ears pricked. 'Um, this's serious with Randall if he's coming all this way to visit?'

Felicity grimaced, annoyed at herself as she had just told the local gossip information that would speed like wildfire through the neighbourhood. 'His business is changing direction, so he's taking time off before he gets too busy.'

'What's he do again?'

Felicity deflected the subject to the low-pressure systems expected to bring rain over the weekend and how their lives would be so different if there were more drenching falls.

As Bill was leaving, he said, 'I'll drop over while Randall's here. I'd like to meet the bloke.'

***

Felicity, like a caged cocky from her vantage point on the lounge, barked directions at Mia for coffee. It spilt and Mia watched mesmerised as the liquid ran across the grimy veranda floor in streaks and sucked itself through the floor's cracks.

'Get a mop. Where is he? Randall's taking too long. I hope he hasn't had an accident.' Felicity repeatedly said. 'I don't want him bogged. Even a little rain can turn those roads to mud.'

Mia reassured her, but it made no difference. Finally, she stormed off, 'I'm going for a drive.'

Crossing her arms, Mia tried to block her passage and said, 'I'll take you. You can't manage a car yet.'

'Leave me alone, I'll do what I want,' said Felicity, banging the back gate and marching to the vehicle. She yanked it open and hit her sore arm on the steering wheel. 'Shit.'

'That's pathetic!' yelled Mia as she watched Felicity try to manoeuvre the wheel with her arm in a sling. 'Stupid bitch. Why don't you give up?'

***

Half an hour later there was a drumming of rain on the tin roof and a pitter-patter on the cleaned windows. Mia popped outside to see if Felicity was celebrating. No ute. In the distance she heard the dogs bark, and a long ribbon of red dust followed a 4WD to the house.

Randall lowered the window and yelled, 'Hey Mia, thanks for the welcome.' He climbed out of the vehicle and gave her a big hug. 'I brought the rain with me, but there's still a hell of a lot of dust. Where's Flea?'

'She has the shits and has gone somewhere in the ute.' Mia threw her hands up. 'You know what she's like. Too impatient, and not allowed to drive, so what does she do?'

'Hear you're in charge. How are you surviving?' said Randall looked her over and chuckled as he collected his luggage. 'If you take this bag, I'll pull out the wine. We'd better scamper inside or get drenched.'

Mia was oblivious to getting wet and hammered on about Felicity. 'She's so testy and irritable and makes me mad because she won't sit still and rest.'

'Know how she feels. I'm a hopeless patient, give everyone a hard time. Let's make it easy for her and enjoy the next few days.' They scurried to the house. 'This rain's so welcome.'

'A coffee?'

'Hmm, great. Where did you say Flea was?'

Her stomping footsteps approached the kitchen. 'Here.'

Randall studied her and laughed. 'How can I cuddle you when this apparition's an injured and wet duck?' His face softened as he raised her good arm and pressed his warm cheek to her hand. 'How do you feel?' She lifted her head to kiss him and buried her shoulder into his body.

'Get a bedroom! Watch Flea's collarbone doing that. I'll make us something to eat.'

'Don't worry Mia, I'm on top of it.' Everyone laughed.

Over lunch, they organised the jobs and Randall told Felicity he would put her out of her misery and finish the lawn when the drizzle stopped promising to be careful.

'I'll supervise!' said a stern looking Felicity.

'Is she always like this?' He said, looked over his reading glasses at Mia.

Mia chuckled and threw her hands in the air.

The drizzly rain stopped, and they filled the afternoon with chores. Felicity tried to keep up, but the others ganged together and sent her off to rest.

Mia and Randall drove around the paddocks laughing and joking, and when he stopped the ute to check a sheep, she remained in the cabin. She turned the radio loud and thought of how Randall treated her well but was too blunt if he believed she was exaggerating or acting strangely. She wondered what he would be like as a father, maybe okay, but a control freak and a dickhead sometimes.

'Are you deafening me or the animals? You can hear that crap for miles,' said Randall as he jumped in the ute, banged the door and turned the radio off.

Mia pulled a face and shot daggers at him as they drove in silence in the scorching heat to sweep a dirty water trough.

She rested on her broom and swished her hand, but it made no difference to the persistent buzz. 'Bloody flies stick to you out here,' said Mia, squinting at him, trying to build her courage to say something. 'Can I thank you?'

'What for?'

'For listening to my raves when I first came here.'

'That's okay. You've done so well and I admire you for getting off those pills. What's happening now?'

'I can't get through to Flea.'

Randall raised his eyebrows and laughed, 'That's Flea. One thing, she always thinks she's doing her best and we may not like it, but her heart's in the right place. Few people would open their home like she has to you. I know I wouldn't. I was shitty with her for doing it, but she hung on to her way of doing things.'

'Should I be more... grateful?'

'Grateful? You should jump for joy, you've somewhere to stay, three meals a day and someone to care for you.' He placed his hand on Mia's shoulder and squeezed it. 'Later, this'll be a dream, the good and bad parts.' He moved towards the ute. 'Let's get back to her, I don't want to leave her alone too long. She won't admit it, but she's suffering and needs lots of TLC.'

'What's that?'

Randall roared with laughter, 'Tender loving care.'

Mia and Randall tumbled into the kitchen, laughing to meet a stony-faced Felicity rigid in her chair. 'Where have you two been?'

He frowned and said, 'Out cleaning your shitty troughs.' He bent to kiss her. 'How do you feel?'

'My arm hurts. Had to take something for it.' Felicity rubbed her fingers in the sling with her other hand. 'Must have done too much this morning.'

'Fragile superwoman. Now you sit there and talk to us while we get dinner. Mia, you can organise me after I wash.'

Throughout the evening Felicity frowned at Mia's warm glow and her darting gaze watched Randall's contact with her like a poker player. Her jaw was clenched, her own anxieties making life difficult.

Chapter 26

Two weeks later Felicity rang Randall, and tried an upbeat tone on the phone, but it didn't work.

'I've had a hell of a time with that girl since you went away, she's been bossing me around, not listening.' She paused. 'What a moody bugger, and she only does jobs when she wants, even left the washing in the basket for days. When I lost my temper, she told me to nick-off and I can't believe in my drug-addled state at the hospital, I said I loved her.'

Randall chuckled, 'You're not a perfect patient, are you? Time for you two to part company and it's your home so you can ask her to leave any day. No good complaining, just do something.'

'Yeah, but my gut tells me she needs an extra stint here to recover. I don't want her to relapse as soon as she hits the temptations of Canberra and go to the next level of drug taking. It's been so hard for her to get off the pills.'

'But what about you? Isn't Bill's son coming back to stay? Pay him to work with you or get him to share farm. Mia's much better, but she's hard going.'

'Yeah, yeah. You're right. I must set a date for her to move.' Felicity struggled to find her words. 'I'll miss her, but I need a break. Let someone else take the responsibility.'

'You've done so much for that girl, now you're the one needing help. When can you remove the sling on your arm?'

Felicity sighed. 'The doctor wants me to keep it on for a while. He knows me too well, and says if it isn't strapped, I'll try to do too much. The exercises for my rehab have started, but everything's a mess with her here.' She closed her eyes. 'Oh, to be alone again.'

'That's it! I'm coming this weekend and we'll set a date for her to return to Canberra. She's got to grow up sometime. You don't have to carry this load.'

'Would you...visit?'

'Flea, what did I say? We can do this together.'

The tone of her voice was flat and hollow as she said, 'It'd be it easier if you were here in more ways than one.'

'I can't wait to get there.' He chuckled. 'No more arguments with Mia, promise?' She imagined he was wagging his finger at her and laughed.

***

Felicity grinned, and a lump rose in her throat when she saw a 4WD race towards the house with someone in the passenger seat. Randall to the rescue with a helper?

'My knights in shining armour,' said Felicity as he gave her a kiss and a gentle hug. 'Wonderful to see you, Merv, I'm so pleased you came. Did you have an interesting trip?'

'Wild backblocks out here, Flea.' He bowed to her. 'Mallee country, kangaroos, emus, you name it, we saw the lot. It's so different since I visited this part of the world, dry in parts even after the rain. Hope you don't mind the extra guest.'

Felicity's eyes danced as she giggled and grabbed him by the elbow. 'Enter at your own risk, Mia will be glad to see you, but she's cooking dinner and there's chaos.'

Eskies, boxes of fruit and luggage crowded the kitchen floor as Mia pulled a lamb roast from the oven to check if it was ready. Her cooking gear included a bright pink midriff top; tight green pants; with a shovel load of blue eye shadow and kohl, and her hair was piled on her head.

'Mia, you're a wild parrot, but I didn't realise you were a chef. Is this a hidden talent?' Randall dropped his luggage. 'Come and give me a hug. I brought your mate.'

They smiled at each other and had a long cuddle. Felicity stared and clenched her teeth, and when she saw him touch Mia's exposed back, she interrupted and said, 'Let's sort out this mess, we'll put your bag in my room now.'

Merv unpacked the Eskies and presented the women with a big tray of sweets each. 'These'll make you both better.'

'Thanks.' Mia gave him a peck on the cheek.

'That's thoughtful of you,' said Felicity as she placed her good arm around him. 'Come and I'll show you where to throw your gear and Mia, could you prepare the fold-up bed in the office later, for our guest?'

Bang, bang. The kitchen hummed as Mia ordered Merv to chop vegetables, sharpen knives and carve the roast while she banished the others, each with a drink, to the veranda.

The best silver, serviettes and rose-coloured glasses appeared on the dining room table and, Mia as host, served the wine with a tea towel over her arm. Felicity sat close to Randall and watched the proceedings like a hawk.

Following pavlova and berries for dessert, Merv said with a wicked look, 'What a superb cook, Flea's so lucky to have you here.'

Mia glowed and winked at Randall while Felicity drew in her breath, then laughed to herself about her imagination running riot.

The conversation changed to Mia's travels and how she had lived in Kenya as a child and loved the country. She appeared ecstatic when she described the animals and birds and her former life there.

'I've always wanted to go,' said Randall with his arm around Felicity's shoulder. 'What's it like there?'

She started to explain but Felicity interrupted and with a strained smile said, 'Mia, you'll clean up, won't you? I want to spend time with Randall.'

'I'll help you. Not bad on the dishes these days,' said Merv as he stacked the plates.

When they made themselves comfortable on the veranda lounge, Randall looked at Felicity and frowned. 'What's the matter with you? You've been attacking Mia throughout the night.'

Her gaze flitted around the room, dithering before she answered, 'I'm harassed, hassled, doing nothing sends me crazy and there is so much to do on the farm. I'm cranky, everything worries me.' She added sarcastically, 'How come your ex isn't ringing all the time?'

Randall lay his arm over the back of the lounge and grinned. 'Didn't you see me turn my phone off when I arrived?' He stroked her face. 'Superman and his mate to the rescue, we'll run through a few of the jobs for you over the weekend, but you must take care of yourself. Promise me?'

She twisted and turned her necklace, and her sigh was weary. 'I'm so used to being boss, I hate having other people do tasks I can do.'

'You're a perfectionist and like to be in control so now sit back and enjoy it,' said Randall hugging her and rubbing noses, making her laugh while they stayed locked in one another's arms. 'When did you last have a holiday?'

'Have to think…I drove to Sydney when Emily flew overseas. A whirlwind week.' She choked on her words. 'Then the fateful journey to the festival… supposed to be a relaxing quick break.'

'See, you need to relax. Your trip to Adelaide wasn't fun, you kept running after Mia, not me.' He tickled her and laughed. 'Then our blissful weekend in Canberra.'

'Yes, that was fun,' she whispered, closing her eyes and cuddling into him.

They sat together in silence, each one feeling the other's heartbeat.

Five minutes later, she tapped his thigh and said, 'Don't know how it'll go when we talk to Mia about leaving. I spoke to the counsellor the other day, and she gave me tips and told me what to arrange in Canberra.'

'She's on her best behaviour and Merv will entertain her. Enjoy tonight and we can talk to her tomorrow.'

An ominous shadow fell over them and Mia said, 'What are you going to say tomorrow?' She crossed her arms, and her foot tapped as she glared at them.

They searched one another's eyes, hoping for clues.

'Pull up a chair,' said Randall, pretending to be officious. 'Then we can talk.'

Mia dragged a wooden stool from the kitchen and sat like a cat poised to attack, twisting her hair.

Felicity gulped and started her sermon in a faltering voice, 'Mia, you've worked hard at getting off your pills.' She steadied her hand on Randall's leg. 'Since I hurt my shoulder, you've really helped me and I can't thank you enough. I'm very grateful, but it's now time for you to return to live in Canberra.'

'What? What will I do there?'

Randall leant forward on the lounge and cleared his throat. 'Get on with life, find work, relax and have fun with your friends. It's no fun living in the middle of nowhere.'

'I've no friends and no job,' said Mia with hurt written over her face as she jumped to her feet, sending the stool flying and yelled, 'I don't want to go and you can't make me.' She crossed her arms, gave them a menacing look, then stomped out the door to the back gate, calling Whiskey, and they trudged into the night.

In the uncomfortable silence, Randall moved first and when Felicity thought he might follow, she said, 'Leave her, Whiskey's there and she's used to the dark.'

'Well, she deserves an award for that performance.' He scratched his head, stared at Felicity with a clenched jaw, and they both laughed with embarrassment. 'Hey, Merv, can you pour us a wine?'

He arrived with inscribed goblets. 'Best I could get for me, Lady and Lord.'

'Have never drunk from these,' said Felicity, studying the inscription. 'These were an award for my prime sheep.'

'Something to celebrate at *Neerea*.' Randall raised his glass. 'Thought I had finished with kids and their hissy fits and now I understand what you've been tolerating.'

'She hasn't been too bad. I was naïve at the beginning, didn't see the challenges lying ahead.' She placed her sling over her heart and whispered, 'I've told her many times how proud I am of her getting off those pills. It's taken a genuine effort, will power.' Felicity halted. 'But if she behaves this way… it means she's still touchy.'

'You've done enough,' said Randall, ruffling her hair. 'She has to leave, get on with her life so it's time to call in other support.'

'Who? Her father has only called a few times. Then her friend Brad who calls regularly but she says he's preoccupied with his new boyfriend.'

'That doesn't mean they won't help if Mia asks them.'

'You think she would?'

Randall shrugged his shoulders. 'Does she use the counselling services for drugs?'

'Yes, on and off, she's told me about using the apps and there's one counsellor she likes. They are fabulous support and I don't know how I could've put up with her without their help.'

The lounge sagged as Merv joined them, and they updated him on the saga. Randall stuck his finger in Felicity's ribs. 'You must be firm. Set a date for her to leave and then tell her your decision.'

'Yeah, I don't mind helping but I want to be "good cop",' said Merv, saluting them. 'Give me a job on this case.'

Felicity's head drooped with weariness. 'Okay. I'll consider when she has to go.'

'No, she may never be ready. It's very comfortable here - food and the board laid on and you don't ask her to do too much so you must set a date,' said Randall, raising his voice.

'You're right. I'm so pleased you both came.' Felicity threw her good arm onto Randall's knee, knocking the goblet from his hand, and it shattered. 'Oh no. They awarded this for first prize for my sheep and it'll be the last one after this drought.'

The shards glittered in the subdued lighting as the men scrambled to collect the bits of glass while she sadly searched for a broom to sweep the debris away.

'From dust to dust,' said Merv toasting with his wine and they laughed, but for Felicity a sense of longing crept upon her, losing something that once had been so important. She had fought hard for this award, a recognition that like her father before her, she could win prizes for the quality of her sheep. Now it had disappeared.

Merv agreed to wait for Mia while it was an early night for the lovers. They lay in bed and when Mia traipsed into the house, they overheard her say being alone at night made her scared.

Felicity cuddled into Randall and kissed him. 'It's so much better having you here.'

Randall rested on his elbow, gazing lovingly at Felicity. 'Um, a perfect world.' He stroked her arm. 'Seems she's always on her own. What's her father's responsibility? You should contact him again.'

'Yeah, you're right. Wouldn't like to be him, juggling Mia and a new baby at our age.'

'The joys of older fatherhood. Not for me, I get into enough trouble with this old gal,' he teased, and she tickled him till he squirmed, knowing her injured arm was her protection.

'Over the years, my ex and our kids have dragged me into their troubles. Wasn't rapt, but at least I contributed, and their lives settled. I've a decent relationship with the kids now, it's their mother who's the problem.'

'What's wrong with her? Is she ill?'

'Since the bust up of her relationship, she's become obsessive, ringing me all the time and even threatening to harm herself, and I'm concerned she might be heading for a breakdown. My daughter's staying with her this weekend, trying to convince her to see someone apart from her doctor, perhaps a good counsellor or psychologist.'

'Well, you've got your own, Mia?'

'Looks that way.'

He closed his eyes and for the first time Felicity noticed the deep worry lines on his face. She stroked his forehead and ruffled his hair, and they began their intertwining love making dance.

***

Good-hearted laughter filled the kitchen as Randall made a quick breakfast of toast and tea, and Felicity gave instructions on the day's jobs while Mia remained in bed. The men offered to make a gourmet feast that evening if Felicity rested during the day.

In the paddock, Felicity perched herself against a tree and closed her eyes as she waited for the men to fix the water pipes. Bloody men always think they are best with farm work. Many people in the district had ignored her when she had returned to the property. The stock agents deferred to Alan, which annoyed her because he knew nothing about animals or farming. They side-lined her as though she was invisible. But when her sheep topped the sale yard and won prizes, there was a strained, grudging respect for her work.

She laughed to herself as she thought of how she would be a match for them again if she did not have an injured shoulder. And her old school mates Bill and Crowbar always stood beside her in strife.

Images of having someone, perhaps Randall, to share the load, came to her, but there was a poignancy in not knowing how this would ever happen. The Mia dilemma needed immediate attention with a resolution suiting them both and getting Mia's father involved made sense. Maybe he would offer to take her to India to recuperate further. The men interrupted her thoughts as they returned to the ute to drive to the next job.

'Let's work out a spiel for Mia before we arrive at the house,' said Felicity. 'I'm worried. She's fragile and will need confidence when she gets to Canberra.'

'Had a quick chat to her last night,' said Merv, adjusting his cap. 'She's worried about going back home.'

'Yes, she hasn't mixed with anyone except Bill and me. Ant, Bill's younger son, came over the other day, and asked her to the pub. He's a great kid and she agreed to go, then when he arrived, she said she didn't feel well. I understand she was frightened of what people would say.'

'Confidence problem there and I'm not sure what you can do,' said Merv scratching his head. 'Maybe get someone to talk to her, one of those counsellors you mentioned.'

'When do you want her to leave, Flea?' Randall swung the ute to check a sheep was okay.

'Today...No, in two weeks. But I can't just dump her in Canberra.'

'It's time for others to step up now,' said Randall, rubbing the back of his neck as he glanced at her. 'You've done enough.'

'Um, I'll chat to her, perhaps she has ideas herself,' said Merv.

'Would you mind? She's easily hurt, it's like stepping on eggshells. You talked to her when we were at Shirl's, so you know what to avoid.'

'Okay, I'll be walking in treacle but will find the right moment.'

***

A colourful array of socks appeared when they dumped their riding boots at the back step and laughed at their odd hidden attire. As they walked through the kitchen sliding door, Felicity gasped and grabbed Randall. 'What on earth are you doing, Mia?'

The hallway was in bedlam with a strewn shoe resting on a spilt make-up bottle, and multicoloured bras, a black and red corset, and shorts, T-shirts and dresses covering the floor. A stream of rings and bangles littered the mess. It was a scene from an Indian bazaar.

'I'm leaving,' said Mia with defiance.

'When?' asked Randall as they picked their way through the labyrinth of clothes, jewellery, and coloured plastic bags. 'Who's taking you?'

Mia did not answer.

'Okay, let's have something to eat and you can tell us more,' said Felicity crossing her arms, battling to keep her agitation at bay as she stared at the mess, and with her good arm, she went to the fridge to choose a few items for a salad.

'Don't, Flea, I'll get lunch.' Randall gave her a meaningful wink as Mia dragged around her belongings with downcast eyes. 'Now, where're you putting that luggage?'

Mia dropped her bags and paced the hallway, examining her phone. 'Brad's sending me a message.'

'Okay, we can't help you until you hear from him,' said Felicity, pulling an old tin with a cocky brand from the cupboard. 'Anyone for Mia's biscuits before lunch?'

Merv studied the biscuit and called to Mia, 'These are delicious, what a cook.'

'Don't flatter her,' said an annoyed Felicity, and she yelled, 'Mia, take that stuff out of the corridor and pack your gear in the bedroom.'

Merv surveyed the jumble in the hall and asked, 'Can I help?' Mia raised her eyebrows in disgust and joined them at the table. She glared and flung words at Felicity, 'You want to get rid of me.'

'No, I don't. There's nothing for you around here. You're young and attractive with many good skills,' said Felicity, sweeping crumbs away with her palm. 'Ant left to study and work and it's time for you to embrace life and find your niche in Canberra.'

'Yes, it's too boring to stay, you'd be out of touch with everything, your industry, your job, people your own age. You'll end up like Flea,' laughed Randall, reaching for her hand.

'What do you want to do?' said Merv, trying hard to keep the peace.

Mia snatched a section of her hair and examined it. 'I don't… know.'

'Any ideas?' He stood, put his arm around her shoulders and pulled her body to him. 'It's your life.'

There was a sudden blast from her phone, and she sprinted out of the room while they organised the afternoon tasks in whispers, Merv to stay and talk to Mia and the others to carry out farm jobs.

'Fight or flight. I've had enough, and it's time she moved back to Canberra.' Felicity wagged her finger at him. 'She has to figure this out.'

'Am I the right person?' said Merv, gathering the cutlery for lunch. 'Suppose I'll give it a go.' He pointed the tip of a knife at Felicity. 'No saying "told you so" if it doesn't work. I need a few facts before I tread this treacle.'

'What do you mean?' said Randall, wrinkling his brow.

'Her experience of life - where she grew up, her parents, where they are, and her circumstances in Canberra?' Merv threw his hands in the air and the cutlery fell to the floor. 'Who'll look out for her there?'

'Don't know, ask Mia.' Felicity's eyes glowed, his thought-fulness would bring out Mia's best and help everyone. 'Thanks, thanks so much.'

Chapter 27

After lunch, Merv grabbed a beer from the fridge and sat on the veranda lounge surveying the garden. He found his reading glasses, engrossed himself in a book, and helped himself to another drink.

On his return Mia called to him through the half-open door of her bedroom, 'What are you doing?'

'Having a grog out the back. Do you want to join me?'

Ten minutes later Mia plonked herself on a wicker chair wearing a bright red sarong and her hair pinned to the top of her head. 'Where're the others?'

'They've gone to do jobs around the farm. Do you want a drink?'

Mia flicked her mane and buzzed off to get a cuppa.

'What've you been doing?' said Merv.

She shrugged her shoulders and curled her legs into the armchair, dangling the tea bag in water, and wondering whether he would repeat everything she said to Felicity.

'What's that piss?'

'Herbal stuff. Good for digestion. Flea found it.'

They talked of music. He described how he loved haunting, heart-rending sounds and how he blasted it through his house and out into the night, all the way to the stars and Mia laughed, in return telling him how she was hooked on the rhythms and drums of the African continent. She sipped her drink as she gave the details of her life in Kenya and how each week her nanny made her listen to tunes as they ambled along to the colourful markets.

'Africa's a wonderful place, I travelled there with Bett a few years ago,' he said as his eyes watered. 'I'm sure it's different now. The Chinese have interests and there are many refugee camps. You enjoyed your time there?'

'Yep, I didn't want to leave. I wept and howled and had tantrums when my mother left, and then my father dragged me to England and I hated it.' Mia looked at her bright red toenails peeping from under her sarong. 'I was so cold, I had chilblains and that first winter in boarding school almost killed me.'

'Bloody boarding school nearly killed me too. All those rules and I had a few fights at the beginning, as some kids had more money than sense, so many smart Alecs.' He paused and stared into the distance. 'I wanted to be in my tinnie, back home on the Barka with my Indigenous mates. But my father said he was trying to toughen me up, show me the world. A hard way to do it.'

Mia murmured in sympathy, 'I'll get Whiskey.' The dog followed her to the veranda, and he lay on the floor beside them.

'Everyone needs a wonderful companion.' He relaxed and lay his arm across the top of the lounge. 'Have you ever had one?'

'A dog? No, moved too much.'

'I have Dexter, a little Jack Russell and he follows me everywhere. But I miss my Bett.' He blew his nose with his huge tartan hanky. 'You know, she was the love of my life.'

'What do you mean?' said Mia with a bemused smile.

'If you ever find your true love, hold him or her tight and don't take it for granted.' He blew his nose again. 'When you return to Canberra, you check around and no hobos, drop-kicks because you deserve the best. Someone who realises how special you are, a man or woman you get along with, somebody to talk to, not only on a superficial level but on those things that really matter to you. You're a bright lady, use those brains. Now enough of my sermonising. Do you want a beer?'

'No, but I'll find us something to eat.'

They brought a table from the side of the veranda and spread olives, cheese, savoury biscuits and dried apricots and nuts across it and Whiskey stirred, sniffed the snack, and moved away.

'Ah, this is the life. Fine food, good company and a beer.' He tipped his bottle to Mia in celebration. 'You'll make me healthy yet with these nibbles.' He snatched a handful of nuts and shoved them in his mouth. 'Now tell me…' He patted his chest as he coughed. 'What'll you do in Canberra?'

Mia shrugged her shoulders. 'Don't know. Brad's on the lookout for a job. Should organise myself, but it's all too much as living here makes everything so distant and unimportant and there are no worries about money or work.'

'The good life! My son thought he might hide away too,' said Merv strumming his braces. 'I booted him out before he became useless. Made him make his own way.'

'What did he do?'

'Beat a retreat to Melbourne, found himself a job. A high flying one, just to spite me, I'm sure.' He chortled. 'Maybe a "chip-off-the-old-block"? I hear from him sporadically from exotic places around the globe. He has his Indigenous mates and keeps me up to date on their performers, he likes Casey Donovan, Thelma Plum, Xavier Rudd and I always argue that Gurrumul's music is much better.' He winked. 'We battle and he hasn't settled with a family yet, but he's fine.'

'What about your daughter?'

His face fractured into tiny pieces of bright light as he said, 'Ah, just like her mother, and she lives in Broken Hill with her hubby and my grandkids. She's busy, runs a business there and comes out to see me when she can and those kids love their Poppy, Dexter and my place.'

Mia bent to play with Whiskey's ears, waking him. 'My Dad has only rung me a few times since I've been here, and my mother's a nightmare, only interested in herself. She has two ex-husbands and is onto the third. Never hear from her, and I don't wish to contact her. Your kids are lucky to have had wonderful parents who stayed together, I didn't.'

'It's a tough way to start. But you must be strong, you got off those pills, and that's hard yakka.' He scratched his jaw. 'I'm sure your choices will be different if you have children. Now when do you intend to leave for Canberra?'

About six o'clock that evening, Felicity and Randall tiptoed past the sleeping trio. Whiskey rose and shook himself while Merv snored through an open mouth with Mia's head resting on his lap, her hair spread across the lounge and down to the floor and beer bottles, plates, and cups littering the room.

'Everything's pear-shaped here, so much for leaving him in charge,' said Felicity, nudging Randall, and they both chuckled.

'Where did you two get to this afternoon?' said Merv when he woke and tried to deflect questions on what happened with Mia.

They looked at one another, grinned, and Felicity explained how they were doing repairs on the front fence when Bill's wife came along and insisted they visit for a drink.

'We were on our best behaviour as they were really checking out Randall.'

'Yep, I had a few beers with Bill. Seems okay, he gave me the "look-over." Thinks Flea's his girlfriend.' He winked at Merv, put his arm around Felicity and squeezed her.

'Don't worry, I've known him all my life and he's been so good. His wife sends him over here to find out the gossip. Most of the time my place is boring, but with Mia and you lot, the bush telegraph's working overtime.' Then an inquisitive smile etched her face. 'Now what's been happening here?'

'Ah, we've been making plans,' said Merv with a smirk.

'Doesn't look like it,' said Randall with a wicked grin.

'These are Mia's ideas. She can tell you.'

Mia flicked her hair and averted her gaze. 'I've decided to leave you Flea, return to Canberra with Brad, he can come and take me back in a few weeks.'

She then rose from the table, kissed Merv on the side of the face and marched to her room with her musky perfume lingering as silence washed over them.

After Mia had banged her door, Felicity whispered, 'What's a few weeks?'

'Beginning of next month? She must get moving if she wants a job,' said Merv. 'Think Brad's helping her but wasn't sure what she meant.'

'I'm more interested in what you two did.' Randall nudged Felicity.

'None of your business.' He placed his palm on his chest and had a twinkle of mischief in his eyes. 'A pillar of virtue.'

'Well, Romeo, time to fall to earth, get the beers and help me make dinner,' said Randall. 'Flea, what do you want us to cook?'

***

'Thud' went the tissue box, a hand trying to reach it in the still of daybreak. With extra care, Felicity bent over the side of the bed and found the tissues. She wiped her tears and blew her nose and lay listening to the first of the birds chirping their good morning. Her mind was topsy-turvy and having Randall and Merv seemed to make it worse.

Randall stirred beside her, and in his sleep, he reached out and put his arm over her body.

'Ouch.' Pain charged through her. 'Darl, can you move?'

'Ah, what?' said Randall, his early wake-up time kicking-in. He sat up, peered around the room, not sure where he was. 'What happened?'

'You squashed my sore shoulder,' said Felicity sniffling and dabbing her nose.

'Oh, darling, I'm so sorry.' He enclosed her in his embrace and kissed her lips. 'A cuppa will make you better.' He fluffed up the pillows and pecked her cheek, and she smiled as he covered his nakedness with a towel.

As she did her hand exercises, she looked at the ceiling wishing everyone would go home. She was tired and jaded, her shoulder hurt, and it was all too much.

Randall juggled two mugs to the bedroom, gave her one and rested the other on the side table. He dropped his towel, jumped into bed, and pulled the sheet up and wriggled next to her, resting against the bedhead.

'Just like Ma and Pa Kettle.' He laughed as he reached for his tea and she stared at him blankly. 'Ah, you don't understand. It's an old story…Now, is it still sore?'

She placed her head on his shoulder, and with her voice choking with tears said, 'A bit.'

'Are you okay?'

'I'm fine, really,' she said as she clutched the tissue tightly.

'Here, I know what's good for a girl like you.' He held out his cup and gave her butterfly kisses across her shoulders and face.

'Watch out, you'll spill that.'

He grabbed her mug and set it on her side table alongside his. He wiped away the tears, continuing his patient kisses with intervening feather like stokes to her body.

'Is this making you better?'

She saw his devilish grin from below her navel, her watery eyes glowed and with her good hand she ruffled his hair.

She quivered as he massaged and stroked her, kissing her with his lips, his tongue, soothing her body as she squirmed, breathing heavily until the flame lit bringing her to a loud passionate climax.

The pillow hit the floor as their fervent kisses consumed them. Mounting him, she rocked back and forward. Her breasts teased him, and her tongue kissed his face and licked the salt from his skin. She arched for him as he moved, and they found a rhythm that freed them to come as one.

Two bodies laid damp and spent with happiness. She gently stoked to his body and played with his hair. 'That was so good.'

'Hmm, the research I've done on your clitoris has really helped,' he said with a wicked grin.

She playfully hit him and they turned, spooned each other, and slept.

Felicity was the first to stir and whispered in his ear and toyed with the hairs on his chest. 'You make this so enjoyable. What'll I do when you leave?'

Randall kissed her on the forehead, stroked her naked body and cleared his throat, 'I'll miss you.'

'Me too. You'll be even further away when you go to Adelaide. What are we going to do?'

His face shone as he ran his fingers between her breasts and around her stomach. 'You can live with me.'

Felicity shrugged off what he said. 'And leave the farm?'

'Why not? You're the one telling Mia to change. We'd set up in Mildura or in Adelaide. Don't think it'll matter.'

'But what do I do with this place?'

'What everyone does — sell it or lease it. You always said it was the agreement with your father which kept you here. That's over, you've lasted through the best and the worst times and he couldn't expect much more. Things change,' said Randall without drawing breath. 'We could have so much fun together. There's plenty for us to do - travel, go to the movies, the theatre or just hold hands and get old.'

'Are you proposing?' She gave a startled laugh and wriggled her finger at his nose. 'You know I'm not available.'

'We're over that marriage business. I want you near me, that's all.'

She stared at him. 'I don't understand, I'm surprised and confused. Not sure what to say. What about your Ex, she's still annoying you, isn't she?'

'Surprised, confused? Flea, we've known each other for years.' He played with her ear lobe and stroked her face. 'I care for you and want you with me. You've had a shitty time. Look, it's only a matter of time before your divorce comes through, we can shack up together while we wait.'

'Yeah, but everything's so new.'

'Stop making excuses. We're not in our twenties and we both like a bit of mischief,' Randall teased, pretending to bite her.

They turned to each other and lay in their nakedness and discussed what his offer might mean. Felicity was not sure whether her anxieties would abate or increase with this announcement. For now, as the new light of the day skipped across the dawn sky, she'd enjoy the moment.

***

'Breakfast is on me this morning.' Merv diving into the fridge and finding eggs and bacon. 'I'll get Mia, she can be my assistant.' He raised his eyebrows and his eyes twinkled.

He knocked on her door. 'Mia, Mia. I need help with brunch.' No response.

The smell of brewed coffee filled the house and they saw a figure scamper to the bathroom. 'Ah, there she is,' he said with relief. 'I wonder what delicacies I can tempt her with.'

'Merv, you old perv. You concentrate on our food,' said Randall. 'I'll get the herbs in the garden for your menu.'

'Let's eat on the veranda as it's cooler there,' said Felicity, giving instructions for the table to be moved.

'Much better here. We can see how dry your little oasis is, Flea,' said Randall.

Mia looked like a bright tropical flower when she joined them with green eyeshadow and a long pink floral skirt and black flowing top.

Felicity cast her eyes downward to her jeans and blouse, glanced at everyone and laughed. 'At least they're clean.'

Mia cradled her computer under her arm. 'I'll liven you lot up.'

She fiddled with her music until the drums and stamping of Africa blasted and enveloped their haven into a cocoon. Breakfast was a symphony of banter, colour, and chaos, with Merv leading the dancing, pulling Mia to her feet, and making the others join them. They danced, they laughed and told long stories as the flies buzzed at such a feast. In the afternoon booze appeared, and later the lively atmosphere disappeared as everyone napped.

'It was amazing this morning the house was so full of fun and happiness and I can't remember when it was last like that,' said Felicity as she drove with Randall around the paddocks after their nap. 'Mia's been on her best behaviour.'

'So have you!'

She gave him a thundering glare as he lay his hand on her leg. 'Now, I was serious about you coming to live with me. These matters take a while to work through, but I want to be with you.'

'Oh, Randall.' She moved closer to him in the ute and put her arm around his shoulder. 'Thank you, you're a darling, I don't know what to think but I need time and space. You realise I haven't finished sorting out stuff with Alan?'

'Time…we can't wait forever. Here's our big second chance, so let's take it.'

She studied him for some time, then said, 'Be realistic, we both have our own issues to work through and yes, they take time.'

Chapter 28

A hollowness, an emptiness settled on Felicity as she waved goodbye to Randall and Merv. Their dust exposed the mosaic of her life, the conflict in her heart. While Mia was unwell, she had buried parts of herself and now they had resurfaced, uncovered and raw. Her thoughts whirled as Randall's outrageous insistence they move in together troubled her. She had to talk to someone, so she slipped into her office and dialled Shirley's number. After their greeting, Felicity updated her on Randall and Merv's weekend visit.

'Ah, how did it go, did Missy behave?'

'Fortunately, we finally got Mia to see it was time to move on, to return to Canberra. And it'll happen in a few weeks and I won't know what to do with myself.'

'I'm sure Randall will take up more of your time if you let him.'

'That's the problem, he wants me to move in with him.'

'What, it's too soon, isn't it?' said Shirley, raising her voice. 'Sorry, you're old enough to do what you like.'

'I agree with you, but Randall's decided, he wants to be with me. His kids, apart from teasing him about my nickname, Flea, are happy to have me move into his place. Think they must feel a little sorry for him with their diabolical mother ringing him all the time.'

'Cas was always strange, never understood why they married. She never liked me, probably jealous because I knew him before they met.'

'Those bloody calls, he seems oblivious to the strain on himself and those around him. The worse his ex seems to get, the more obstinate he becomes,' said Felicity, jabbing the desk with her finger as she ran her words together. 'He won't listen to me when I tell him to turn off the phone, and he wants me to move in with him!'

'Don't get excited, not good for the blood pressure,' said Shirley. 'What are you going to do?'

'Don't know.' Felicity paced up and down the room. 'Living in Mildura scares me. I'm so used to the bush now, and playing homemaker isn't my style, he's so fastidious. Alan tried to control me and I hated it so I won't let Randall boss me around.'

'Time to make a few decisions and it sounds like Randall won't like the outcomes?' said Shirley. 'I've got a meeting shortly so give me a ring if you want to chat again.'

In the kitchen, Felicity made herself a cuppa but couldn't relax. She needed to be alone, to grieve, to cry. Her sanctuary called.

'I'm going for a walk, Mia,' she yelled through the house, and called for Whiskey.

Slices of sun filtered through the needle leaves of the she-oaks and as she strolled, she tuned into their ancient eerie sounds, saying, "look after me".

The scarred tree supported her back, and its distinctive smell sustained her. Ah, the nothingness of life, she thought as she closed her eyes. The trees sang in unison as her mind echoed with thoughts of her parents, losing her mother at an early age, and her father's trust in her going so wrong. This, followed by Alan's betrayal and manipulative ways threatening her livelihood, making life so difficult. Now decision time approached, she needed to fill or expose those papered over holes of pain.

Tears threatened as she dived into the darkness of what was bothering her.

The naysayers like Randall thought she was mad to bring Mia to the farm to, but he didn't understand that she was so fragile. Felicity wanted to give her a second chance, to offer her a refuge to heal and to get security, love, and kindness. Her own anger was irrational and came from stress, even though she knew there was no easy road to recovery for Mia. Many times, she had whinged and moaned to the access line counsellors and they helped Mia and herself battle their way through their differences, to beat their self-destructive tendencies. The counsellors deserved medals for their patience, as it was hard going for everyone.

Felicity's skin tingled when she thought of Mia's wonderful fortune in recovering so well. The medicos advised there was only a "tiny window of possibility" to kick the habit. Despite one or two lapses, she had not touched pills for weeks. With her chin on her knees, Felicity hugged herself. Was Mia a "natural recoverer"? A person able to recover mainly on their own without treatment or self-help groups. Or was she so bloody minded, or was it a Miracle? She would never know.

She laughed to herself at how difficult it had been for her to give up drinking while Mia battled her demons. From what she read, there was no quick fix for addiction and people tried many times. Her intake of grog had stopped at the height of Mia's battles. Now she had days without, and sometimes one or two drinks a night, but no more. She didn't want to go through her own withdrawal again.

A lingering wave of sadness swept over her at the thought of Mia being overprescribed opiates and how they had created pain, anxiety, and uncertainty for her.

'Mia, please, please don't relapse,' she called to the trees, wishing her to reach out for support when she returned to Canberra.

Felicity wondered whether she had been as overprotective of Mia as Randall had said. Maybe she had to let her go, put the energy into her own life. The date for Mia to leave was looming, and Brad had agreed to take her home.

Swishing the flies away with eucalyptus leaves she had broken from a tree, she smelt the lingering aroma and thought of the challenges ahead. Decisions circled her like bees.

Her shoulder still hurt, but she didn't know how much longer the healing process would take. Bill's son had agreed to help with the farm as he was marrying soon and could do with the extra money, but it was only a band aid solution as Bill wanted a manager for his place.

She watched a trail of ants. Her biggest quandary was her relationship with Randall. In her view, he was pressuring her to live with him, but there were too many obstacles; she was the one who would have to sacrifice the most. Her settlement with Alan was in a state of flux, and his lawyers continued to pester her. Emily's contact was intermittent as she blamed her mother for her parents' marriage ending. She smiled through her tears when she recalled her daughter's tantrums, not taking her calls, and the announcement that bastard Alan had made to her, "Your mother's a whore."

Randall was more pragmatic. He understood what he wanted and had considered their future together. With a small, warm smile, she thought of the many times he had told her he loved her and she was never certain how to respond. Love involved courage, and she didn't know if she was up to it again.

To be with Randall meant leaving this property she had loved since she was a child. She shifted positions against the tree and remembered how excited she was when she took over the farm. She couldn't believe her naivety, the cost to her marriage and the unexpected never-ending drought. In the first few years it was tough, but everything flourished, nourishing her, and she was so overjoyed and optimistic. Now the constant work around the farm with no reward, just survival, depleted her. Life on the land had become so difficult, and as she watched the sand slip through her fingers, she realised her emotional well was dry.

'Do I care enough for Randall?' she called to the colourful budgies in flight over her head and heard a gentle swoosh in return. She grinned, thinking of him and the opportunity of mysteries to be explored. 'Can I live with him for the rest of my days?' A distant crow cawed in reply. She laughed and ruffled Whiskey's ears. 'Let's get home, storms are brewing. I must go to town tomorrow.'

Her smile broadened as she hugged the tree in thanks for listening to her rants and raves. Decision time loomed.

***

The radio blared as Felicity sped along the road. Warm tingles flowed through her body as her thoughts of Randall dipped in and out. She removed her sunglasses and twisted the mirror to view her eyes, to see if they were red from an attack of tears in the middle of the night.

What a fabulous weekend she had had with Randall and that crazy man, Merv. The brightest, most humane person she had ever met. His knowledge and wisdom could fill an encyclopaedia, and he made life fun. His presence touched everyone, and she thought of how much they had laughed at his antics.

Felicity still had a niggle about where Mia stood in Randall's world. She had seen her pout her lips when he was around, but more and more, Felicity believed he had tried to help them both by listening to her woes. She smiled to herself, her doubts only surfaced when she was anxious or feeling low.

Perhaps Mia wanted a father figure. She loved the attention of older men, and Merv was always glad to spend time with her. He couldn't be so foolish?

As Felicity drove, the wind picked up, forming and re-forming whirly tubes of dust, the trees beside the road bent with twigs and branches losing their grip and falling to the dry earth. The clouds became bulbous, ominous with flashing sheets zigzagging through the sky. She heard the grumbles and groans of thunder and as the unseasonal autumn storm moved closer, the loud booming cracks overhead followed the streaks of lightning. Will there be fires from the lightning strikes?

At the front gate, big drops of rain messed with the dusty windscreen and the wipers worked full throttle across the window, but visibility was poor. The drumming on the roof drowned out the sound of the engine as she drove cautiously up the track.

Felicity parked the car near the house, picked up as much as she could from the back seat and ran to the veranda, with the drenching downpour stinging her.

'Mia, where are you?' she shouted, as she dumped her gear in the kitchen and shook her hair to remove the raindrops. She banged on Mia's bedroom door and peered at the mess on the floor and noticed Mia's velvet bag sitting on the antique lowboy. She searched the rest of the house and called out in the yard.

No answer, but she can't be far away, thought Felicity. She secured the windows, made herself a coffee and sat on the veranda lounge, watching the storm move over the farm. She bit into the delicious looking, but tasteless salad roll she'd bought in the café. Where is she? Surely, she didn't go out in this mayhem?

'Whiskey, Whiskey,' she yelled. The other dogs barked but he didn't answer.

For the next hour Felicity, lost in thought, cleared out limp vegetables, mouldy fruit and out-of-date cheese and condiments from the fridge, not wanting the putrid smells to spread if the storm turned and blew out the electricity. She laughed to herself as she made a pot of tea and thought of Merv's freezer. She had forgotten to ask if it was okay.

The wind rattled the louvres, and the sky darkened as her concern grew. When the rain stopped, and the blast had died, she found her torch and checked the animals. Mia must have taken Whiskey and she jumped in the ute with the other dogs leaning like sentinels on either side of the back tray.

Felicity cursed. Wasting bloody time in the dark. She drove the road to the gate, then along the boundary. The rain had sheeted across the land, but when it petered out, it left a slight impression on the parched earth. Lightning struck one of her favourite trees, and she groaned with sadness at its huge, jagged trunk now standing naked amongst the fallen branches.

'Shit, stupid woman,' Felicity yelled to the sky as she searched the trees near the dry creek along the fence, then crisscrossed the scrubby bush. She travelled back and forth because of unexpected dips, and the wheels spun in the bare dirt before each hollow released her. The lack of visibility and the terrain made driving slow. A sudden barking of dogs and the appearance of Whiskey's friendly face relieved her concern.

'Whiskey, where's Mia?' shouted Felicity as she abruptly applied the brakes. Whiskey jumped up on her and she hugged the dirty wet dog and when she released him, he darted forward and kept checking behind to make sure she followed.

After five minutes he stopped, barked, and let out a mournful howl. Old decaying branches rose like ghosts in front of her. She struggled through them, and the smell of dust and crumbling leaves filled her nose as she stepped into a circular patch of ground. Shining her torch, she caught Mia in the beam, propped against a tree, wet and covered in dirt. Elevated on a log in the clearing was her right leg.

Felicity's immediate thought was of the snakes resting in the log's hollow.

'What happened to you? Are you okay?'

'I fell over this branch.' Mia appeared dazed as she put her hands on her leg. 'My ankle's twisted.'

'Why were you out in a storm?'

'I hit the road for a walk and when the lightening appeared, I tried to run back using the short-cut and became lost. You don't understand,' she said with pouted lips. 'Everything looks the same.'

'The same! You foolish girl. Check out the sky. Do you need a sign saying?

S...T...O...R...M? You're too busy tripping around to notice.'

'I've had NO pills for weeks,' said Mia her eyes flashing as she clenched her fists. 'You can't even see what's going on under your nose. You hate the bush. Best thing you can do is leave.'

Tiredness, fear and anger surged through Felicity as she tightened her arms over her body and drew in her breath. 'You don't appreciate the bush!'

'Well, why do you whine every day? Bloody sheep, they need shooting.'

'You're such a grateful imp, gratitude oozes out of you and I've put up with you for weeks with never a thank you.' She pointed her finger at Mia. 'You spend your life here lying around doing nothing and flirting with every man who appears.'

'Stop behaving like a drama queen. Flirting! There's been no one worthwhile here. Fuck you. Stick yourself up your bum.' She attempted to stand while Whiskey barked. 'I'm leaving. Enough is enough.'

'Run! The further you go, the better. I'd thought you'd changed.'

Mia squeezed her hands on her bowed head and whimpered. Felicity knelt and pressed her ankle and jumped back with surprise when Mia screamed.

'Well, suppose we have to get you home.' Felicity cleared her throat. 'I'm sorry I carried on, it scared me you were really hurt. I'll help you to the ute.' She offered her uninjured shoulder as the dogs stayed with them.

Felicity bowed her head in relief once they were in the ute's safety and turned the key in the ignition while Mia snivelled. As they drove, the ute's light beams gave the newly washed trees a gentle hue, a mystical touch. No one spoke. Mia hobbled from the vehicle and plonked herself on the dusty lounge on the veranda.

'Here put this on your ankle, it'll reduce the swelling.' She handed her a frozen bag of peas from the freezer. 'Just keep your leg up on this chair. I'll get you water.'

'Sometimes I slip up. I'm sorry,' said Mia, sobs racking her body. Her hair dripped, so Felicity threw her a towel. 'Whiskey stops me getting scared. I don't bother with the weather when I go for walks with him.'

The phone rang and as Felicity ran to answer it, an ominous flash went through her body.

'There's a lightning strike on that big gum tree on our boundary, we're off to check it,' said Bill. 'It's dry enough for the fire to cause havoc unless we have more rain. You might have to get your water truck out but wait till we ring. You know your mobile phone's not working?'

Felicity closed her eyes and gritted her teeth. 'I'll wait here for your call.'

'Let's hope we can put it out straight away.'

She checked on Mia, who was innocent in sleep, then went out the back gate and searched for an unwelcomed glow on the horizon.

For the next hour, she paced the house and fiddled with the TV channels, beside herself with concern for Bill and his son and the damage to the land if the fire spread. She went through all the possibilities as she waited for the call.

At midnight, Bill rang. 'It's okay, we've done what we could, and it should be okay for the night.'

'Lightning struck one of my favourite trees. There didn't appear to be any problems when I drove in, but I'll check it before I go to bed. Bloody mobile phones, always drop out in an emergency.'

Chapter 29

Mia sat cross-legged on the floor of her room, examining the clothes she had to sort and pack over the next few weeks. She grinned as she thought of her how she had thrown everything into the hallway when Randall and Merv visited. It won everyone's attention, but in her madness, she had flung the bags into the bedroom and left them lying in a higgledy-piggledy mess but now was reckoning time.

With a toss of her hair, Mia recalled Flea's treatment of her when she fell in the storm. Medusa. It had reminded her of the dark and stormy music Flea always played, Gluck's *Dance of the Furies.* The moment for settling former scores. Felicity had screeched and screamed about her being ungrateful and accused her of flirting. Was it with Randall or Merv? She had rocks in her head as they were old enough to be her father but she did have fun stirring Merv.

Chuckling, she shuffled on her backside to the long wardrobe mirror, catching her knickers on the carpet. Her lips curled in distaste as she identified unwanted hairs and zits. Vengeance the only cure, she attacked her eyebrows and dabbed balm on her pimples.

Next, she checked her clothes in the light, and the discarded pile grew, the bright colours producing vivid patterns against the carpeted floor. Her assortment of bags lay scattered throughout the room and she pulled the largest aside and packed the items to go with her to her new life.

'Flea, where are you?' Mia called through the house.

'Fixing the wire on the chook pen.'

'That crocodile Fred's not there?'

'No! He won't eat you, but he'll take a nasty bite.' Felicity's face lit with amusement as Mia, wearing no shoes, traipsed towards her with a large bundle of clothes. 'It's time for him to bunker down for winter.'

'Here's a pile I don't want. What'll I do with them?'

'I'll give them to Vinnies,' said Felicity. 'What's this sudden rush to get rid of your stuff?'

'Um, my new life in Canberra.'

'What do you mean?' Felicity removed her hat and wiped her brow.

'I'm not the same. I shouldn't have taken those pills from that doctor. They numbed me and I couldn't face myself, reality. Yes, I have a shitty mother who doesn't care and Dad's distant. But people like you, Brad, Merv and Randall love me. You're all bossy, but your hearts are in the right place.'

'Good.' Felicity stared at her with misty-eyes and her voice wobbled. 'Sorry, I'm a little overwhelmed.'

'When I go home, I'll be more carefree, not so serious,' she teased, flipping her hair.

'Oh, really?' said Felicity, glancing over her sunglasses.

'Brad's man has a job for me and there'll be new friends and I won't see the old crowd.'

'Will you stay in the same place?'

'Ah, yep. I'll get rid of lots there too.' She dropped the clothes on the ground and ducked into the chook pen. 'A make-over of my life,' she babbled, holding three eggs. On the path, she tilted her head and did a jig. 'You won't know me. "A new woman hits Canberra".'

Felicity's body quaked in laughter. 'Good for you. I'm so proud of you and let's celebrate with a cuppa.' She pointed to the pile of clothes. 'Don't leave your castoffs out here, the animals will ransack them.'

It was as though Felicity was seeing the kitchen for the first time when she looked around. The old cuckoo clock on the wall had not worked for years. As a child, she had loved its consistent sound and the way it came out to greet her every hour. Her grandmother had bought it for her mother on an overseas tour. The women had died and the cuckoo too, but no one had removed it.

Peering into the crockery cupboard, she said, 'There are more things to clean out here too, but they must wait. Now what will you do in Canberra.'

An exuberant Mia laid out her plans. 'Brad's man has organised a job with a magazine publisher doing IT stuff. Only three days a week to start so I'm joining a gym and getting fit doing yoga and dance classes. Maybe meet some new friends.' She paused, her face resigned. 'I'll miss Whiskey, so I'll get a dog to keep me company, to watch TV with and walk.'

Felicity's head whirled. 'Brilliant. How'll you care for it with so much to do?'

'Plenty of time. It'll happen, I'm better after my stay here and know what's needed.' Her tone dimmed. 'In the first few months, I'll find a good counsellor and a support group to help. I promise I won't return to taking pills, it's too hard to give them up.' She pounded her chest and laughed. 'They have to be conquered forever!'

'A group, how will that work?'

'Ah, I had a look at the net and found stuff in that book you gave me. There's no temptation out here but I'm stronger now.' Her voice faltered. 'If it's a supportive group, they'll help me understand what to expect.'

'Wonderful to hear, you've changed and worked hard to get where you are today.' Felicity lifted her cup to Mia. 'You've had your share of demons with those pills and I know it's not finished. But you've come a long way.'

'Flea, you let me stay here and watched over me like the mother and father I never had. Okay, sometimes you gave me a tough time, but thank you. Meeting you was the best thing.' She raised her cup and toasted Felicity. 'At the beginning, I was out of control and hurt myself and everyone else, but you didn't give up on me. Both Merv and Randall told me how lucky I was to have you and they were so right.'

Mia could see Felicity bite her lip and tears slither down her cheek and into her voice. 'Thanks. We've had rough patches, but I'm glad you're feeling better. I'm excited for you but I'll miss you so much when you go.'

'Flea, I'm coming back. You're my family now, Merv, and Randall too.' She hugged her. 'Blood isn't enough. Felicity, the most decent, kind and generous person I know, who cared for me during my worst time.'

They stood in tears, wrapped in each other's arms for the warmest hug each could give.

Chapter 30

Felicity sniffled, then dissolved into tears at the back gate as Mia drove away, shouting goodbye and banging on the door of Brad's over-packed red sports car. A tidal wave of emotion crashed over her as she sobbed and wailed as Whiskey stuck his chin on her legs and whimpered. A sense of loneliness infiltrated her soul. For many months she'd hung on, fought and calmed Mia, placing her own life on hold. Now she was alone, and she wasn't sure she liked it.

She dawdled around the garden and smelt the intense fragrance of an old-fashioned deep pink rose climbing on the side wall. Pressing her face to a flower, she inhaled the scent, getting giddy. Her roses were one of the few flowers thriving in the dry conditions. Felicity smiled and her eyes blurred when she thought of the care she'd given them, dead-heading the faded blooms, pruning and watering. Through the fence she could see the long-neglected orchard her mother had planted where the fruit was hard and withered. Tending the roses was like caring for Mia, prickly and tough, but the reward of an exquisite bloom or a young person on the way to releasing her addiction to pills made it so worthwhile. She wished the best for her in Canberra.

A few nights later, Randall rang. 'Hello, how's life without Mia?'

'Why do you want to know?' she growled.

'Well, I didn't expect that response. Are you okay?'

'I bawled my eyes out this afternoon. I wanted her to leave, but now she's gone, I'm crazy. Sleep will make it better.'

'Darl, I'll come over next weekend, okay? I can help you with work and cook dinner-for-two. We'll be on our own. A first for a long time.'

'Isn't there talk of a lockdown for this new virus? We're not supposed to travel,' said Felicity.

'I don't give a hoot and if I get caught, I'll make up an excuse.'

'You sure? Aren't they fining people?'

He huffed and puffed on the other end of the phone and ignored Felicity's advice.

When they finished their conversation, Felicity sat at her desk writing a list of over-due jobs. She thought of how reckless Randall was to be travelling when there was a travel ban between regional towns. But she needed his help to fix the wrecked fence. The fast-flowing water from the storm had knocked out the fence posts, and she was worried stray sheep from the stock route might mix with her animals and take hours to muster.

She laughed to herself about her catch-up with Emily, and the rest of the family members and friends she had neglected over the past few months, the gossip she'd missed while Mia was staying. Bill had told her stories, but she was so self-absorbed that she hadn't listened. She caught herself whistling and singing with the birds as she returned to the mainstream of farming life.

Her daughter screeched with happiness when she heard Mia had left and chatted for half an hour with no sighs or drama, only saying, 'I hope she hasn't ruined my clothes.'

Felicity had the upper hand and made a mental note to wash everything in the cupboard and throw out items of no use, knowing Emily would make trouble with whatever she did.

Simon was harder to track down, and she tossed and turned in bed, worried something had happened to him. When he rang at midnight, it scared her. Phone calls late at night always spelled doom and gloom. But he was excited and talked and talked, explaining why his work was going to keep him in the States.

Then he dropped a bombshell and said, 'Mum, terrific news for you. I've got a girlfriend, Elise. She's American and lives near Chicago.'

She spluttered, 'Congratulations, I hope I get to meet her soon when this virus is under control. What's she like?'

When she finished the call, the update trickled through her veins. It floored Felicity, her little boy on his own across the world, with all those riots and that dangerous virus. Now he had his first girlfriend, or the only one he'd mentioned. What would happen if he lived in the US and raised his children there? She might not see her grandchildren. She realized Simon was not coming back to run the property she had committed herself to working, and Emily certainly wasn't interested in farm life. There was no one to pass the farm to.

***

Felicity slept restlessly at night with worry about Randall's visit. On one hand, she wanted to show him the things she loved about the farm and, on the other, she was so uncertain of how she felt about him. He was pressuring her to move in with him, but this idea was not exciting for her. It was such a commitment, and she didn't want to feel trapped in a relationship again.

Randall had stopped mentioning his ex and their difficulties and she didn't know whether to be relieved or worried. But there were other unsettling issues. The thought of living with him scared her. He was so fastidious, always wanting everything clean and in the right place, which was not her way. And living in town with initially no job after her independence on the farm could be a nightmare.

Perhaps working together around the farm during his visit might bring them closer and help their understanding of one another.

'Whoopee, we're on our own,' said Randall, grabbing her and hoisting her from the ground in an embrace. 'How are you, Darl?'

She threw her head back and laughed. 'Good, I'd say. The police didn't pull you over for travelling, did they?'

'Didn't see any police along the way. Told you I'd be right getting here.'

Felicity stared at him in annoyance, and mumbled, 'I wish they'd got you! Suppose you want lunch after that trip.'

'There's only one thing I'm starving for.' His eyebrows lifted, and a wicked grin crossed his face as he grabbed her. They tussled together until she broke away, giggling, and moved to the back of the 4WD to help with the luggage.

As Felicity prepared chicken and salad sandwiches, Randall made the coffee and chatted about his business and Merv's latest visit to Adelaide.

'Hey, let's do your jobs after lunch. I'll cook dinner tonight and tomorrow we can have a leisurely breakfast.'

'Sounds good.' She pointed to a notepad and laughed. 'There's a list of work I want done, a month's worth of jobs.'

'You're organised. You want me to stay that long?'

'Couldn't resist it, having a slave here,' she teased.

Fencing was not Felicity's best skill, but with Randall by her side, they soon had the posts in and were straining the wire.

'I'm surprised you've lasted so long on the farm when you don't know how to fix a fence. Here let me do it, you sit in the ute.'

Randall's flippancy as he tightened the wires reverberated through Felicity.

'Did you mean that?'

'What?'

'What you just said.'

He shrugged his shoulders and continued working.

Felicity caught her breath and stared. She was speechless, baffled, and livid. How dare he, he doesn't understand how to run a farm himself. Was she over-sensitive or was he having a go at her?

During the visit, Randall talked and talked about them living together, and his intensity scared her. The more he spoke, the more Felicity vacillated, not able to discuss the conflict she was in. She knew he was generous and loved her, but she couldn't shake the shadow of Alan's manipulating and double-crossing lifestyle.

'You don't seem your normal self,' he said as they lay together on Sunday morning. 'I go to touch you and you turn away. That's not the Flea I know.'

'I'm whacked.' She stroked his arm and heaved a sigh. 'Mia's only just left, and I've been buzzing like a mad bee catching up with people and getting jobs done.'

'Um, come here.' He wrapped his arms around her and whispered, 'It'll be much better when I don't have to travel to be with you.'

***

The week after Randall's departure, Felicity sat under her scarred tree. It was a confusing day; it had rained in the morning, the leaves shimmered, and the birds chirped overtime, but it was still hot. Whether to sell or lease the farm and move in with Randall weighed on her. She noticed her jaw was sore from grinding her teeth as she tried to gnaw away the knots of what to do. There was still no resolution. Randall was handsome, and it was enough for her to hear the timbre of his voice and see his ocean blue eyes to lose herself. He had been Mr Fix-it after Alan left her in financial distress. She'd thanked him many times and was so grateful for the direction and support he offered. But he hadn't changed or eased up when they became lovers. Her identity would disappear if she lived with someone too controlling again. Was he controlling with his ex, too?

After contemplating her predicament, she covered her face with her hands, closed her eyes and screamed, 'Oh, no. I don't think I can live with him.' It hit her hard and the realisation scared her.

What Randall wanted for them was so straightforward, but not for her. She must extricate herself from this relationship or continue as they were and pretend it was rosy. Either way was fraught.

Retribution at the thought of leaving him was swift. It was as though the furies unleashed, and waves of doom and gloom filled her head as she came to terms with what it would mean if she told him they couldn't be together.

***

The house glimmered with the winter light, wisps of silver-grey smoke danced from the chimney, and the trees and bushes sang gentle lullabies as Felicity drove the ute with the dogs in the back into the yard. The scene made her nostalgic for the wonderful times she had experienced at *Neerea*. After her accident, she'd realised she needed more help around the farm, especially with an ageing body.

Picking up firewood to carry to the house, she thought of how her options were closing. Simon didn't want the place, and his new girlfriend in the States meant he'd live in a different country. Randall wasn't a candidate as he had his own business; and there was Bill's son, who might share-farm. She wanted to stay independent and fit, but if she became ill or too old, there was no one to run the farm and she had no stamina to go through another drought.

Felicity heard the buzzing of the phone as she stepped into the kitchen. She saw the name and held her breath before answering, 'How's it going, Randall?'

'A quick call. I'm worried about you after my last phone call. Are you okay?'

'I'm fine,' said Felicity, gritting her teeth, holding back words she might regret.

'Thought I'd come over this weekend. Friday at lunch time, and I'll cook and we can celebrate my birthday together.'

'What an excellent idea. Love the cooking part. See you soon.'

***

Her predicament with Randall muddled her thoughts and when he stepped from his 4WD, she gulped and held her stomach. He gave her a relaxed and playful greeting kiss as he retreated to the back of the vehicle.

'What have you brought here?' said Felicity in surprise. 'How long are you staying?'

'Remember, I said I'd cook. Knew you wouldn't have the ingredients so brought my own.'

Felicity rubbed her forehead as it miffed her because he should've remembered that Mia had stacked her pantry with exotic foods. When she became their 'chef', she had insisted they have oils, herbs and other foodstuffs, and he had even used them when he and Merv prepared the meals. Maybe she was being unreasonable? Having someone to cook for her was a luxury, and there was no point in spoiling the occasion by saying something to him.

'I'll make you the finest meal ever,' said Randall, giving her an air-kiss as he laid the boxes on the table and pulled out a notebook. 'An Italian theme, we'll have *Arancini with Taleggio Cheese* for entrée tonight and a good old *Chicken Cacciatore*. Tomorrow's dinner, *Osso Buco* is best cooked in a slow oven.' He winked at her. 'I went to my cellar and picked out a few McLaren Vale and King Valley reds to wash it down. Even found bubbles, so it'll be an amazing celebration.'

Felicity squeezed her hands together, flabbergasted as she had never seen Randall so animated with food and wine.

'We won't have time to do any jobs, you'll be cooking, and I'll be drinking,' she said, running her words together.

'We'll be fine,' he reassured her. 'What have you lined up for me?'

She ran through a list of tasks she needed help to do. 'I'm your slave.' He grinned as he folded his arms together and bowed.

That evening, while he deftly cooked, Felicity sat at the kitchen table with a glass of bubbly in her hand. She was the chef's apprentice and followed instructions. "Chop this, get me that."

When the food was ready, they savoured the Arancini on the back veranda and watched the glow of the day diminish with the sky's pink and purple striations, Randall's arm around her shoulders.

'Let's eat the Cacciatore in front of the TV. We can catch up with the world and see what the weather's doing,' said Randall, standing to get the meal underway. 'Tomorrow we celebrate.'

The next night, his theatrics had Felicity hooting with laughter.

'Tonight, I'm Mario, the chef, and I'll spoil you,' he said, spinning a tea towel in front of her and bowing.

He fed her titbits from the antipasti plates of cheeses, salami and olives, poured her drinks in style and cuddled her throughout the meal. Nothing was too much trouble as he served a delicious osso buco with greens, which he had prepared earlier in the day and had cooked for hours. Felicity made fun of his gestures, and he laughed with her. She couldn't give this up, could she?

They skipped the birthday dessert and sat side by side on the lounge, teasing and toasting one another with their wine.

'You make me special,' said Randall, hugging her with tears in his eyes. 'I can't wait for us to move in together.'

Felicity untangled herself and stared at him with surprise, knocking over his wine.

'I'll get a cloth to wipe this.' He tried to grab her, but she had left.

Romance and light-heartedness disappeared at breakfast the next day. It was as though she'd removed a mask and everything Randall said rankled. Anger rose in her throat as she remembered all the nasty comments he'd made about her farming and housekeeping.

Her mouth tightened, and she crossed her arms. 'What's happening? You spend so much time chastising me and criticising what I do around here. It's hard enough farming without your cutting remarks.'

'What cutting remarks?'

'You know, how you said last night my house is always untidy, or what you just said before about how I care for my sheep, and how I can't fix a fence. Those words you say to ridicule me.' She turned and stared out the window.

'I'm teasing you. You're too touchy.' He came behind her and squeezed her in a hug, but she stood staring into the distance.

After a few minutes, she asked Randall to sit at the dinner table. 'Look, this won't work if we keep commenting on the worst in each other.' Her lips narrowed, and she glared at him. 'Okay, I admit I'm a lousy housekeeper, but I always have an enjoyable meal for my guests. As for my farming practices, you might not like them, but I can assure you they worked before the drought.' She pointed her finger at him. 'I don't go around bad-mouthing you… I'm so grateful to have you in my life, you've done so much for me, and we've had fun together.' She paused. 'But I feel trapped into moving in with you, and I'm not ready for it. I want a break to figure out my life and it'll take time. There are so many pieces jumbling through my mind.'

He lifted his eyebrows and gave her a disbelieving stare. 'What? You're crazy. I don't understand you. Let's get these jobs done.'

'No, you didn't listen.'

An angry sound escaped from his pursed lips as he ran his hand through his hair. 'You mean to separate, not see each other?'

She fiddled with her watch, rubbing it along her arm.

He moved toward her and pleaded. 'What are you worried about, that I'll take care of you? We'll both decide what to do with the farm and where we live.' He grabbed her in a tight hug. 'I want to be with you, no one else.'

There was a lengthy silence.

'I need space away from you to work out what to do. Mia's just left and I want to work through everything on my own. We won't survive if I jump into moving in together so soon. Please, please give me time.'

'I'm not sure what to say. I just want to be with you, I love you.' He grabbed her hands and searched her eyes with a sad frown.

'Look, you're making it hard for me as I don't want to be trapped nor do I want to be like your ex, ringing you all the time.' She paused and tried to reason with his beautiful blue eyes. 'All I'm asking for is a break to sort out my head.'

'Sounds like there's not much I can do.' He put his head in his hands on the table. 'Do you want me to leave now?'

She nodded, and he stood to walk to the bedroom.

'Where will you go?'

'Home.'

'I'm sorry, but I guess that's it,' said Felicity as she put her hands to her face.

***

Felicity moped around the farm, every job seemed hard and useless as she questioned whether she had done the right thing by stalling her involvement with Randall.

A family friend had died in Canberra, and as he was an enormous part of her childhood, his family expected her to attend the funeral. She was on her way as the first golden rays of the sun spilled across the paddocks. Felicity threw on the music she always played, driving to requiems, Purcell's *Music for the Funeral of Queen Mary*. It mirrored her anguish and melancholy. The trees in their receding shadows bent in the gentle breeze as she sped past, and tears formed, and soon she was bawling, exposed and raw.

She pulled into a rest-area away from other drivers and dropped her arms and her head on the steering wheel, her body shuddering. Her obsessive questioning of herself grated. What would she do alone? In her inner most heart, she knew changes were necessary to survive and thrive if she was to be the person she wanted to be. Otherwise, she'd be embroiled in a more tortuous situation. It meant reconsidering her relationship with Randall. She closed her eyes, trying to stay calm but a wretchedness bordering on despair racked her body.

At the next large multi-purpose service station, she wiped her cheeks with a torn tissue, rustled in her handbag for sunglasses and strode into the café to get a coffee. She slid herself down on the car seat, trying to make herself invisible in the vehicle as she sipped the ghastly drink.

Donning her dark glasses and bright lipstick, Felicity attempted to disguise her drawn face. She signed the funeral register and sat in an empty pew at the back of the church. The funeral service was a blur, and she scampered out before the coffin, fleeing to her car. A funeral flight.

She wanted lunch and to escape her misery, she decided on a visit to the National Gallery. She joined the COVID queue at the entrance and looked around at the other visitors, all drawn and probably wondering when this social distancing would end. When she arrived at *Blue Poles*, she clasped her hand across her mouth and the tears rose. Randall was with her when she'd last been here. She thought of how they had laughed and teased one another after she had recovered from her hissy fit about his interest in Mia. She washed her face and sought refuge in a bowl of pasta and a glass of wine in the café overlooking the Sculpture Garden, before she began her slow, disheartening trip home.

There was no one to greet her, no one cared if she arrived home. Nobody to talk to who knew she had attended a funeral. Whiskey and the other dogs jumped around, thrilled to see her return, but it wasn't enough.

Chapter 31

Months later, winter's icy weather had almost broken on the farm, and record-breaking rains had made the paddocks lush. Little blossoms appeared on the fruit trees and a new kamikaze magpie attacked anything that moved near its young, so Felicity was a comical sight when she fed the chooks with an ice cream bucket on her head.

She sat on the laundry steps in her nightie and UGG boots, surrounded by her snoozing dogs, and looked with nostalgia at the yard. *Neerea* had been her home for so long, and memories of childhood flooded her mind. The wonderful times she had with her parents and sister and she remembered the seasons matched the rhythm of her father's work. A simple life. Now everything was a complicated maze, and time galloped. The drought had hollowed her and many others in the district out. She counted on her fingertips the number of properties changing hands, farmers no longer able to sustain their livelihood.

It was easier when Randall was around to discuss the options and find solutions to her dilemmas. He loved her, but she couldn't accept his need to control her as Alan had tried, and she'd hated it.

Felicity closed her eyes and remembered the moment of her 'Randall epiphany' under the scarred tree. There were many phone calls as they had tried to work through the knots in their relationship. She had hurt him; he was indignant and couldn't understand what was happening. Things deteriorated from there. She had missed him and longed for intimacy, someone to share the load, and to laugh with.

'Whiskey, why do I make it so hard for myself?' He shook himself and came to her for a cuddle, and the other dogs followed. She observed them with sadness. 'Don't know how you'll go with Bill's son and his new wife. You must behave.' She lifted their paws to search for burrs and patted them as they nuzzled into her. 'Now, I'm going inside for a cuppa and boys you're moving outside the fence.'

The noise of a motorbike disturbed her peace, and the dogs barked. Puzzled, her ears strained as the gate squeaked and she heard an excited voice arriving at the door.

'Flea, where are you?' The words rose as a song as the unexpected intruder called and the veranda fly screen door flew open and Whiskey raced in, barking.

'Mia…' Felicity received a wild embrace. 'It's too early for you, isn't it? What are you doing here?' She glimpsed a lanky young man with inky hair and an enormous smile striding up the path carrying two bike helmets. 'Ant. I'm still in my pyjamas!' She gave him a hug. 'Whiskey, out you go.'

'Don't worry. We're here for the clearing sale,' he said as Mia grabbed the dog, cuddled him and ruffled his fur.

'Perfect, I need more support,' said Felicity, pulling out the sides of her blue tired-looking nightie and looking at her boots, making everyone laugh. 'I'd better change. Help yourself to something to eat.'

When she returned to the kitchen, Felicity chuckled to herself as Ant looked sheepish when he stepped away from hugging Mia.

'A new woman, you look wonderful. I haven't seen that dress.' Mia pulled her hair into a ponytail. 'Sit, I'll make you brunch as I'm playing mother this time,' she said as she took items from the fridge. 'Think I owe you that.'

'What happened, I didn't expect you to come for the sale?' said Felicity.

'Brad made me guilty. He said, "After what Flea has done for you, you must help with the move". Ant rang last week and said he was coming through Canberra, so we made the big decision to ride out here early this morning.'

'Good on Brad,' said Felicity, raising her thumbs in thanks. 'Most jobs are under control. But I'll need some help to make sure I get everyone's details in case that virus is lurking. The entire district will be here, now auctions are possible. Thanks for coming, I need some moral support.'

'When do you leave the farm?' said Mia, placing the teapot and cups on the table.

'The sale goes through next month, but Bill says I can stay as long as I wish.' She glanced at Ant. 'Don't think your brother and his bride-to-be would agree, as I'm sure they'll want change a few knickknacks when I move out.'

'And what's happened to Randall?' called Mia from the stove. 'I thought you two were shacking up together.'

'Hmm, he wanted me to move in with him, but there were a few issues, and they scared me. I didn't want a repeat performance, Alan was enough and Randall had problems of his own with his ex.'

'Hey, let's get down to the drama.' Mia served the food. 'I've missed your mates, Randall and Merv.'

Felicity crossed her arms. 'That's all I'm saying. Randall's coming today with Merv to help with the sale.'

'Wow, what a surprise. I'd love to see them. Will you get back together?'

Felicity lowered her eyes, picked up the cutlery to eat and smiled, knowing there was a thaw or was it a breakthrough. Her phone conversations with Randall were more regular, and they'd met once or twice for lunch. Too risky to say anything further, but things were progressing.

'Something incredible happened with Ant and me. It's good.' Mia's face glowed, and her eyes flickered with happiness.

He dropped his head, and his fringe fell across his forehead. 'I haven't told my parents yet so I'll run home later, sleep there and come and help tomorrow.'

'What wonderful news,' said Felicity, placing her hand over his. 'Don't worry, I won't discuss it with your father if you don't want me too.' Whiskey wandered in looking for titbits. 'Outside! Mia, could you get rid of him?'

While Ant and Mia bantered and pulled the dog into the backyard, she spied the cuckoo clock still withstanding the ravages of time on the wall and made a note to remove it to the junk pile for tomorrow.

Her thoughts lingered on Randall. The angst and doom and gloom she had experienced when he continued to insist on them moving in together was no longer there. She grinned with pride, having made her own life-changing decisions to sell the property and pay off Alan. Somehow it strengthened her, made her more aware of what she wanted, and it reinforced her ability to negotiate for what she required. Her increased use of the word, "No", defined how far she had come.

Running her hands through her hair, she laughed to herself. The last time they had met, Randall had showed signs of wanting to control her, and she was forceful, "Enough of that, I make my own choices". He had stepped back and chuckled.

After lots of discussion, they had rekindled their relationship, and they were cautious, there was no mention of living together. They were more sensitive to each other's needs and committed to unravelling the knots. His ex seemed to have accepted there was no getting back with him and was getting proper psychological support. She had stopped ringing him. Felicity realised the toll Cas's behaviour had had on their relationship, and now both she and Randall were free and more relaxed.

'Mia, I've got something to tell you, 'said Felicity when she returned to the kitchen. 'I had a surprise the other day. Remember Adrian we met at Mungo National Park?'

'Not sure, that was when I was in my drug addled-brain stage and I've forgotten a lot from that time or maybe I don't want to remember,' said Mia, looking downcast.

'He rang me a few months ago before the lockdown. He was on the way to Sydney for a conference, so we met in town for a coffee as I didn't want him coming out here and having an accident like you on my rough road,' said Felicity, laughing.

'Wow, two blokes on the go. How did he get your number?' said Mia.

'Protective Barney from Mungo rang and asked if it was okay to give Adrian my details.' Felicity gave a self-conscious giggle. 'Yes, I always wanted to find out what he and those other scientists were up to out in the bush, but events overtook me, and I never followed it through.'

'Is he potential?' said Ant.

Felicity put her hand under her chin and gave a distracted look. 'He said he'd help me get a job so I might look him up when I'm next in Adelaide. But those scientists were so secretive at Mungo and I got annoyed with him when he told me they were searching for somewhere to dump waste in the outback so he may not want to see me again. Now, how's Brad and work, Mia?'

'The job's challenging, and I'm learning other skills. My workmates are okay. Only see them in the office twice a week, the rest of the time work's online.' Mia flicked her hair back. 'Brad, as usual, is painful.' She whined, '"How did you get yourself involved with that? what about this? why did you miss yoga? why don't you eat that?." I love him, but he drives me crazy, like you.' She threw her arms around Felicity.

Felicity disentangled herself and grinned. She knew Brad could be bossy, he would do anything to stop Mia from hurting herself. When she had stayed on the farm after their fateful trip to Adelaide, he had often rung to give her a reality check. On the one hand he was gentle and kind, but he often made remarks to Mia and Felicity that no one else dared say and Mia adored him.

'I'm not taking any pills. I live the life of a saint.' Mia raised her eyes and joined her hands together in prayer. 'The support group's fun and my counsellor's wonderful, she gets me, and I use the access line if I get anxious or upset.' The words gushed out. 'It's first to bed and early to rise, and I might become a vegetarian, but maybe I'm too lazy and fast food will always do.'

'What, I can't believe it,' said Felicity, and everyone laughed and hugged one another. When the group dissolved, Felicity asked, 'Do you still dance?'

'Not as much, Brad now lives with his partner. Maybe Ant can dance with me.' She blushed and grabbed Ant's hand and raised it in the air, and they grinned. 'And Dad's coming to Canberra for Christmas with his new wife and my half-sister if this virus stuff is over by then. I'm going to play tour guide.' She examined her fingernails. 'I've forgiven him. He was useless when I was trying to recover, so I'm glad I had you, Flea.'

'Really? Even though we battled and tore each other apart?'

Mia reached across the table and clasped her hand. 'Yep! I wouldn't be here with Ant if it weren't for you.'

Felicity choked back tears. 'Have you heard from your mother?'

Mia bristled. 'We've spoken once, but I'm not seeking her out just yet. Did she contact you? I gave her your address.'

She shook her head.

'Yeah, she's caught up in her own world.' Mia propped her hands on her hips with a mischievous look. 'Flea, let's tell Ant the story of my start in the wilderness here.'

Roars of laughter reverberated through the kitchen and Ant chuckled as Mia flapped her arms and recounted the tale of her first stay on the farm, chased by old Fred, the goanna, both trying to escape.

'I didn't tell you then because you were so scared, but goannas will inflict damage if you don't get out of their way.' Felicity had a deadpan face. 'Their tails swing the same as a crocodile and their bites are very nasty with lots of bleeding.'

The uproar died and Ant asked, 'What are you going to do, Flea?'

'Well, COVID-19 has changed things. No firm plans, but when the border re-opens, I'm off to Shirl's place in Adelaide where I'll spend a few months, then go to the States to meet Simon if they allow us to travel. There are decisions about what I do next, but I'm not ready to make them yet. A holiday first so I'll have time to recover from the difficulties of the last few years.' Her voice dropped. 'Emily's in Sydney so I'll visit her too.'

'Won't you get homesick for the farm?' said Ant, playing with Mia's hand.

'I know your parents and brother will always welcome me.' She splayed her fingers across the table. 'It's interesting, when Mia came to stay, I had to think to myself why I chose this battle.' She pointed to the cracked photo of her father on the sideboard. 'Dad wanted me to continue his legacy, and I loved the challenge but now I want a different life, farming's too hard, the drought sapped me.' She drew in her breath and closed her eyes. 'I want a home with easy access for my kids, and a place where there's life, to go to the movies, listen to music, travel when we can, all that stuff. But I'll always miss *Neerea* and my special scarred tree.'

'It's payback time so you and Whiskey can come and live with me in Canberra,' said Mia.

Bellows of laughter filled the room.

THE END

Acknowledgements

In writing and researching this story, I worked and travelled in different parts of NSW, Victoria and South Australia. In the spirit of reconciliation, I acknowledge the Traditional Custodians of these areas and their connections to land, sea and community and pay my respects to their elders past, present and emerging.

Building a story into a novel takes time and effort and a dalliance with experience matched to imagination. One highlight of the journey has been the contribution of so many people to this work. To the wonderful people I acknowledge below, please accept my gratitude for your contribution. There are many others who have added a richness and depth to my story. A big thank you to you all.

I would like to thank Anita Heiss, Barbara Neil, Sally Richard, Michael Star for their inspiration.

For reading and commenting on chapters in various drafts and encouraging me in the right direction, the members of Randwick Writers' Group: Garth Alperstein, Susan Beinart, Dina Davis, Helene Grover, Marie McMillan, Anne Skyvington.

To the Celestial Writers' Group: Julie Janson, Sarah Sasson, Nicole Sheridan, thanks for the laughs, insightful feedback, and support.

To those who read various drafts and provided comment, clarity, and support: Sue Doran, Christine Campbell, Meredith Garnsey, Lesley Turnbull.

For providing support and editing my manuscript: Elaine Stewart.

For providing insights and information on medical conditions: Garth Alperstein, Wayne McDonald, Sarah Sasson and Gayle Murphy for her knowledge of the rural Area Health services in NSW.

To Writing NSW for the excellent courses which started me on this journey.

To my parents whose life adventure took them to a farm on the Hay Plain where the flatness of the land and nature combined with distance enriched my imaginative life.

Author profile

Geraldine Star's stories live and breathe the Australian bush, the majesty, intrigue, how people are drawn to work and live there, and the complexity of their relationships. She leaves no character untouched by the beauty and gnarled harshness of the environment, weaving unforgettable stories.

Geraldine is an educator having worked in schools; tutored at University and in the world of communications and writing; coaching and mentoring a culturally diverse group of Australian creatives through her business, Star Monde Communications. She is a graduate of Sydney University and has a Graduate Diploma in Writing from the University of Technology, Sydney.

Geraldine is a writers' group enthusiast and a member of two groups. Recently, she complied and contributed to *Sharing Writing Skills*, published by Ginninderra Press, about the enjoyment of collaborating with other writers.

She grew up in country NSW near the Hay Plain and now lives and works in seaside Sydney, Australia.

Contact
author@starmonde.com.au
www.geraldinestar.com
Instagram: geraldinestar2

www.ingramcontent.com/pod-product-compliance
Lightning Source LLC
Chambersburg PA
CBHW030528120726
47904CB00005B/1674